THE
ANCIENT

A NOVEL BY

NICHOLAS RUSS

Edited by Marcus Busekrus

Artwork and Design by Nicholas and Brennon Russ

To Catherine and Brennon

————————————————

Marcus, this book wouldn't be what it is without you

NORIDRAN
LAND OF NO KING

GREAT
SWAMP

YOG
DWARF TERRITORY

DAIN

GREEN
HILLS
FORT

CAPITOL

RIVER

BROKEN PLATEAU

THE
ANCIENT

Your Majesty Egan,

One of our messengers has returned to inform us that the northern kings will not be sending support. I fear that we will get the same response from the rest.

Concerning the other business, lately there's been an unusual calm over the lands. It seems a good time to begin.

I have a feeling I won't be returning to Capitol any time soon.

- Strom

Chapter 1

RAIN

He stood at the railing of the cannon tower and looked out over the swamp forty feet below. Raindrops drummed quietly on the roof shingles, though now he swore his ears detected something less rhythmic out there in the gloom.

"You say somethin'?"

His mind brushed away the question like a hand would a fly. It had been like a low snort he'd heard; the first strange sound since he'd been brought to this place. He waited to hear it again.

"Five."

"What?" He couldn't help but ask.

"Five of 'em."

At last, Gehn turned to regard the tangle-haired soldier squatting on the floor nearby. His confusion turned to annoyance when he saw the man's reason for distracting him.

Below the sword in Fisher's meatless fingers, carved into the splintery panels between his crossed legs were four vertical lines topped by a horizontal one. "For five days out here and not seeing nothing."

Gehn turned back toward the rain. "Fisher, you can't even make a tally right." He quietly said.

"I make a tally the way I like to." Fisher grumbled defensively. "My pops taught me the best way."

A third voice, sharp in tone, broke in: "He teach you how to dress and comb your hair?"

Fisher turned toward the heap of scratchy, brown blanket on the cot and scowled. "As I was sayin', rotation'll be back out here day after tomorrow to pick us up. Captain told us seven days, 'member?"

Gehn was only partly aware of the question being directed at him.

"'Member, Gehn?"

"Yes, I remember."

This affirmation only eased Fisher's mind for several seconds. "It was seven he told us, I'm sure. A marsher's week."

Oswin, the blanket-shrouded veteran, spoke up yet again. "It's a merchant's week, you imbecile."

"Quiet. I wasn't asking you."

"A marsher's week." Oswin mocked. "That's almost as bad as you loading your rifle backward."

Fisher leaned over and pushed the cot.

An arm darted out from beneath the blanket and grabbed the tower's wooden rail, keeping the cot from toppling. The veteran righted it beneath himself and half-rose, his wrinkled, scar-stippled face filled with murder. In a flash, he took a handful of Fisher's hair from behind and twisted a wail out of him.

Gehn shot a sidelong stare back at them.

When Oswin's eyes met Gehn's, the veteran immediately let go.

"Old fool!" Fisher's paralysis broke and he gave an exaggerated flail as if he'd fought off his tormentor.

"Keep your hands off my cot." Oswin warned.

Fisher scooted away a bit on the floor. His threat came out like a cough. "Touch me again I'll kill you."

Gehn released a soundless sigh.

"I was manning a post out in the deadlands once," Oswin started, cocooning himself in his blanket again, "maybe fifty miles southwest of Cortos. This is back when that land still belonged to us and not the dwarves. Dry, desolate place. Two whole

6

months we got left out there, forgotten. Our water supply was nearly empty within a week."

"No one cares." A sneer revealed Fisher's yellow, rat-like front teeth. He picked up his sword and began to add to the artwork in the floorboards.

Oswin turned and looked directly at him. "I watched men shrivel in the heat." He said, squinting with a smirk. "A few of them were desperate enough to set off across the wasteland, but there's no way they could've made it to Cortos before the sun beat them down."

"And you survived?" Fisher's tone bristled with skepticism.

Oswin chuckled, tapped at his temple and smiled before rolling over to face the rain again. "You really think the General cares whether we live or die?"

"How *did* you survive, Oswin?" Gehn asked, also skeptical now.

There came no answer.

Gehn knew that the man had heard him, but he also knew that if he pushed the question he would be doing it out of spite. 'I'm turning into one of them.' He thought.

Suddenly, a stream of water came shooting down from the ceiling and onto one of the barrels of gunpowder, splashing Oswin's head.

"God almighty!" The veteran rolled over awkwardly and got to his feet, looking around wide-eyed as if he'd been soaked in some fiendish prank. He ran a hand through the center of his wispy hair, leaving two dry tufts like stubby horns.

It was Fisher's turn to smile.

Gehn took hold of the barrel and pulled it out from beneath the leak.

Oswin came to his senses. "Don't let it get through to the powder charges."

But already Gehn was turning the barrel onto its side, freeing the water that had been trapped at its top and darkening the wood around Fisher's tally.

Oswin eyed the leak's new, thudding point of impact near the cot. "We need something to divert it toward the edge."

7

Righting the barrel again, Gehn briefly pointed toward the neat pile of armor against the far rail.

Oswin went to it and began digging through the metal pieces. "Don't help us, Fisher." He growled. "We've got it under control."

When Gehn opened his eyes the next morning, his first thought was that the rain had stopped. He found himself propped against the cannon, his rifle angled across his thighs and his left boot jutting out over the forty-foot drop.

A thin mist hung low over the swamp for what seemed miles. Clumps of black mud broke through here and there like tiny mountain peaks.

The silence ended with a single *ponk*, a drop of water into the makeshift gutter: a down-faced breastplate, supported on one end by a bracer so that it slanted toward the tower's edge.

He turned to see Fisher curled up and slumbering on the floor. "Fisher."

Fisher mumbled.

Gehn jabbed him with the muzzle of his rifle.

The scraggly soldier sat up with a jerk. By his twisted, frozen expression and drooping eyes he might have still been asleep.

"You were on watch." Gehn said, waiting for the soldier to look at him, wanting the soldier to see his displeasure.

Fisher never looked. He rubbed his face with two filthy, spidery hands. "We ain't seen anythin' for seven days." He said. "What we need to watch for?"

"I'm going to flog him." Oswin muttered from his cot, staring intently toward the roof as if he were imagining the act.

Fisher persisted. "You really think we're going to see something now? There ain't nothing out here."

Gehn stood up, his eyes on the mist-veiled landscape, and he placed his rifle on the tower's rail to push it down with both hands. He was sure he'd heard something out there, the same low snort he'd heard the day before.

"It was your job, Fisher." The veteran said. "I've known soldiers killed by their own comrades for failing to do their job."

"Tell me another story, old man."

Oswin flung his blanket aside and sat up. "How about I throw you over the edge?"

Gehn focused on the ruins of a lonely, long-dead tree roughly a hundred yards out. Whether by some beast's force or by the suction of the mire, its slender trunk was tilted, and its branches seemed to reach out in the opposite direction as if it were trying to right itself. Perched on the highest branch was a crow. The bird shifted restlessly, turning toward the northeast now to give a quiet *croak*.

'You're not what I heard.' Gehn thought.

"It's a fool like you that gets his fellows killed." Oswin lectured. "You're far more dangerous to Egan's army than any dognar."

"Only one in danger is you, if you don't shut your mouth."

Gehn watched as the crow turned away from the northeast and leapt from the branch, flapping twice and gradually fading into the distant fog. When he saw what had spooked the bird, his eyes slowly widened.

"I could break you in half. I could rip your head clean off its..."

A deep, guttural rumble cut the veteran's threats short.

Oswin joined Gehn at the rail.

"Oh my God." Came Fisher's whimper from behind them. "It's two of those... those *things*."

The two great shapes moved in like prowling wolves, their heads low and their dark, spiny tails lashing gently against the mist. They arrived at the angled tree and began searching around it with an unsettling swiftness.

Fisher put a shaking hand to his mouth. "Do they see us?"

"I think they smell us." Gehn softly said. "We're upwind to them."

"What now?" Fisher asked.

Gehn was already adjusting the tower's short cannon, swiveling it and dipping its muzzle toward the closer of the two beasts,

9

bringing the jagged, scaly shape into the weapon's crude sights. At last he took hold of the tiny cable at the cannon's rear and wrapped it once around his hand. Glancing once to check and see that the creature hadn't yet moved away, he began to pull. "Cover your ears." He said.

The cable went tight.

Fisher waited and watched with bulge-eyed interest.

Oswin's rugged face hardened with anticipation.

"It shouldn't be this... difficult." With Gehn's final word, his clenched hand jolted back with the sound of a *snap*. Now he looked toward a broken cable hanging from his fist.

"Never seen that happen before." The veteran muttered.

Gehn tossed the metal braid aside. "We'll have to do this the old-fashioned way." Instantly his eyes and hands went to the small, black plug just below the weapon's failed firing mechanism. "Oswin get me a fuse."

Within a few seconds, the veteran had scanned the tower's visible supplies three times over. "Where are they? Shouldn't they be next to the cannon?"

"Check the trapdoor."

Fisher had retreated to the opposite rail by this point. Hugging to himself, shivering in sporadic jerks, the soldier pressed a hand against his mouth as though he were about to vomit.

"Snap out of it." Oswin hissed as he pulled the square of panels up from the floor's center.

"Oswin." Gehn quietly pressed.

The veteran snatched a brass box from a nest of leather bags. "It's a shock he made it through training." The man said, glaring briefly at Fisher before putting a yellow-headed fuse into Gehn's open, expectant hand.

Gehn had the fuse in place in less than a second. "Light it." He said, and as he looked down the cannon's length and toward the dark creature beyond it, he was sure now that the creature was looking back at him.

With the *pop* of a match, sparks crackled their way up the short, white cord and promptly died with a curl of smoke.

10

For a moment, Gehn could only stare. He took the open box from Oswin and scrutinized the neat and seemingly untouched collection inside. "Did the rain get to these?"

"The box was sealed tight." Oswin replied. "It's waterproof."

Gehn snatched out a second fuse, but when he turned toward the distant, spindly tree, he felt his stomach lurch; the creatures were no longer in sight.

"What are you waiting for?" Fisher practically shouted.

"Tshht." The veteran aimed an accusatory finger before putting it to his own sharp-edged lips.

Gehn stood and peered over the edge. "Too late for that." He said as he beheld the two visitors that sat at the tower's base: two dognars leering up at him like black cats at a bird in a flimsy cage. Tales drifted up from the depths of his mind, hushed stories of living horrors that looked like dragons but moved like dogs.

One whispered voice drowned out the others: "They don't breathe fire, but one look into their eyes can freeze even the bravest hero's heart."

Focused now on a pair of roiling, scarlet spheres, Gehn waited for a supernatural dread to well up inside him, and though everything around him seemed to fade to a shadowed blur, it wasn't terror that he found.

Fisher's scream sliced through Gehn's thoughts.

As if in an excited reaction to the sound, one of the dognars reared up and dug its claws into the bricks, its fanged jaws wide and its hanging, carmine tongue glistening with slaver. Its massive tail whipped back and forth.

Again Fisher screamed, and when Gehn glimpsed Oswin's face, he was sure that the veteran was going to join in.

"That isn't helping." Gehn stated.

After a violent, snarling bark, the dognar dropped back down from the tower's side. With slow patience both beasts began to circle the structure's base, each scaly head tilted to keep a glowing eye on their intended prey.

"The cannon won't aim that steep." Gehn grunted to himself just before his attention fell to his rifle resting on the wooden rail.

11

Cocking back the hammer of his own sleek firearm, Oswin aimed down at one of the massive, moving shapes. The weapon fired with a welcomed *bang* but made only a spark on the creature's stony, black hide.

Despite having never heard of a dognar falling to anything less than a cannonball, Gehn snatched up his rifle and aimed with confident purpose.

"You've got to hit them in eye." The veteran fit another iron ball into the side of his weapon's barrel, followed it with a powder charge and closed it with a *chack*. "Either that or a gap between their scales."

Certain that he had a bead on one hellish, red orb, Gehn's finger tightened on the trigger when the beast abruptly turned away and rushed out into the hanging, gray clouds. Puffing a frustrated breath, he searched for the second creature in vain. "Where..."

"He's going to knock us down!" The veteran yelled.

Gehn saw the movement out of the corner of his eye. He swung his aim for the monster now as it charged full speed through the mist and mud, its head low and its teeth bared.

Bang!

His shot glanced off the dognar's spiny back just before the impact.

BOOM!

The tower shook.

Fisher's frantic breaths heightened to a string of groaned, unintelligible words. The man stared straight down at the floor with his hands open near his head as if he held the sides of an invisible helmet.

"Knock it off or I'm throwing you over!" Oswin threatened.

Chack. With his rifle ready for another shot, Gehn spotted the other dognar standing some ninety feet out and facing the tower with the stance of a challenged bull. Knowing how little time he had before his target moved, he brought the weapon up and fired.

Through the spurt of gun smoke, he saw the beast suddenly jerk and drop slightly lower on its front legs. Its red eyes locked with his as it gave an angry, roaring bark, and now he was sure that he could see a dent between the scales at the top of its head.

Gehn's attention hardly left the beast as he opened the rifle's chamber. "That one hurt?" He whispered through his teeth.

With a snarl, it bolted toward the tower's base.

"Here he comes!" Gehn warned, taking one hand off his rifle to grab a wooden support post.

While Oswin scrambled to do the same, Fisher dropped down to plead and beg with the backs of Gehn's boots.

BOOM!

The tower swayed from the impact.

"Bloody hell." Oswin growled. "We won't last two seconds if they keep that up!"

"Fisher!" Gehn yelled, nearly tripping over the bent soldier behind him. Snapping the next iron ball into his weapon's open side, he reached for a powder charge and then froze when he saw the two barrels. He went to them and set his rifle aside.

"What are you up to?" Oswin asked.

Fisher's panic momentarily faded as he watched.

Gehn took hold of the round, iron piece that kept the barrel's lid firmly attached. "We'll drop these on them." He muttered as though to keep the two horrors below from hearing. "Use a short fuse and get each one as they come."

"And if all of the fuses are bad?" Oswin looked out into the fog again just as one of the dark shapes came with the speed and force of a loosed boulder down a steep mountainside. "Incoming!"

BOOM!

The veteran gripped the rail as the top of the tower lurched. Bricks tumbled as the structure's wooden skeleton creaked like an old ship.

"We'll makeshift a fuse if we have to." Gehn answered.

"Even if it works," the veteran argued, "if the first blast doesn't level the tower, the second one will."

"I'm open to a better idea." Gehn at last removed the lid to expose a tightly-packed circle of cannon charges resembling perfect, cylindrical apples. He took the end of one, but as he

13

attempted to remove it, the entire layer of explosives rose until he saw something beneath them, something attached and emerging with them like a slab of dried clay.

Furrows reached across Oswin's scowling face.

Gehn heard the fourth strike coming, the heavy claws in the mire and the rapid, snorting breaths, but now he couldn't pull his eyes away from the barrel's true contents before the impact came.

BOOM!

He caught the object before it fell and held its open edge as though it might attempt to escape him. Handing the circle of affixed charges to the veteran, he brought his free hand up and now raked his fingers across small, pale shards of stone.

The word stumbled off of Oswin's tongue: "Gravel?"

Already, Gehn had moved to the second wooden container. He pried the lid and tossed it aside and now tried one of the cannon charges to find that it too was attached to the surrounding cylinders of red. He took the layer with two hands and as he ripped it out it snapped in half. Dropping the pieces to the splintery floor, he stared at the countless stones within and said: "Who would do this?"

"We're dead." Fisher's voice wavered as he struggled to his feet. "We're DEAD!"

BOOM!

The tower rattled and swung like a faulty pendulum, throwing one of the barrels onto its side to spill a torrent of skittering, gray fragments.

As Gehn moved to the rail, the nearer of the two attackers met his stare and showed its fangs with several thunderous barks.

"What did I tell you, Fisher?" A grinning Oswin calmly said. "We've been left out here to die."

Gehn spotted the more-distant creature just as it flung itself forward through the mist with a snarl. As he gripped the wooden beam and braced for the coming impact, his attention caught a hint of color on the dented, ebon scales atop the creature's skull: an unexpected trace of red.

'Blood...' He thought.

BOOM!

14

The structure lunged. Deep inside the column of bricks, wooden members groaned and popped.

Certain that another strike would bring the tower down, Gehn turned toward the surrounding weapons and supplies. His eyes leapt from object to object, the useless cannon and its fuses, the munition barrels with their insidious weight, and nothing caught his interest until he saw the coil of heavy rope near Oswin's cot.

Fisher's tone was almost sane. "What are you doing?"

"Gehn?" Oswin said.

Gehn secured a knot to one of the posts and tossed the rest of the rope over the tower's southern side. Slinging his rifle over his shoulder, he snatched up his sword and linked its sheath to his belt before climbing nimbly over the rail. "Just stay alive." He said with quiet earnest. Then he slid down, the rope's angry bristles cutting like tiny scimitars at his hands as the tower's slate gray surface flew up past him.

When he heard Fisher's shrieked question, the sound was already high above.

"*What is he doing?!*"

When his feet were just a few yards from the dark muck, he let go of the rope and fell. His boots sank to the ankles.

"*You're out of your mind!*" The veteran cried.

Thunder rumbled through the clouds as Gehn pulled the rifle free and moved out from behind the tower, his boots collecting more clinging sludge with his every step. At last he knelt to loosen them and now yanked each foot out to plant it, wincing, in the freezing mire. Raising the weapon, he gave a shout. "HEY!"

The closer of the two dognars whisked around and found him with its menacing, red stare. As it bent its snout low to issue a lengthy growl, Gehn tightened the weapon's sights on the bloody dent in the center of the armored scales atop its skull. From distant, drifting fog, the other beast watched him like a hound at full attention.

Crack!

A dark fragment tumbled from the wound on the nearer dognar's head. Its growl became a flurry of roaring barks as it charged toward Gehn, and as he turned to sprint into the emptiness of the swamp, he was chased by Oswin's angry cry.

The small, dark ridges of ground seemed alive as they rolled beneath him like waves on a restless lake. The surface was ever hungry for him, a futile trap for his flying, naked feet.

Over the ripping snorts of the beast's pursuit, a second peal of thunder boomed above and was followed by a rifle blast.

'That's it, Oswin.' Gehn thought. 'Don't give up.'

Ahead in the haze, the roots of a massive, long-dead tree suddenly appeared. Between the largest of its pallid projections, Gehn noticed a V-shaped space that he knew his pursuer wouldn't fit between. He veered through the gap just as he heard jaws snap behind him. Looking back, he caught a glimpse of a jagged shape stopped briefly by the natural blockade.

He brought his rifle up and popped open its side. He shoved a powder charge in behind the small, iron ball and closed the chamber. As he stopped and turned and aimed, the beast smashed through the rotting edge of the fallen, old tree and came for him.

Crack!

The shot missed the wound in the center of the creature's head and sparked against its stony brow.

Once more Gehn turned and sprinted. Once more he loaded the rifle with deft fingers, the barks of the beast just behind him, but when he tried to close the weapon now it wouldn't budge.

"Come on." He urged. "Just one more shot." But his attempts to force the chamber shut were fruitless.

After several more strides he stopped and spun.

Through the mist the monstrosity came, its mouth wide with ravenous anticipation, its fangs agleam like ivory spearheads. As he looked into its blazing, scarlet eyes, his doubt melted away.

Swiftly he tossed the rifle aside and unsheathed the blade that had been waiting at his hip, but instinct told him that the hole in the horror's skull would be too difficult a target. As its snarling form closed the final few yards, purpose darted through Gehn's

16

arm to the ends of his fingers and now he plunged the sword through scales and taut muscle.

Lightning struck the distant tree with a brilliant burst of flame.

Tingles crawled across Gehn's flesh as he fixed his eyes on his open, empty hand. To his right, the beast's unmistakable tracks passed him, and when he turned, he saw a fallen, motionless form.

He made his way around the creature, its body and tail like a ridge of hellish spines and its legs like thick, charred branches. His stare never left the half-submerged head, the once-burning eyes now empty caves, and then, at last, he saw the weapon's hilt level with the mud and seemingly attached to the side of the scaly neck. The blade was buried all but entirely.

He stood for a while, thunder mumbling as rain began to lightly fall. Then, he went forward and planted a mud-painted foot on the side of the dognar's head before pulling the sword free with barely a grunt. He stared at the length of wet, red metal expecting at any moment to wake from a dream.

He remembered his companions just in time to hear a crashing sound that he knew hadn't been made by the oncoming storm. With a last look at the dead creature, he made back across the sea of mire in the direction of the tower.

Through thickening sheets of rain, Gehn saw the other monster digging into a heap of gray bricks and broken, wooden beams. From the rubble, the beast extracted a body and shook it wildly in its jaws; by the lack of Fisher's scream, Gehn guessed that the hapless soldier was already dead. The creature dropped and sniffed its prize and then began tearing through the bricks again to find a certain second victim.

'That first kill was a fluke.' A voice inside him whispered, yet it could do nothing to quench the fire that drove him now. He moved toward the monster from its blind side with his sword ready, his every step quicker than the last.

It saw him coming. He tried to dodge its lunge but suddenly found his left arm trapped in a vise of enormous fangs. The beast threw him to the muddy ground and slammed its claw

17

down onto his chest. As it started to pull him apart, he tightened his right hand on the sword handle and his searching eyes fell to the beast's throat. He stabbed.

The monster's vehement movements stopped.

Blood spurted from the wound and coated Gehn's face and chest. He could see the center of his blade inside the dognar's mouth, its tip protruding from the top of its head like a single, silver spike leading the row of black ones. Its eyes were closing now, the red glow in them fading like quenched coals.

Its final breath came out in an echoing sigh, an icy wind against Gehn's pierced and mangled flesh. He managed to slip out from under the oppressive claw only for the beast's weight to fall heavier on his arm. Despite its death, its jaws remained as tight as a bear trap.

Mud bubbled and crept up past Gehn's left shoulder now. He yanked the sword free with another outpouring of blood and then jammed its razor edge tight between the rows of teeth at the back of the creature's mouth. He levered the blade now with all of his strength, the cold sludge rising up past the side of his bloodied neck and toward his face. The moment that he felt the evil jaws budge, he tried to pull his arm out but the teeth still had him. As the mud consumed his mouth, he heard a soft and steady sound, a rumble echoing from the depths of the beast's throat, and when he looked toward the dark orb of its eye, he saw, within it, a growing dot of red light. With a final jerk on the sword's hilt, he released his left arm and fought his way out of the mire's hold. Panting, he stood and now took several steps backward, but the stillness of the beast before him did not change.

Gehn flung bricks aside and at last he could see a leg. "*Oswin.*" He exhumed a twisted, battered body from the last of the crumbling pile. The veteran's hair was a helmet of drying blood, his head tilted back and his mouth open in a semblance of eternal sleep.

"Oswin say something."

The lips barely moved. There rose a quiet, groaned word: "Gehn?"

"Yes."

"You're... alive."

"Yes." Gehn stated as he inspected an ugly cut that ran down Oswin's partly-exposed flank. Even in the pouring rain, it bled in thick, crimson runnels. He turned and moved carefully across the debris to stoop over Fisher's lifeless body. He tore a section from the corpse's shirt.

"He's dead?" Oswin asked casually.

"Yes."

The veteran chuckled, winced, and then released a sigh. "I knew he'd be the first to go."

A distant peal of thunder drowned the noise of the pattering rain.

Returning to his comrade, Gehn placed the bunched cloth he'd acquired over the open wound. "Here." He gently positioned the veteran's arm to hold it. "Try not to move otherwise."

"Are they dead?"

Gehn heard the question but said nothing. He scanned the wooden members around him with a plan, and just as his eyes stopped on a patch of pale and scattered gravel, Oswin spoke again.

"Someone meant for us to fail."

Molten anger flowed through Gehn's veins as the treacherous events returned in full to his mind. Nearby, jutting at an angle from a pile of bricks, the cannon's dark, round muzzle gaped stupidly at the cloudy sky.

"We might've had a chance," Oswin struggled to make the words, "but they screwed us good."

"Strom." Gehn voiced with quiet spite. "Why would he do this?"

But the veteran had no answer.

Gehn worked quickly.

19

When he was finished, he gave the shelter a last, scrutinizing look, his eyes hunting for any break in the camouflage of shrubs and mud-slathered planks hidden within.

"They'll sniff us out." The veteran remarked as Gehn squeezed into the dim structure and shoved a mass of springy branches into the gap behind him.

Sealing away the mist and rain with a section of roof shingles, Gehn moved then to peer through the crack he'd left to serve as a peephole. He could see the dead beast out there, a hulking mountain in the gray, and he couldn't help but picture the shape rise up by some godless force. "First one that comes sniffing here is going to get a sword straight up its nostril."

Oswin chuckled weakly at this and then abruptly stopped to cough. "You killed them." He said when he'd recovered. "If that's true, it was luck. Leave me here. You're only wasting your own time."

"Rotation comes tomorrow." Gehn reasoned. "They can help you."

"You really think *rotation* will come?" The old man snapped with sudden vigor. "Use your head, boy. All bets are off."

"I doubt Egan's entire military was in on this."

"Not the entire military, just one man with control." The old veteran slowly shook his head. His words became delicate again. "If rotation does come, they won't be coming to take us home."

Gehn thought of the General. "It doesn't make sense."

"It doesn't have to. The men of Dain have become desperate to ensure their own survival. For all we know, we were a... a tactical experiment."

Gehn remained silent. Outside, the rain had gotten heavier. Drops were finding ways through the low, assorted roof to trickle and fall.

"Leave." Oswin said. "Flee from Dain."

"I'm not leaving you to die. I can risk waiting one more day."

Oswin sighed and looked away before muttering something beneath his breath. He fell into a fit of hoarse coughs.

20

Gehn realized that he was touching the wounds in his upper left arm. The holes from the dognar's teeth stared like many, sunken eyes as dark and as dead as those of their inflictor.

The holes had stopped oozing. The only blood around them had long dried.

Night had fallen.

Darkness hung inside the shelter like thick smoke. Gehn sat deep in thought as Oswin lie sleeping nearby. Sometimes the veteran's breathing would go still, and Gehn would wait and listen and prepare to give the man a good shove if the silence lingered too long.

But the quiet rhythm always resumed.

"You killed them." The old man's words echoed. "If that's true, it was luck."

Gehn recalled what he'd seen in the dognar's eyes in that initial moment. He'd felt not terror itself as the men in the tales did, but instead a sense of familiarity, like an obstinate riddle that his mind now strained to answer.

He recalled the power he'd felt and could not suppress the tremor that ran through his body now.

There came several rapid, muffled sloshes from outside.

Gehn moved to the peephole and tightened his grip on the handle of his sword. He saw only blackness.

His comrade's faint voice took him by surprise.

"Your eyes..."

It was too dark to see anything, but Gehn looked to where he thought the man's face might be. He was sure Oswin was talking in his sleep.

"Your eyes were blue flames." The man said, and then began to softly snore.

Chapter 2

(12 years earlier)

THE STRANGER

"All of you have come on short notice and even shorter information." King Linus began, his gray beard an even mixture of pure blacks and whites. Even in the dense, crimson fabrics that dominated the throne room, his words resonated on the strips of dark, exposed stone. "Many have traveled far," He added, and now, any air of warmth disappeared from his demeanor, "but only one will be chosen."

At this, the group of robed figures began to whisper to one another.

"The rest of you," Linus added, "will be compensated for your time."

With a deep breath, Alcris rolled up the scroll in his hands and set it onto the pile of documents that currently occupied the corner of the throne platform. Whether daylight still existed beyond the chamber's lofty curtains, he couldn't guess, and as he looked down toward the crowd, he heard the grumbled question: "What's this about?"

"I've one requirement." The king's pitch-black irises studied the faces below him. The corner of his mouth pulled back to form something halfway between smile and sneer. "None of you will breathe a word about what is discussed here tonight. If any man thinks he might have difficulty with that stipulation, he can know that I have spies in every kingdom from here..."

"From here to the North Sea." Alcris whispered the words to himself in perfect accord with the king.

"Close the doors from the outside." Linus ordered.

Alcris looked toward the doors now to see a cloaked, hooded man slip between them, pass the two guards and stop just beyond the glow of the muttering braziers. He watched as the two armored, spear-toting figures moved in and took the newcomer's arms.

"Hold it." One of them voiced.

"Wait." The king squinted. "Leave him be."

The guards obeyed and then closed themselves out of the chamber with a gentle *kathunk*.

The man in the cloak pulled his hood back, revealing lengthy, dark hair, and Alcris glimpsed a semblance of his own father in the hard and hawkish profile. For a fleeting moment, the stranger's eyes locked with his own.

"Now then." The king scanned the chamber as though he suspected an intruder behind one of the blood-hued curtains. The tips of his ringed fingers drummed on the throne's gilded, lion-paw armrests. He shook his head slightly now, as though displeased by his own thoughts. "There's an intriguing rumor making its way around, one that claims that the western dwarves are working to build a machine that will be capable of raising a body from the dead. It is my intention not only to build it first, but to answer yet another riddle with the very same stroke. That is why you are here."

A brief span of silence followed. As quiet chuckles rattled in the crowd, Alcris read amusement on every face there except one.

"Impossible, your Majesty." One of the men finally blurted with a fading smile as the king's focus fell upon him. "What I mean is that these rumors have no validity."

"Fallacies." Chimed another. "Death is a boundary that technology simply will never cross."

"The rumor may hold truth."

At this statement, the robes turned toward the man who had spoken, the dark-cloaked newcomer, to stare.

23

"I've read in detail about devices that can heal devastating wounds in a matter of days." The man went on, his dim, gray eyes and cadaverous expression set on the king. "There is even talk of the power to restore lost limbs."

"Nonsense." A voice from the crowd challenged.

"Tell us, friend," one of the more garish robes addressed the stranger now, his words thick with specious good will, "what exactly is your area of expertise?"

Never looking at his inquisitor, the dark-haired man answered: "Science."

This time, the men laughed without restraint.

"I'd assume that's why you've come." The robe replied with a toothy, well-maintained smile. "But whether you truly belong amongst *us*," he gestured to the crowd with a brisk sweep of his hand, "is a thing that remains to be seen. And as you've spoken about the works of others, perhaps it's time that you disclose what you yourself have accomplished. Yes? Tell us, what would you consider your greatest scientific feat?"

The stranger said nothing.

Alcris glanced up at the king to see him watching intently.

"Well?" The robe pressed. "Have you nothing at all?"

"Once," the stranger started, and by his downcast visage it seemed as if he were about to share a long-kept secret, "I cured a young boy of his illness."

Alcris felt his mouth break open to a slit.

"Illness?" The robe said impatiently.

"He asked too many questions, you see." As the stranger's unblinking eyes lifted to meet those of King Linus, they seemed to fill with life. "So I fed him a phial of acid."

There was a moment of wordless tension in which Alcris could see the rage steadily rising in the robe's face like froth nearing the brim of a boiling pot.

A smile appeared within the king's blended beard.

Alcris spoke now. "What is your name?"

"Eleazar."

"And have you brought anything along with you?" Alcris touched one of the scrolls to denote. "Any testament to your abilities?"

Reaching into his cloak, Eleazar produced a small, leather-bound book and stepped forward to place it in Alcris's waiting hand.

Alcris turned through a few pages, glanced up, and then shifted closer to the throne so that the king could also see the book's contents. "You have an interest in the Ancients."

"They're the last great mystery." Eleazar replied.

Alcris brought the book inches from his eyes for a moment. "Between eight and ten thousand years. I think many scholars might disagree with you. And you theorize here that their disappearance was linked to a certain catastrophic event."

Eleazar said nothing.

Skimming through the booklet before handing it to Linus, Alcris asked: "Where are you from?"

"Far away." Eleazar said.

"He's a swindler if there ever was one." The garish robe injected. "I'm sure I saw him ride in on his snake oil wagon just this morning."

Eleazar couldn't help a smug smile. "Come see me when you need a refill, friend."

At this, the robes' whispers rose nearly to a clamor.

"*Quiet.*" King Linus spat, his lightless irises still locked on the book in his hands.

The throne room fell silent but for the gentle snapping of the brazier flames and the king's careful turning of the worn, browned pages.

"These drawings," Linus finally said, "you've built these machines?"

"All of them." Eleazar answered.

As Alcris turned again to regard Linus, the king handed him back the booklet, and then looked at him with a near-imperceptible nod.

Beyond the lantern's circle of light, the city streets were colorless beneath the gaze of the moon. Alcris led the way between the dark and deathly-silent buildings of stone.

"I expected such a large city to be noisier." Eleazar voiced behind him.

Alcris looked up from the cobblestones to see a dot of amber hovering above a distant archway: the torchlight of a watchful sentry. "There is a curfew." He replied. "No one ventures out past sundown unless they enjoy being interrogated."

"You have special privileges?"

"As do you, though it will take some time before the guards know you."

Eleazar seemed to ponder this for a moment. "Capitol has a problem with crime?"

Alcris pulled a deep and inaudible breath. "It has a troubled history." He said at last. "Let's just say that the king is a firm believer in loyalty through limitation."

Eleazar chuckled. "I wouldn't have guessed."

A tongue of orange flame shone suddenly from a nearby alley and caught both men in its light. Beneath it, a half-armored figure stared from the shadows of a glossy helmet.

"Grand Magus." The sentry said. "You're out late tonight."

Just moments later, Alcris passed his lantern to Eleazar and fumbled with the iron lock hanging from the center of the storehouse doors. "Having seen your knowledge of the Ancients, I assume that you're familiar with what lies in the clifflands south of here."

"Yes." Eleazar said. "I've heard of it."

"A discovery was made several miles away from it." With a *click*, Alcris removed the lock and pulled one of the two broad doors outward to reveal darkness. He continued speaking once the door was closed and secured behind him and his companion. "Two bodies were unearthed." He gestured for the lantern back.

Eleazar handed it to him. The man's face was a statue of expectancy.

26

"Despite being as hard as stone, both are impossibly well preserved." Alcris explained, leading Eleazar through angled, needle-thin moonbeams and echoes indicative of empty space. "I might've tried to dissuade Linus, but I was too curious."

They came now toward the structure's center where two wooden crates appeared in the dim light, one roughly the size and shape of a coffin and the second massive enough to have housed an entire carriage.

The two men stopped before the objects now, and as Alcris eyed the larger of them, he encountered an inexplicable chill that raised the hairs on his arms.

After a moment, Eleazar stepped forward and touched the wooden panels of the same crate. "Something tells me, Grand Magus," he said, nodding once slightly, as though to himself, "this is going to be your greatest work."

Chapter 3

(Present time)

THE FOREST AND THE DREAM

Gehn trudged through drying mud. The rain clouds were dormant, the low fog unusually thin, but without a compass, he found judging direction impossible in this place. Having no clear view of the sun and no road to follow, he could only move with the hope that he was heading south.

It'd been two days since the beasts' attack. This morning he'd awakened to find Oswin pale and lifeless, the old man's stiff hands having clawed deep into the wood. Whatever terrible pain the veteran had suffered in his final moments of life, he'd suffered it in proud silence.

"Not the entire military," the past words of Oswin echoed, "just one man with control."

"Why?" Gehn whispered angrily to no one.

He'd been walking for many hours now, and he'd begun to believe that he was heading the wrong direction when the sight of some verdant bushes told differently. A wood materialized in the mist ahead, the twisted trees bearing smooth, white bark and leafless branches that resembled bones. Somewhere nearby, a crow fussed like a peevish, old woman.

As he went, he discovered that the ground steadily inclined and seemed to tilt the forest toward the sunken lands at his back. He climbed an embankment infested with roots and rusty moss as thick as wool, and, at last, he came to stand on solid ground.

He could see now, beyond the haze and the most distant bone trunks, a deep green that could only be pine trees.

Heat. Intense heat. He felt as if he'd been submerged in a vat of boiling oil.

Gehn opened his eyes only to have them scalded. With a drowned cry, he closed them again, thrashing desperately now against what felt like a smooth surface curved around him.

The burning agony intensified with every second.

He woke with a hissing, indrawn breath. Night had fallen, and he found himself sitting on the forest floor in a den built of foliage, his back against a sturdy sapling. He twitched at the sobering touch of the crisp, evening air; he had not planned to fall asleep here.

There came a sudden crashing from the bushes a short distance away. Expecting the worst, Gehn felt for the sword at his belt, the rifle strapped to his left shoulder having become second choice. Unable to discern anything through the screen of starlit leaves, he gripped the sword's handle but didn't yet unsheathe it. The crashing rose again, closer this time, and then, abruptly, stopped.

Moving silently into a crouching position, he listened for a dognar's heavy, grating breaths, but his ears made out only the hypnotic chorus of night frogs. Seconds passed, and now, as he focused, he was sure he could see movement.

The beast made an inquisitive snort and then broke away through the foliage with a squeal of terror.

Relieved, Gehn let go of the hilt and settled back against the sapling. 'Just a boar.'

Crash! Crash! *CRASH!*

Gehn jerked forward at the new sounds, his fingers digging into the cold, spongy earth. There came the squealing again, more frantic this time, and then the *crack* and *smash* that spelled the ruin of a small tree. What followed was an unequivocal snarl.

With a noise like crunching bone, the squealing immediately ceased, and now, an unseen monster gorged upon its prey.

Heart racing, Gehn crept forward and pushed a cluster of leaves aside to behold, some thirty strides away, not one but several pairs of dognar eyes like a swarm of red fireflies. As the creatures snapped and snarled greedily over the kill, Gehn followed the wind stealthily away.

The morning sun's rays were brief through the clouds, but just a glimpse was enough to reinforce his sense of direction.

For as far as he could see, bright ferns dominated the forest floor. Above them, densely-packed pines stood like endless, indifferent spirits.

Gehn went warily, often pausing behind a trunk to watch and listen.

Not wanting to attract the attention of the beasts he'd managed to avoid in the night, he resisted an urge to use the rifle when a family of speckled ground hens crossed his path and stopped to nervously observe him. He instead tried to appease his empty stomach with three crackers and a strip of dried meat, and while it worked for the present, he knew that there was barely enough food in the pouch to last him two more days. Traveling on foot, he gauged that the Green Hills Fort was a week away.

'Rotation.' He thought bitterly.

Taking a gulp from his canteen, Gehn thought of the dream again, of the boiling pain that he could still almost feel. He'd never known a dream to bring pain the way this one had.

The sight of azure through the branches above stole his attention. There were fewer ferns and bushes here, and the pines were more widely-spaced. He now glimpsed, broken by the black silhouettes of the farthest trees, a stretch of golden countryside, and he couldn't keep the smile from his lips.

Beneath open sky, Gehn strode through tall, yellow stalks. A gust caught him halfway up the hill and brought the surrounding grass into a thousand shifting waves.

As he came to the top, the confidence he'd previously felt in his whereabouts changed to puzzlement. Dain was primarily green, but from here he could see only the perpetual, golden hills of an unknown land. Even the distant mountain peaks, so far away that they seemed translucent in the whitish haze that clung to the horizon, appeared alien to him.

He stood here for a while, scanning for a landmark that would not be found. Instead, he spotted a trio of dark, bristly objects jutting up from beyond the crest of another hill. Something about their appearance struck him as artificial, and as he squinted now he thought that he could see holes in them like small windows.

He started toward the half-hidden shapes, never noticing a series of craters in the shadowed valley behind him.

At closer sight, the fortification had the appearance of a colossal insect nest. Between the cannon-ports like countless, staring eyes, great spikes of black charged the multifaceted walls. It occurred to Gehn that no dognar would have an easy time breaching such a shell, and while this should have been a welcome thought, he only felt unnerved by the stillness. The fort was no ruin. If it had been abandoned, it had been abandoned recently.

Several lookout spires rose from the outer wall, and a single massive tower stood in what looked to be the center. Other than the flapping bronze flags and the two, curious ravens leaping from perch to perch, there was no activity.

He stopped some fifty yards from the open entrance. Even from here, he could see that the archway was so low that he'd have to duck to get under the pointed teeth of its fully-raised portcullis. Peering now at the gate is if it were the gaping jaws of a trap, he called: "Is anyone there?"

Only the wind answered, ripping through the metal spines ahead with whistles and screeches. Then he heard something like the *creak* of a hinge, and he spotted, pointing toward him from one of the hollow circles, a rifle's muzzle.

"*Don't sh...*"

The weapon's echoing *crack* drowned him out, and there was a short-lived droning noise before the pain struck his lower left

31

leg. He looked down to see, not the mangled hole he'd expected, but a feather-finned dart buried in his flesh like a metal parasite.

He leaned down and pulled it out easily, eying its narrow, crimson-coated head for a moment before dropping it to the dust. Then he felt what he thought was warm blood filling his boot until he realized that the sensation was also flowing upward, reaching up through his veins in tingling, numbing tendrils. Within seconds, his entire leg succumbed to uselessness.

Gehn stumbled forward onto his hands and turned his eyes up toward the gate, seeing a blur of figures like child-sized shadows emerging to approach him.

He thought to reach for the sword, but he no longer had arms or hands to do such a thing. His body no longer consisted of bone or muscle but had evaporated into churning vapor, and then the world drew away from him at ever-increasing speed.

UNWELCOME

"He's waking!" A strident voice cried.

Regaining his senses, Gehn discovered that he was half-curled on his side, on the circular floor of what appeared to be a bronze cage. Afternoon sunlight shone in through the bars, slow-burning his exposed forearm.

"That dose should have kept him out until nightfall." Another voice chimed.

He propped himself up against the bars and saw that he was not alone in the cramped prison. A gaunt, scruffy-bearded man in dirty rags stared back at him from the shadier side.

With the sounds of a clinking, clanking chain, the cage abruptly lurched and began to rise into the air.

Gehn didn't have to check to know that the sword and rifle were gone. Grunting, he made to stand. This was a shaky process due to the unstable floor and to his own lingering dizziness, but he'd soon gotten to his feet and now had each hand on a rounded bar of bronze. All around him, watching or

32

waddling here and there across the flat, dry ground were short, thickly-bearded people.

Dwarves.

"Well look at this fella!" The closest of them, ruddy-haired and leaning on a rifle as if it were a staff, exclaimed. "Been awake a few seconds and he's already on his feet!"

Gehn scanned the interior of the fortress. Lined up behind the wall's crowded cannons were massive, iron catapults, each one's bomb-loaded thrower fashioned to resemble a titan's gripping hand. Sentries wielding spyglasses stood atop the towers that had once appeared empty.

"I was the one to tag you, so you know." Red-beard smiled and brought his free hand up from his belt to give the rifle's barrel a flick.

"What do you want?" Gehn calmly asked as his prison continued to ascend. He spotted the dwarf doing the work, stout and young, bearing a cropped black band of facial hair. The dwarf drew in chain by cranking a wooden wheel.

To Gehn's left, most of the small audience observed from atop a few stacks of crates that had been assembled like tiered seats.

Red-beard answered. "We want to know what you're doing on this side of the Yullid."

'Yullid?' Gehn wondered. Then he recalled the river that separated the human territory from that of the dwarves. 'The Ulad.'

"My friend here can sniff out a lie." Red-beard gestured to one of his nearby companions: a helmet-wearer with a beard like a scraggly raccoon tail. "We don't appreciate fabrications."

At last, the young dwarf stopped turning and the cage now gently swayed some ten feet above the ground.

Gehn had already spied the tall, steel lever behind the crank-wheel. "Didn't realize that I was on the wrong side of the Ulad."

"Oh, no?" The sharpshooter tilted his head forward and raised his bushy, red caterpillar eyebrows in mock surprise. Behind him, a dwarf gave a high-pitched chortle.

33

Despite just how preposterous Gehn knew his tale would sound, the thought of making one up on the spot somehow felt even more foolish.

"I haven't got all day." Red-beard pressed.

"I was sent to man a tower in the Great Swamp." Gehn explained. "My companions were killed when two dognars attacked us."

The sharpshooter squinted skeptically as Raccoon-tail whispered into his ear. He spoke again: "A tower in the middle of the Swamp? That's a risky venture, even for you humans to take. What's the payoff?"

"I'm a soldier." Gehn dryly replied, though the very same question had been haunting him. "I only do as I'm told."

Red-beard turned to look up at Gehn sidelong. "So the dognars killed your companions and you somehow escaped?"

"I was knocked unconscious when the tower came down. When I woke, the beasts were gone."

The sharpshooter simply squinted up at him now. The dwarf turned toward the helmeted Raccoon-tail, who offered nothing more than a subtle shrug, and then looked back up at his captive.

Hearing a stir behind him in the cage, Gehn glanced back to see the ragged human rise to his feet and take hold of the bars at his sides. The man whispered something that Gehn couldn't make sense of.

Red-beard looked toward the young dwarf at the wheel and nodded.

"Wait." Gehn said.

But the lever was pulled. With a *chank* the wheel spun wildly and the cage went into free fall.

Gehn tightened his grip on the bars. His stomach had fully occupied his chest just as the cage hit a sudden jounce mere inches from the ground. He'd managed to keep himself from collapsing, but by the loud curses at his back, he guessed that his fellow prisoner had failed.

While the audience of dwarves howled with laughter, Red-beard only smiled and took several steps closer. "So." The dwarf said at the sight of Gehn's savage glare. "Your true feelings

34

come out. Don't lie to me again, or next time it goes all the way to the ground."

"You idiot." Snarled the haggard man. "You fool. Tell them the truth."

Gehn thought if he reached out quick enough he could take the dwarf by the beard and satisfy his ire, but he guessed that this action would be suicide.

With the sound of clanking, the bronze prison started to ascend once more.

Deciding that he didn't care whether his captors believed his story or not, Gehn gave a deep breath through flared nostrils and finally spoke. "I slew the beasts."

"How?"

"I put my sword through them."

The cage stopped at Red-beard's hand signal.

Dwarves that had been passing by or paying half attention now watched and listened intently. Any mirth had vanished from their bushy faces. "Impossible." One of them uttered.

The sharpshooter's expression never changed. He turned to one of his companions, who had produced Gehn's blade, and he took it. While it was almost too heavy for the dwarf to hold with one hand, this didn't stop him from scrutinizing its double-edge as if he might catch a clue that would attest his captive's claim. He chuckled quietly. "You're even crazier than that other one in there."

"No." Taking hold of his left sleeve and the crude bandage beneath it, Gehn pulled both up past his shoulder and revealed the two rows of large, red holes in his flesh.

For the first time, the sharpshooter appeared dumbfounded. He passed the blade to Raccoon-tail and now approached his prisoner for a closer inspection. Several other dwarves followed cautiously, as though the cage contained a dangerous animal.

Still glaring, Gehn knelt to accommodate them.

By the movements of his lips, Red-beard appeared to be counting the wounds. Then his eyes rose to meet with Gehn's and he said: "You could have done those to yourself."

The haggard prisoner broke in nervously: "I think he's telling the truth, Chief. I really do."

"Hush, you." Raccoon-tail croaked.

"Those were made by dognar teeth." One of the closer dwarves stated. "I'd bet a week's wages on it."

"Never seen anyone make it out alive with such wounds." Added another. "Not when a dognar gets *that* close to you. A giant might survive. Not a man. Can't be real."

"Alright." Red-beard said. "I think we've had enough. Hoist em' up and let em' sit for a while."

As the bronze cage rose and the cluster of dwarves hesitantly dispersed, Gehn stood. "How long do you plan to keep me?" He inquired, but received no answer.

"Make yourself at home." Suggested his fellow prisoner.

Gehn half-turned. His question was not for the sake of small talk. "How long have you been here?"

"Not really sure. Few months maybe."

Gehn's eyes drifted down past the cannons and catapults and toward the sandy ground to which a few stubborn patches of golden grass still clung. "Tell me that's a joke."

"Wish I could."

Spotting Red-beard and his helmeted companion speaking near one of the immense, black catapults now, Gehn called out: "Hey!"

The haggard man shushed him.

"Release me, and I'll make sure you're compensated for it!"

Red-beard answered Gehn without looking at him. "That's doubtful! Now quiet down!"

Gehn felt rage building inside him once again. The desire to express it, to spit out words like bitter poison from his mouth, was restrained only when he saw the young dwarf return to the crank-wheel and, smiling, wrap his stubby fingers around the release lever.

"I'll let you down if you like." The dwarf said.

"You make them drop us again," the haggard man breathed, "and I'll kill you."

Chapter 4

(10 years earlier)

THE PROVERB

Two years of intensive experimentation flashed before his eyes in an instant, every soul-taxing failure and every small yet glorious success; every glass tube and crude drawing and tiny, intricate tool seemed to dance from the shadows before him. Legions of bolts rolled to their designated places over great, candlelit shapes of glass and steel. Somewhere, the sound of a furnace bellows could be heard, air rushing in and out and in and out, louder and louder like the breathing of an unspeakable beast.

Alcris woke with a jolt. He was exactly where he'd left himself, sitting at the desk in the basement laboratory, a single candle burning at its corner. His right hand rested on his open project journal and clutched a purple feather pen. The past years of hard work began to settle inside him, to dissolve into the months and days and hours that had risen from the archives of his mind.

Standing from the desk, Alcris took the candle in his hand and approached the object that towered in the corner of the chamber: the eight-foot cylinder of glass. He made slowly toward it and toward his own lengthening, distorted reflection in its rounded surface. As he drew close, the fluid inside reacted to the candle's light and began to glow faintly blue. There, suspended as though in an ocean's serene depths, a partial silhouette could be discerned: a manlike shape as toned as any hero sculpture.

Placing his hand against the warm glass, Alcris turned to face the arched, shadow-filled corridor leading into the laboratory's second chamber. Even from here, he could feel the creeping, cold air as though the passage were an open doorway to the wintry streets above.

Then his eyes moved to Eleazar's desk and he saw a note consisting of two words:

Palace

tonight

"Friends," The king's hard-edged voice saturated the dining hall, continuing only once the boisterous stories and the clinking of knives and forks had fallen completely silent, "ever since the dawn of time, man has sought to take the power back from God. I've brought you here tonight to tell you that man, at long last, has succeeded." Linus scanned his guests with coal-black eyes. "I make no exaggerations when I say that we have arrived at the most monumental human achievement of our generation, and of likely every generation to come."

At this, there came an outbreak of whispers that spanned the table's length.

Alcris glanced across the table to see Eleazar staring at the king, his head tilted forward slightly with the look of a modest man uncomfortably anticipating public praise.

"There is little more I can say now except to give credit to the talent and skill," The king raised his goblet, "to the endless hours of toil and dedication that it took to forge this reality." His pleasure slowly manifested within his blended gray beard. "Here's to the two greatest living wizards in this realm or any other... to Alcris LeQuinn and Eleazar Dauntille."

The people clumsily, merrily stood and raised their gold vessels. "TO ALCRIS AND ELEAZAR!" They resounded, and drank now as the king did.

As the guests sat again, steaming dishes floated down by the hands of servants. From the chamber's far end, a chorus of female voices began a song of Dain's rolling, green splendor.

Cutting into a slab of tender meat, Alcris looked once more toward Linus. At the king's left sat his Queen: a strikingly-beautiful woman with porcelain skin and hair that all but matched her red lips. At the king's right sat Prince Egan, the raven-haired son not quite in his teens, watching the goings-on with keen eyes of faded blue. A pale complexion seemed only to enhance the boy's already-handsome features.

"It's truly amazing what you've done." A voice caught Alcris's ear: Eleazar's plump, fuchsia-faced neighbor at the table, clutching a goblet of wine as closely and awkwardly as a young child would a toy. "Wizard's work. Truly astonishing."

"How could you possibly know what we've done?" Eleazar's words were listless, his eyes fixed on his surgery with a fork and knife.

"Astonishing." The guest repeated, seemingly oblivious to this question. He gulped more wine and followed it with a lip-smack and a breath of satisfaction. "I assume you both heard about our visitor."

Alcris suppressed his curiosity.

"Claims he's come to share information with us." The man went on. "Secret technologies."

"Secret technologies?" Alcris grumbled. "For a price, I'm sure."

"That or a peek at our work." Eleazar crisply added, severing a square of meat to prop it up on the end of an angled, gleaming fork. "A devil often comes bearing gifts." He glanced up at Alcris briefly before placing the food between his teeth to chew.

About to take a bite of his own, a shock of frigid adrenaline suddenly filled Alcris. He found himself transported back to his youth, to the vision of a lofty silhouette against an archway filled with golden sunlight. His fork slowly fell as he aimed his focus at his cohort. "Where did you hear that?"

Eleazar stared with confusion.

"That proverb." Prince Egan inserted. "Is it well known?"

"...Oh." The dark-haired wizard finally muttered. He squinted and shook his head dismissively. "I'm sure I've heard it a hundred times."

"I've never heard it before." The prince stated.

"Do you know the one about children?" Eleazar asked without looking at the boy.

Egan's answer held no shame. "That they should be seen, not heard?"

"No. I meant the one that says they're a precious gift."

At this, Linus chuckled.

Conversation continued all around Alcris. The words became meaningless to his ears. For several seconds, he merely stared at the man across from him. When Eleazar's eyes met his again, any friendliness in them had been replaced by a glimmer of quiet hostility.

Snowflakes tumbled gently from the night sky as Alcris made through Capitol's empty streets. He turned the corner just in time to see a cone of yellow brilliance draw thin and then vanish from the cobblestones directly in front of his house.

Seconds later, he came down the last of the steps and into the dim basement lab and the soft bubbling of its pipe-fed machines.

Beyond the glass cylinder and its silent occupant, the passage to the lab's deepest chamber held a trace of light. A shadow passed the far, clay-red wall on which tools and other iron hardware hung like pieces of art.

Alcris felt his heart thundering in his chest now, his blood a toxic mixture of fear and rage. "A devil often comes bearing gifts." He said as he entered the arched corridor of stone, his breath meeting the frigid air around him to make curling, silver tufts. He could partly see the man he'd known for two years as

40

Eleazar. The hooded shape faced away from him and toward the chamber's massive centerpiece: the lab's second cylinder, so large that it nearly filled the entirety of the space. Its surface gleamed like a core of pure obsidian.

"Before tonight, there was only one man I'd ever heard use that phrase," Alcris said as he stepped into the candle's light and stopped, "and that was our father."

The shape before him didn't turn.

"All the precautions you must have taken..." Alcris couldn't help a tiny, bitter laugh, "your face, this new identity you created for yourself. What are you here for? Revenge?"

"Not on you," The man replied now, "despite your cowardly actions."

"I was only a boy." Alcris said through his teeth. He shook his head so slightly that it could have been a tremble. "You weren't the one they questioned."

"I would've had the sense to keep my mouth shut." The man that called himself Eleazar turned his head back, but he didn't look directly at Alcris. "Your words doomed our entire family."

"So what now?" Alcris asked. "When the king finds out who you are, he'll likely kill us both."

The man looked again toward the curve of glass. He spoke with quiet confidence. "He won't find out."

It was then that Alcris glanced at the nearby wall and noticed a tall, T-shaped emptiness amidst the tools there. He didn't see the object in the man's hands until it was too late.

The sledgehammer struck his cheekbone with sickening force.

He hit the cold floor, blood drooling from his open mouth as he tried to push himself up. The last thing he saw was his brother standing over him, eyes wide and teeth bared, lifting the hammer high for a second strike.

The iron drum was heavy, its contents sloshing lethargically as Eleazar made the last few yards and set it down beside the others with a solid *thud*. He moved then to the center of the mostly-

41

empty level of the house, the acrid smell of chemicals settling around him as he dropped one knee onto the floor's stained, wooden panels. His fingers slipped into the man-made holes and his hands tensed, and with the steady creak of an old tree straining against a breeze, the basement's golden light shone up around the edges of a monstrous trapdoor.

Below him, a surface of dark liquid quivered and shimmered with the air's displacement. Seconds passed as he simply peered into the cylinder's depths, and when the pair of scarlet orb eyes appeared to stare up into his, it was with the swiftness of a being that had only been half asleep.

MONUMENTAL ACHIEVEMENT

Except for the scattered patches of snow still clinging to the shadows of the pines and the few pale boulders, winter's presence was strangely absent from the hills southeast of Capitol. High in an all but cloudless sky, a bright sun ate away at the air's remaining chill.

King Linus turned his ambling horse off of the snaking ridge trail and toward an open stretch of hillside. He brought the animal to a halt. From here, the view on his kingdom was one of his favorites, due mainly to the distant palace's lofty towers being visible, as well as the very top of Capitol's steadfast wall. He would have enjoyed the moment more if it had not been for the vulture-infested stag carcass some twenty strides below him in a bed of grass and snow.

Linus caught a glimpse of his son speeding down through bushes and trees on his dark steed. Egan triggered an explosion of screeching birds before veering out of sight.

'At least he's good at something other than reading books.' Linus thought.

"Sire."

The king had almost forgotten about his rifle-toting escort. "Yes what is it?" He mumbled.

"Someone's coming."

42

Linus turned his black eyes down the path behind him and saw another rider approaching through the slanted rays of sunlight. He knew by the man's bright and elaborate armor, mainly the golden helmet topped by a maroon plume, that it was one of his couriers.

"Highness." The man stopped and dismounted to tromp the last few yards on foot. He removed a gauntlet and used his bare hand to delve into the bag attached to his belt. "I was told that it's important." He produced a tan envelope.

Squinting with interest, Linus took it and flipped it to regard the perse-hued wax seal. Instead of a horizontal line, the imprinted "A" held a single staring eye fringed by sharp leaves.

Linus opened the envelope. He pulled out a rectangle of paper and unfolded it to recognize the fluent handwriting of the Grand Magus:

Your Majesty,

You'll be pleased to know that the Sleeper has begun to stir.
Before we share this monumental achievement with the realm, it is only right that you be the first to see the fruit of your wisdom.
I humbly request that you would meet us at sundown.

 -Alcris

The sun had begun its dive below the horizon when the party reentered Capitol, the land's mass shadow steadily climbing the western wall as the season's cold swept back in like floodwater.

Prince Egan rode close behind his father, his ebon hair feeling to him like a trampled crown from all of the wind and sweat. While the king's skilled escorts were ghosts in the field, here, clomping along on the mostly empty street in a somewhat jumbled arrangement, the boy thought they looked amusingly awkward.

43

Linus led on without word or expression, but with obvious purpose.

Finding himself now on an unfamiliar street lined with tall, narrow houses like oversized pickets, Egan asked: "Where are we going?"

The king gave no answer.

"Evening, Sire!" A jug-cradling man called from the steps of a corner building.

One of the king's escorts threw a stern "*Hey*" at the culprit, but the commotion had already attracted a host of new eyes in the windows and doorways. Shutters creaked open one after another.

The sun's last light lingered on the tops of the chimneys as the party came halfway to the street's end. Egan spotted, on a rooftop's point, a dark gray cat perched and leering like a gargoyle.

"This is it." Linus pulled his steed to a stop only to blink at the house as though he weren't entirely sure. A rush of wind pulled at his evenly-mixed beard.

Egan turned to look across the many inquisitive faces in the dim buildings behind. In one open doorway, a family of seven stood crowded, each of them expressionless but for a boy close to Egan's age. The adolescent glowered with such intensity that the prince did a double take before timidly averting his eyes.

"Someone knock." Linus huffed.

Then the door at the top of the steps swung silently open. A voice issued from just within the threshold of shadow. "You're early."

"Nonsense, we're right on time." The king prepared to dismount. By his tone, his next words were more command than suggestion. "Maybe you could light a lamp, Alcris?"

"There is no Alcris here."

The king turned to peer up into the darkness of the doorway.

Egan felt his blood run cold even before he saw the riders stiffen in their saddles. He recognized Eleazar's voice, but the contempt in it now was unmistakable.

44

"Tell me," the unseen speaker inquired, "do you remember his father?"

The king's growing sneer revealed a sliver of teeth. "What?" He hissed.

Instantly, one of the riders was in front of Linus and had a rifle raised toward the open door. The other escorts readied their own weapons and shifted their steeds to form a curved wall around their king and his son.

The voice went on. "He was the man they begged to take your place."

Before the king's men could act further, a thunderous *BOOM* shook the house that caused their battle-trained horses to shift and whinny nervously.

BOOM! Windows rattled and dust fumed from the house's lower section. Through the cloud, Egan saw that gaping cracks had appeared. Frigid air tore at the boy's lungs now, his breath coming out in cones of steam.

BOOM!!

"Sire," the leading escort said, "take your son and get back to the palace!"

Linus could only stare in wide-eyed bewilderment.

BOOM!!! Windows shattered. Massive chunks of stone fell. Beyond the haze, from the blackness of a newly-formed hole as wide as a cave, there could be heard a deep, guttural growl.

The men opened fire.

CrackCrackCrack!

BOOM!!! With a final avalanche of debris, the fearsome shape came: a blur of speed and power amidst the riders and their shrieking horses. Hot blood spattered the prince's face just before a hand gripped the neck of his cloak and yanked: his father's flailing attempt to stay saddled on a panicked, rearing steed.

Both of them crashed to the cobblestones.

In his struggle to get up, Egan found himself strangled by the cloak's thin, metal chain. With a grunt he tore free from the garment and scrambled to the center of the street, and from there he turned to watch.

A torn cloak still draping from his fist, the kneeling king seemed to plead with the mountainous horror of scales and spines and dust and blood that glared at him from atop the pile of carnage.

The boy's ears caught a fragment of biting laughter from within the broken house.

"Please." Linus whimpered.

"Think of all the men that have ever pleaded with you." The wizard said. "Did you spare them?"

Linus tossed the cloak aside and raised his palms as if to show that he was unarmed. "I'll give you whatever you want! Please, show mercy!"

After a squint of disgust, Egan spun and sprinted toward the nearby alleyway just as his father's desperate words became screams. With a muffled sound like a roar through tightly-clamped fangs, that screaming stopped.

The prince slipped into the narrow space and turned to see a final, lifeless form drop from the terrible jaws, and though he looked, he couldn't tell where the tattered robes ended and the flesh began. Now the monster's eyes found him, and beneath the chorus of rising shouts and distant warning bells, he could only stare into the shining holes of red as his faith in the alley's safety dissolved away. Abruptly, the creature turned, and with a lash of its tail was gone.

With a *BOOM* that shook the cobblestones, the breached house vanished within a column of blinding flame. Tiny bits of smoldering wood and brick skittered past Egan's boots.

Some time had passed before he moved to exit the alleyway. He stopped at its edge and checked a city street alive with throbbing, orange light. Townsfolk watched nervously from doors partly open. A short burst of gunfire rang in the distance.

At last, he approached the mass between himself and the blaze. When he reached the bodies he simply stared.

He never turned when he heard the sprinting footsteps.

The sprinter halted.

"My king." A guard's panting voice came at last. "Are you hurt?"

Egan knew that the question had not been aimed at the mangled form still wearing the crown, but he didn't answer. Seconds went by filled with the sounds of the flames and snapping wooden beams, and then, gradually, he felt the crowd drawing in around him.

Just above the tangle of hushed words he discerned a single, muttered question: "Did you hear him beg?"

Anger tugged gently at the muscles of Egan's face. Every half-heard whisper became a judgment to his ears, and when, at last, he looked up, it was into the eyes of the same scowling boy he'd spotted earlier.

He heard the rapid approach of riders now, and as the crowd parted for them, it was as though they'd been pushed aside by a single, unmistakable voice: "Out of the way you sheep! Out of the way! And someone get those flames under control!"

Chapter 5

(Present time)

U-TURN

In the falling sun's light, the land of endless golden hills had turned a copper hue. Through it Gehn raced like a messenger with urgent news. His direction was sure now: he was heading straight east and straight toward human territory. His shadow reached out ahead of him, elongated in the tall grass like an otherworldly mimic, often bending and merging with the darkness that accumulated in the valleys as the day sank ever into the west.

When the sun vanished, Gehn gave in to his weariness and slowed to a jog. He'd hoped to find some kind of shelter for the night, but in the fleeting light, the hills of the horizon could've been barren sand dunes. At last, he stopped and stood panting, and was reminded all at once that he had no water to refresh his parched throat.

'The River.' He thought. He guessed at the distance he'd put between himself and the dwarves and he recalled the words of one of the bearded imps: "*Forty-five miles to the Yullid.*" He sat down in the grass and hung his head. He pictured the cool, dark water for a mere moment before an image of his escape overtook him: his hands on two bronze bars glowing like fired branding irons.

Then the evening's air grew cold. Gehn was certain that he felt the ground trembling softly beneath him, and the echoing bark he heard next came like a bitter knife.

He saw them when he looked up.

As swiftly as a pack of wolves they moved, following the ridge of the next hill from north to south, crossing his path almost exactly. Thinking that they hadn't yet seen him, he went flat on his stomach and now peered through the grass.

All but the last two creatures passed. The pair halted and turned in his direction, black silhouettes against the dim sky, their heads high and their red eyes fixed.

Inch by inch Gehn's hand crept toward his belt for the sword. But there was no sword; the dwarves had taken it from him before they'd thrown him into the dirty, stinking cage to rot.

"No." He whispered at the distant beasts, certain by this point that they were looking directly at him. "Not now."

The two dognars moved closer and then stopped again. One of them tilted its snout upward like a wolf searching for a scent on the air.

"*Not now.*"

All at once the monsters charged.

"Perfect." Gehn growled as he leapt up and fled back into the west.

High in the air he'd been, each hand on a sturdy, bronze bar, gently rocked by the breeze and by his own occasional shifting. Stale beams of afternoon sunlight hovered in the cage. Below him, the sounds of the dwarves had devolved into a less-than-intelligible din.

Opposite Gehn in the space, the haggard man snored, spittle oozing down from the man's mouth to hang from his beard in glistening stalactites.

Gehn's face had formed its own stubbly copse by this time. For five days he'd been a prisoner, and he was certain at this point that his captors had no plans to release him.

Again his mind drifted back to the swamp.

Strom stood before him in the air; the General was a frequent visitor. "Nothing personal, you understand." Strom said, a smug smile hidden partly beneath his gray mustache. His form began to dissipate in the wind. "Simply an experiment..."

Gehn's fists tightened on the bars. As he pulled, he never noticed the hairs rising on his arms.

The General's voice and frosty blue eyes were the last to fade. "...and for you, a matter of plain bad luck."

The metal gave.

For a few seconds, Gehn stared dumbly at a space between the bars easily large enough to fit his head through. He let go, glancing at his open hands and then back to the bent, bronze rods from which threads of white smoke rose.

He turned to find his fellow prisoner still fast asleep. A glance down through the bars confirmed that his captors were oblivious.

Sure that he'd already tested the metal's strength in the hours of tedium, he inspected the bars again before placing his rough hands on them. He pulled.

"*Hey!*"

With a twitch, he looked down only to see one dwarf calling to another. Breathing deeply, he brought his attention back to the bars and now readjusted his grip.

"It was a fluke." Came Oswin's hushed assertion from within. "A defect."

Gehn ignored this as he strove to widen the space before him, his brow furrowed and his taut arms trembling. He thought back to the two beasts he'd killed and the power he'd felt flowing through his body. As his doubts scattered like insects, warmth flickered to life in the muscles of his upper back. It crept through his shoulders and into his arms, and when it reached his hands, visible red heat spread through the metal nearest his closed fingers. The bronze again began to bend. Grunting he pulled, and seconds later found he'd made a gap so large that his knuckles touched the next bars out.

Gehn reversed the direction of his strength, forcing the rods back to their original positions. The moment he relaxed his grip, the metal lost its glow and faintly smoked.

50

The amazement he'd felt was nothing compared to the overwhelming prospect of freedom now. His eyes touched on the fortress's open gate before settling on the lever near the chain-coiled wheel.

He put his hands on the bronze bars and tightened his grip until a hint of glow again inhabited them. "Hey!" He called.

The gentle snoring behind him ceased.

"Let me down!"

"What are you doing?" Came the gruff voice behind him.

"*Hey!*" Gehn called, smiling now as he watched one of the dwarves approach the lever. "I dare you, you ugly little stub! I bet you can't even reach it!"

"*Stop you idiot!*"

Gehn felt the hand touch his back. He heard a loud *snap*, and saw a small, azure flash hit the bars around him. The haggard prisoner made a shrill cry of pain.

Then the lever was pulled, and as the rim of the spiked wall rushed upward, Gehn's eyes were on the open, golden hills beyond.

Twilight.

Under steadily-brightening stars, Gehn ran. He'd taken into the winding valleys in an attempt to lose his pursuers, and while this forced them to keep their snouts to the ground to sniff for him, he knew that they were getting closer.

His legs had depleted most of their strength in his sprint from the dwarven citadel. He now found himself heading back toward that place, hoping every time that he crossed a ridge that he would see the barbed towers above the dark and distant terrain, but all the miles he'd put between himself and his prior captors had turned to betray him.

Rounding a stony, barren turn, he glanced back and saw the first pair of malicious eyes emerge from between the hills behind.

He'd made it nearly to the top of a broken, crevice-scarred slope when a rock caught his foot and he came down hard onto

51

his hands. Seconds passed and he remained there, each breath seeming only to fuel the roaring fire in his lungs.

The grass shifted around him in a sudden rush of wind. Above the stalks' whispers there rolled a clear voice.

"Gehn."

He turned to see no one. Instead, his eyes discerned it several yards away and partially hidden under a tangle of curling, white weeds: the upper half of a corpse. It was unmistakably dwarven, and above the bearded, yawning skull, a fallen spire of a helmet bore, in its center, a blazing, upturned fist.

Gehn saw no sword, just a rusty pistol in one fleshless hand.

After a glance back, he came to the skeleton's side and snatched up the pistol to find its muzzle bizarrely fat. Knowing its purpose at once, he nimbly popped open the chamber to check if it was loaded.

A string of furious, snorting barks filled the valley behind him. Gehn closed the pistol with a *chack*.

He sprinted to the top of the hill and gasped with relief when he discerned, in the distance, the peaks of two familiar towers beyond the rolling landscape.

Then came the rhythm rising steadily behind him: the rapid thunder of heavy claws like war drums, and he knew that trying to evade the creatures without help would be fruitless.

Seeing the inevitable stretch of valley ahead, Gehn aimed the gun skyward and sent the flare with a hollow *crack*. He cast the pistol aside. High above, the burning projectile began to scintillate, blanketing the nearest hills with its white brilliance again and again like rapid bursts of lightning.

When he came to the top of the next ridge, the fortress could be seen almost in its entirety. Suddenly, up from behind its formidable wall, a fiery orange star ascended, swiftly at first before it slowed and then seemed to hang and brighten.

Gehn risked a look back to see the beasts break off to the left just before a new sound rose over that of his flying feet: a deafening, elemental bellow.

By now, the sky's fiery object had grown into an infernal sun. Certain that he'd sealed his own fate, Gehn veered down the amber-lit slope just as the bomb streaked down like a phoenix and vanished behind him.

BOOM!!!

The shockwave brought him skidding to his hands and knees in the dust.

He looked up toward the fortress to see another orange star rise against the ceiling of night. He sprung to his feet and raced away from a hill crowned in flames, and now, in the curved valley below, he saw the two shadows, great and lunging in avid pursuit.

He hit the valley floor and then was hastily climbing again, often on all fours as he struggled up an incline flanked by steep, grassy walls, and when he saw the pale boulders ahead, they first seemed like enemies, like the final agents of fate having come to hinder his escape. When he saw the fiery missile rushing down, he realized he was wrong.

With a cry, he tackled the barrier of stone and threw himself around it to fall to the dust and tuck into a ball.

BOOM!!!

The ground quaked and a searing wind rushed over him.

For a while, he stayed there curled and listening for any indication that the dognars had survived. He heard only flames.

Pushing himself up, he peered through a cleft in the granite and into the blaze, and he thought he could see, in the swirling column of amber, a heap of black scales and spines.

It was the sound that alerted him: a quiet scraping. He turned to find the other beast crawling low around the boulders like a hellish crocodile.

Gehn thrust himself away just in time from the snap of slavering jaws.

He ran several strides and turned to watch as the dognar straightened its legs beneath itself, its left eye a dripping hollow and a bloody, U-shaped gorge running the length of its side.

"*Stay back!*"

The beast did not stay back. One dragging claw after another it came, a hateful growl in the depths of its throat like a geyser stirring from its slumber. Its chin all but plowed the ground.

After a shake of his head, Gehn made for the top of the hill.

53

At last, he approached the bastion as a flare lanced upward from its torch-rimmed walls, edging the countless spikes and cannon muzzles with hard, white light and accentuating their ominous appearance.

"He's... right behind me!" Gehn shouted. "You can't miss!"

"Dangerous place out there, is it?!" Came the reply.

Gehn's eyes caught movement atop the tower above. Though he could not find the face of the speaker, he recognized the patronizing tone.

"Perhaps you should've stayed in the cage like a good boy!"

Panting, Gehn turned to check the whereabouts of his wounded adversary. Another flare shot skyward and painted the surrounding grass silver.

"Don't worry, he's stopped following you." Red-beard added. "He's in bad shape I'm afraid, so you'll have to be quick."

Gehn heard the whistle of steel seconds before a slender object landed a short distance from him with a metallic *thud*. His sword.

He stared at the weapon for a time and considered the task, doubts forming in his mind like dark, roiling clouds. He approached it and bent to tighten his fingers around its plain handle. When he lifted the blade, it felt to have doubled in weight. "Drop me some water!" He called, head tilted forward as he looked out over the visible curve of the hill. "I'll give you a fight!"

Above him, Red-beard chuckled. "I don't see how that's fair! What's one half-dead dognar to a mighty warrior such as yourself?"

"Get out there, human!" A second dwarf voice chimed. "Maybe you need some persuasion?!"

There came a loud *bang* and a spurt of ground peppered the side of Gehn's boot. He didn't flinch. "If I win," he called, "you let me leave this place without a target on my back! And you give me a full canteen for the road!"

The second dwarf voice was fast to respond. "This isn't a negotiation of terms!"

54

"Make that three canteens!" Gehn shouted. "Do we have a deal?!"

A low buzz of discussion followed and was then drowned out by Red-beard's authoritative answer: "We have a deal! But if you don't get down there in thirty seconds, I'm going to send enough shrapnel at you to turn you inside out! One... Two... Three..."

And Gehn made his way warily down into the dark.

He knew that he was in no condition to escape the hailstorm of catapult bombs that would be unleashed if he attempted to run, but with his every step, Gehn found himself driven less by this threat. There was no hesitation in him at this point, no cursing the situation or frantic grasping of his mind for a strategy. The weight of the sword in his hand was an asset now, and he knew that somewhere, deep down, some small part of him *wanted* to face the creature.

He could see it, a bleeding, hulking form. It sat in the grass some thirty yards ahead, its head down and its body motionless as if it were simply waiting to die. Despite its catastrophic wounds, it seemed almost to have swollen up to a greater size, but Gehn knew that this was a trick of the flare's dying light.

Now he hastened his approach on the horror from the side of its blinded eye. It sensed him, its scaly lips peeling back to reveal its fangs as it slowly turned its head in his direction, its remaining eye a scarlet beacon of warning.

Gehn's heartbeat returned to an ardent drumming. A glint of azure caught his eye, a reflection in the end of the battered sword gliding at his right, but he never looked, because now the beast was on all four claws, spitting barks and thundering forward to meet him.

A few small and scattered flames tarried in the hill's newest craters when the noises of the fight finally ceased. A warm, southern wind tugged at them.

Up the shallow slope he trudged, through the infinite, gently-swaying stalks, dragging the black object by one blood-smeared hand. It seemed to him that the night had grown brighter, that the sky held more gleaming stars than he'd ever seen before, as if the encounter had somehow heightened his senses.

He stopped, and in a final show of strength, he flung his arm out and hurled the severed dognar head to land at the base of the fortress wall, its jaws locked wide and its tongue limp in the dust.

Gehn stared up at the tower and waited. He could hear only pieces of the hushed conversation:

"...give it to him?"

"...we just shoot him right now."

"...you see what he did..."

"...can't be impervious to a rifle ball."

"...one to shoot him then, if it's such a brilliant idea."

"...hiding his strength all along."

"...those days in the cage?"

"...out of it, didn't he? Could be he's..."

"Hear hear."

"...we give him what he wants and be done with it."

Then, after a short silence, what looked to him like a weighted sack flew over the top of the wall and crashed to the grass close to the ugly head.

He approached it and opened it to find three rounded, metal objects. Greedily he drank, emptying the first canteen and half of the second before wiping the water from his chin and looking toward the quiet fortress again. Now he was sure that he could see gawking faces in several of the open cannon ports.

Gehn tied the bag and tossed it over his shoulder, gripping its end with one hand. Hunger rolled through him in sharp, steady pulses. "I think I've earned some food as well!"

"That wasn't part of the deal, demon!" Came Red-beard's stern reply. "You've earned your right to leave! Now leave, and don't return!"

Chuckling quietly, Gehn turned to face the east. He began to walk.

56

SHADOWS

In the hours before dawn, a second blanket of darkness swept high over the hills: a mass of clouds, soaring north as if drawn to the Great Swamp by some supernatural power. Far off, deep in the heart of the ever-marching storm, lightning flashed, revealing quick, monochromatic glimpses of the surrounding hills.

Seeing no familiar features in the landscape, Gehn could only hope that the nightlong journey had brought him close to Dain's edge.

The lone, dead tree served as little shelter from the sprinkling rain. Aching with exhaustion, he sat down and put his back against its trunk, brought his knees to his chest and hooded himself with the empty sack that remained of the dwarves' parting gift. He couldn't remember closing his eyes, only that he was suddenly aware of gray light filtering through densely-clouded sky.

Silence ruled in the absence of wind.

He felt something cold and wet at his right hip: the sword, which he realized that he'd not cleaned well enough of the dognar blood, for now, black ichor oozed from its steel. He watched listlessly as it puddled on the ground, creeping its way toward the headless beast that lie before him like a mass of volcanic rock. Ebon vapors rose from the scales and a shudder grew in the earth. Blades of grass began to curl and wilt. Now Gehn found himself staring into a dark and churning column above the carcass. In it, he could distinguish a solid, manlike shape, a pitch-black silhouette with a drifting mane of hair and arms and hands like twisted iron.

A flash of lightning snapped Gehn awake. For a while, he surveyed the land through the sheets of rain, his dread fading along with the dream. He closed his eyes again.

When he surfaced once more from sleep, it was to a morning sky streaked with clouds. Below him and to the east, the valley he'd thought to be small in the night actually stretched away for many miles, mostly flat and uninterrupted except for a dark and curving ribbon coursing down its center: a river.

'The Ulad.' He thought.

Atop the far hills blanketed with green, he spotted a speck of movement that he knew could only be a rider.

STROM

After staring at the tent before him for several seconds, the warrior in jade green armor drew a deep breath and moved forward to pull the flap open.

From inside, the walls glowed orange with late-afternoon sun. A semi-silhouette sat at the center of the space: a man with white hair and broad shoulders, his tan hands flat on a mess of maps and creased documents that ranged to the edges of the desk but no further.

He appeared to be asleep.

The Captain's reluctance to speak extended a few more seconds. "Sir."

"What is it?"

"It's him."

The figure's eyes opened. He leaned forward an inch in the chair.

"We found him earlier today, crossing the border river back into Dain."

"Where is he now?"

"He's resting in medical."

"And?"

The Captain looked away from his superior. His gaze fell to trampled earth occupied by sparse, surviving tufts of green. "It's not what we expected."

Gehn had done well in hiding the monster's fang-marks in his upper-left arm. His hand made no move to check for the sword this time; he could still remember the exact moment he had been

58

stripped of it and had quietly watched it disappear in the hands of one of the Captain's subordinates.

He opened his eyes to squints. Just outside the shade of the gently-rolling tarp stood his two, current escorts. Clearly, these soldiers had been ordered to watch him, but they hadn't taken this task quite literally enough. No more than a minute had passed and already their backs were to him as they talked to one another, spears in hand as if instead they'd been assigned to guard the medical pavilion from intruders.

The cots were empty but for Gehn's and the one across from his own. In it lay a soldier with a fully-bandaged head and chest. Noting the number of flies this body tolerated, Gehn questioned whether it still held any life.

He looked again toward his two attendants.

Without a sound, he rose up from the cot. They never saw him as he slipped out through the pavilion's far end and made away into the camp.

Gehn had spotted the small, red flag amidst the tents' countless pointed tops. He stood near the temporary structure now, on the shadowed side as not to be given away by the sinking sun, and he listened closely.

"You're certain?" Asked a calm, deliberate voice.

"Yes Sir."

A moment of pause. Then: "When you first spoke, what did you tell him?"

"Nothing."

"Nothing?" The response smoldered with doubt. "You didn't give something away?"

Silence.

The first voice didn't wait for an answer. "And he claims... what, again?"

After another short moment of quiet, the speaker began as though carefully reading from a list. "Two dognars attacked. The cannon jammed. He rigged one of the barrels with a fuse. He dropped it onto them, but the explosion toppled the tower

59

beneath him and his two comrades. He woke up to find himself the only survivor." A pause. "You think he's lying, Sir?"

"Either that or you're completely incompetent."

Gehn could hardly think now as his hands shaped into vengeful claws, his chest shaking with his every heartbeat. His eyes fell to the grass and he somehow discerned there beneath the curved, dark blades, a metal tent spike with a tip as sharp as an arrowhead.

"No, General. I personally went over every last detail."

Pushing into the tent, Gehn saw first the Captain's jade-armored back, and then, beyond it, the General's widening eyes. In an instant, he took a fistful of the Captain's hair in one hand and put the tent spike to the man's neck with the other. "Don't either of you make a sound." He commanded.

Though he remained seated at the desk, the General's right hand had fallen just below its edge. Strom spoke without a smile. "Good to see you again."

"Why did you do it?" Gehn glared.

Strom gave no reply.

"I'll kill him." Gehn said as he pushed on the spike and brought a hissing breath out of his captive.

The General's frigid, gray irises showed no signs of melting. When his reply came, it was in the friendly tone of a man who has thought long and hard and has finally decided against dessert. "I don't think so."

Gradually, Gehn took the tent spike away from the Captain's neck. "I'm sorry." He whispered as he shifted his grip on the object. "I'm sure you were just following orders." With a sneer, he struck the Captain's skull with the spike's blunt end. As the jade suit collapsed, both his and Strom's movements were simultaneous: Gehn rushing forward as the General stood and stepped back from the desk, a dark weapon in his low, right hand.

Click.

"Hold it!"

Gehn halted to glance down into the twin-barreled muzzle of a sleek and lengthy pistol.

60

The General's silvery mustache accentuated his frown. Though he spoke, it never seemed to move. "Now put it on the ground."

He hadn't fought them. He'd been shackled and taken to a small tent in one of the camp's lonelier regions, a place of empty crates and run-down artillery pieces. It was now roughly an hour after sunset.

Outside, two fiery orbs wandered: men with torches. Gehn guessed there were probably more than just two that had been charged to watch him this time, but he couldn't know for sure. His watchers were silent. He could hear only distant voices.

Footsteps approached in the grass.

Gehn occupied a place on the ground at the far side of the tent. Here he watched the flap, waiting.

There came the low "*Uh-mmm*" of a man clearing his throat, undoubtedly Strom. The tent flap opened, and in from the night stepped an umber-bearded warrior holding a ring of keys and a lantern. The General followed, clad in a long, tan coat and keeping his hands behind his back. The two stared at Gehn for a time. Behind them, through the partly-open flap, a torch-wielder peered in like an overly-curious child.

"I'd like to talk." Said Strom. "Will you behave if he unshackles you?"

Gehn said nothing.

"I'd like to trust you, Gehn." The General gestured to his subordinate with a glance and a subtle nod.

The bearded warrior came and knelt, glancing from Gehn's face to his work with the keys and back a few times before the restraints were removed. Then, after a look at Strom, the man set the lantern on the grass in the center of the space and left, closing the flap tight behind him.

Strom moved to a stool in the corner. As he sat, he brought his right hand out into the weak light, revealing in it the same double-barreled pistol it had produced earlier. Though he rested the weapon on his right thigh, his fingers never parted from the burnished, wooden handle.

"Have they fed you?" Strom began.

Gehn said nothing.

"I'm sure you're confused."

"No." Gehn answered without pause.

The General didn't once look away. "Your two companions were killed. I take it that part of the story was true?"

"I suppose their lives mattered to you?"

Strom chuckled lightly. When he spoke again, his face had resumed its deadly-serious demeanor. "Considering that both men were murderers, I'd call it justice done."

Gehn squinted. "Murderers?"

"They thought themselves above suspicion. They never guessed that the tower would be their death sentence."

"Then you admit you planned for us to fail."

"Yes."

"And if I had died?"

A shrewd gleam entered the General's wintry, blue eyes. "But you didn't."

A moment of quiet passed between the two now as they stared at one another, Gehn's expression as hard and as sharp as a tempered blade, Strom's as unyielding as stone.

"There's a place I'd like you to see." The General finally said. "Once we've reached our destination, I will tell you everything you want to know."

"You're serious."

"Mmm." Standing up, Strom pulled his coat aside and slipped the weapon into a holster at his hip. "It's a few days south. Nothing compared to the trek you just made on foot."

For some time, the General waited for a response that never came. At last, he turned to the flap and drew it. "I'll let you sleep on your decision."

With that, he left.

Gehn stared into the lantern's small, serene flame.

Seconds later, he went to the opening and looked out to discover that his prior watchers had vanished. He turned back and gazed down at the lantern again as if it held some secret clue, his hanging hands restless at his sides.

As his fingers tightened to form fists, he never saw the miniature lick of blue flame escape his left hand and disappear.

Chapter 6

(10 years earlier)

THE WRECKAGE

Even in the midmorning fog, King Egan could see the change in the street ahead: a rolling stretch of ash and rubble interspersed here and there by angled, blackened beams like pines after a forest fire.

A short, wooden barricade stood in this street's center, its crudely-painted NO ENTRY sign enforced by a single soldier. The lightly-armored suit pulled a section of the barrier aside to make an exception. "Your Majesty."

Egan stopped his horse just outside but hesitated to dismount. As he stared wide-eyed into the ruins, the animal beneath him abruptly twitched and whinnied, as though it sensed the nervous energy rising inside him.

On his own two feet, the king came crunching to the top of a hill of debris, and now he spotted the General. Strom stood alone with his hands at his hips, looking out across the damage as though it were simply the aftermath of another battle.

"Strom." Egan said, unsmiling.

The General approached. "Sire."

"Anything?"

Strom continued to eye the misty remains distractedly. "No sign of Eleazar."

Egan swallowed dry disappointment. "And of the beast?"

"Not since it smashed its way out through the main gates last night."

Seconds later, Egan followed the General down a treacherous slope lined by sooty, stone pillars.

"Do you know exactly what your father employed the two men to do?"

The young king considered this question, stretching a hand out to grasp a pillar just in time to keep from slipping in the countless bits of charred wood and glass. He realized that he didn't know, but he said nothing.

They reached the basement floor and came to a heap of fallen beams and roof, and here they stopped. A few seconds passed before Egan distinguished the tall, vertical shape from the mess of black. "What is it?"

Strom grimaced and shook his head. "Some kind of tank. There are two of them: one of them large enough to have held the creature you saw, and this narrower one."

"A man could fit inside." Egan uttered.

"Mmm." Strom knelt before the cylinder's jagged, gaping hole. "The glass is two inches thick, but I don't think this damage was done by the fire or the collapse. I'd say something broke its way out of here."

Egan pondered this without word. Nearby, the steady noise of scraping and shoveling was joined now by a gentle commotion of voices.

Strom slowly straightened. When he spoke, it was as though he were still on the topic of the ruptured object before him. "Whatever your father said before he died, I'm sure that he meant it to stall his foe. I knew Linus well, and he was a dauntless man."

The young king did his best to stifle a quiver in his chest. "What?" He said, watching Strom now as if the man had confessed to some unspeakable sin.

The General reached into his coat and brought out his pipe, only to hold it. "I've seen men die, and I know the things that can come out of their mouths. Sometimes they can be..." he paused for a moment, "misunderstood."

"I don't wish to speak about it." Egan firmly said. "Not now and not ever. Do you understand?"

Gazing out into the mist, Strom nodded once, and brought up his free hand to scratch his mustache before carefully filling his pipe. "Alright." He turned to give the empty cylinder a final, grim look as he lit a match.

"General!" A voice called. "We've got something!"

Egan followed Strom through the haze and between the hills of incinerated house. As he approached the two soldiers, each of them stooping low over the crater-like hole, he could distinguish a round shape amidst the ash and pebble-sized fragments: a human face that, despite its horrific state, charred and partly-crushed, he recognized.

Many miles away from Dain, in a dusty, gold-hued expanse mottled by dense tree clusters and migrating patches of cloud shadow, three dark, armored supply carts lie on their sides like fallen buffalo. All around these, the dwarves had been ripped into gruesome halves, some of their faces still locked in soundless screams. The other two beings, however, with long, massive frames and hides like rough bark, had suffered much more, their shackles having rendered them defenseless against the ripping claws and teeth.

Some fifty yards from the massacre, a glinting pair of eyes watched from the center of a group of trees barely large enough to hide the shadowy, crouched shape.

The prodigious being looked back down toward its struggle with the steel chain between its wrists, and now its lips peeled away from teeth like blocks of stone. A groaning growl issued from its mouth, and when the metal finally gave with a *snap*, its arms flew back and smashed through the nearest trees to throw birds into shrieking hysterics.

Chapter 7

(Present time)

FOLLOW THE LEADER

Sunset.

The terrain leveled into a long and narrow shelf, the red-clay ground thick with shrubs and thorny weeds that had smothered all but a wheel-rut's width of trail. Boulders gripped greedily to the barren foothills below.

"Keep on the path." Strom voiced as he led the group across the desolate stretch, his steed's hooves plowing through tangled, brittle branches. "There are hidden pits everywhere. You're not careful you won't see one until it's too late."

Gehn looked ahead toward the next incline — a massive landslide that had consumed the southernmost portion of the shelf — and caught a glowering glance from one of the accompanying soldiers.

Suddenly, something dark and fast crashed through the nearby scrub.

The party stopped. Several of the warriors readied their lances and aimed their rifles toward a thin plume of dust, but the source of the disturbance had vanished.

"Relax." Strom grunted.

"Dognars don't come up this far." One of the men said. "Right, General?"

The General spurred his horse forward. "We're losing light."

Stars pierced a dark sky by the time the party climbed the last of the treacherous stones and settled in the yawning mouth of the abandoned silver mine.

Often, an unintelligible noise like a growling voice would echo through the tunnel, and the men could only clutch their weapons and stare into the lightless depths.

Soon, the sound of snores rivaled that of the hungry fire.

Gehn balled a blanket and placed it on the rocks behind his head.

"Gehn."

He turned to see Strom lean toward him and extend a sword in a dull, leather sheath.

"I'm trusting that you won't try anything stupid." The General said, his expression flat and his heavy, ash-blue eyes on the object itself.

Taking it, Gehn asked: "Are we getting close?"

"We've passed the halfway mark."

Gehn settled back down onto his makeshift pillow. He fell asleep to the row of standing horses, orange firelight dancing on their strong, sculpted forms.

The dream drew him into the tunnel's depths, through the blackness that reached and twisted deeper and deeper into the earth until there existed only a snapping, repeating percussion like an oncoming stampede.

As he awakened to the gentle melody of snores, he thought he heard a childlike whisper rattle in the dark:

"*Don't trust him.*"

Strom woke them at dawn the next morning. After a rushed breakfast, they resumed their journey up the slope's path with little talk. Elevation was more clearly visible by the rising sun, every ridge higher and every cutting abyss deeper, and any sleepy faces in the group quickly sobered.

Between the gusts of wind, Gehn's ears caught the faint, persistent cries of what he knew could only be seabirds. A sour smell haunted the air.

Just as he'd given up trying to anticipate the end of the incline, he followed a rider up and around a rugged edge of sun-etched rock and suddenly before him, there stretched a vast, dusty plateau that might have been the very edge of the world.

The riders stopped.

A bird's scream broke the silence before Strom could.

"Dangerous part is over, boys." The General unscrewed the cap from his canteen, took a swig, and cleared away the stray droplets with the back of his hand and a deftness that defied his age.

As the group followed Strom to the plateau's southern side, Gehn realized that it was not as broad as he'd first thought. Already, a deep blue stripe appeared at the horizon and pushed down against the expanse as they drew closer.

A pale brown tern zipped overhead, banking nimbly left to sing the riders another raspy warning before veering to drop out of sight.

One by one, the soldiers dismounted and approached the edge.

Gehn led his horse to the final few inches of level ground. A pang of vertigo washed through him.

Past the horde of shouting terns gliding to and from their nests on the meager ledges, the cliff face fell away for many hundreds of feet, so far down that the crash of every swell was barely audible. A great, dark ocean ruled to the horizon and for unseen miles beyond it.

Strom took them east along the bluffs, through fat, rounded lumps of stone like melted statues from a forgotten time. By noon, the sky above was clear, and only the occasional trace of wind graced the ridge and the travelers on it.

69

Gehn was splashing water onto his face and neck when he realized that the bandage he'd wrapped and hidden beneath his left sleeve was coming loose. He caught it before it could fall, but after a glance to ensure that no one was watching, he turned his eyes back toward his upper arm and removed the length of cloth. Now, pulling his sleeve up inch by inch, he revealed not the coin-sized scabs he last remembered but a collection of shrunken, near-imperceptible scars.

Stopping his horse, he looked north toward the barren, falling slopes and across the flickers of wind-blown dust. He thought of the voice he'd heard, not the whisper of distrust from the darkness of the mine but the clear calling of his name that had drawn him to a flare pistol in a skeletal hand.

"Gehn." The voice came.

Gehn turned to see only Strom before him; the soldiers had already disappeared among the slumped boulders ahead.

A short-lived gust pulled at Strom's coat and toyed with the mane of his steed. "Something wrong?" The General asked.

Gehn spurred his horse onward. "No."

They went slowly now, the trail gradually declining and curving inland, flanked ahead by a pair of waiting, gray cliffs. Beyond these, clouds hugged the lower landscape like a layer of snow.

Before Gehn ventured into the ravine with the others, he stopped to scrutinize the expansive blanket of white, sure that he could make out a form like a great, dark ellipse peeking up through the vapor. The longer he looked, the more the shape seemed to meld with the soft-edged shadows.

Strom led them single file through the tight crevice. The path descended away into infinity, its rough walls squeezing the sky above into a sharp V. Vines grew out of every crack, some having covered sections of the wall so thickly that there could not be seen a hint of rock behind their leaves and countless violet flowers like bizarre, unblinking eyes.

Ever deeper the path went, dropping into a thin, white mist that the company seemed to notice only after it had enveloped

70

them. Then, unexpectedly, the natural walls pulled away on either side and the men were made to halt before a wide space of murky, mirror-still water. A wooden post topped by an iron ring stood guard at its edge.

After a quiet command from Strom, one of the soldiers dismounted and made off along the narrow bank, disappearing into the gray.

No more than a minute later, he returned holding the ends of two taut ropes by which he dragged two boats, their gentle wake gliding across the glass.

"We'll have to leave the horses." The General said. "Feed them and tie them."

They pushed off. As Gehn settled in his seat at the rear of the less-crowded second boat, he noticed that Strom had kept one of the oars and now pushed steadily against the water.

The shore behind vanished, and now, around them in the mist, just far enough away to be mistaken for imagination, glowing dots like blue fireflies drifted.

A hundred feet or so later, they'd reached the water's opposite bank. A path waited, leading upward between hard walls like the last, only these appeared much too clean and smooth to have been cut by nature's hand. There was no post here, and the boats were pulled up onto a gravelly, ramp-like shore.

They started up the path and were soon faced with a chiseled stairway flanked and gripped by thin, prolific roots.

One by one they came up, as if through a trapdoor, onto a flat landscape covered by vibrant green ferns and a mist pierced through by shafts of sunlight that faded as swiftly as startled wildlife.

The party crunched its way through dead leaves, soldiers fanning out between slender trees with their rifles handy as though they expected an attack.

Calmly, Strom led them, the base of his tan coat brushing fingers of foliage, his head angling up toward the veil beyond the canopy, and then down toward a fallen tree or group of moss-

71

smothered rocks that he was made to step over, and then he would look back up again.

Gehn too found himself looking up, and, for a moment, he was sure that he glimpsed a rising shape against the pale sky, a wide and towering shadow that, though silent and still, seemed somehow alive.

Out of the trees and the ferns they came, and onto a space of hard, moistened earth, and the General stopped. "The Ancients' Wall." He uttered.

Gasps and whispers rose from the soldiers, as well as that word, "*Ancients*", spoken almost fearfully.

Gehn moved closer, past the men and past Strom, and as he did, the mist seemed to clear, revealing before him a surface of smooth, perfectly neutral gray that reached away to the right and to the left and up higher than he could see, and all at once he felt no larger than a grain of sand. In the wall ran two vertical, parallel indentations separated by several feet.

"They believe this to be the entrance." The General explained. "Other than these lines, there are no markings or carvings anywhere to be found."

"What's inside?" A soldier asked.

"I wish I could tell you. Linus's men tried everything: digging beneath it, climbing over..." Strom, eying unseen heights, shook his head. "Their ladders and grapple hooks could never reach high enough."

Gehn extended his hand and touched the petrous surface to find that its evenness in fact consisted of countless, infinitesimal bumps like fine grains of sand. A hot, tingling sensation filled the tips of his fingers. He withdrew his hand and stepped back.

"Can't go through." Strom added.

"Why not?" A voice inquired.

Strom gestured toward the surface. "Be my guest to try."

A soldier with a plume like a single, red spike jabbing from the top of his helmet came forward and pulled a heavy battle-axe out from its sling.

Gehn slowly and distractedly stepped aside.

72

After a smirk back at his comrades, the soldier braced himself, waited, and then quickly cocked back. He struck the wall with a *clang* and the weapon jerked out of his rigid hands and fell.

Snickers rose from the men.

"I'm not finished." The soldier reached down and retrieved his axe. He stood for a moment just holding it and grimacing at the gray surface. Then, bringing the weapon back with a gradual, deliberate gather of strength, eyes wide and nostrils flared, he swung the weapon with enough force to split bone.

The axe head shattered. Shrieking white light burst from the wall like water through a failing dam. As Gehn brought his arms up to shield himself, every soldier dropped in terror from a twisting stream of brilliance. Then, in an instant, the light was gone, leaving behind it a low thunder that faded into silence.

Warily, Gehn lowered his hands. Waves of throbbing energy danced through every part of him, and as he turned to see the black and smoldering branches of a nearby tarquin tree, his mind clung to a single image: a stray thread of the blinding bolt snapping out to touch his forearm.

A thick, hot scent of metal saturated the air.

One by one, wide-eyed soldiers stood up straight, some still gripping tightly to their helmets.

Strom had practically been tackled in the confusion. One of the men reached out a hand in an offer to help him and had it swatted away. With a wince, the General struggled to his feet, his movements lacking their usual vernal fire.

"You might've warned us!" The spike-plumed soldier cried, the other men creeping closer to inspect the ruined weapon in his hands and gape at the seemingly-impervious surface; the wall had not even the tiniest scratch.

After a deep breath through his nose and a subtle shake of the head, Strom said: "That's never happened before."

Gehn caught a stony, sidelong glance from the General before looking back toward his own itching, unburned flesh, toward his palms where the tingling sensation had settled as though he'd just finished clapping. Then, like a snuffed candle, the feeling ceased.

THE WALL

It was dusk when Strom made back through trees as straight and as thin as dungeon bars and found the troops around a simmering pot. Their hushed voices fell to silence as he approached.

The mist had thinned, freeing the firelight to paint the closest vegetation and even a section of the wall's all-but-unfathomable surface.

"Stew, General." One of the soldiers finally stated, dipping a wooden spoon into the pot's restless contents.

"Someone shoot a rabbit?" Strom's white eyebrows formed a crinkled, shallow V. "Or is that just boiled jerky again?"

As he sauntered out beyond the reach of the soldier's resumed chatter, he spotted, past some ferns, a dim, low form: Gehn, cross-legged on a blanket, looking fixedly toward the wall.

Off in the wood, a frog gave a single, bored *crick*.

"Night is getting clearer." Strom commented as he came to the man's side. "Almost clear enough to discern its curve."

Gehn's quiet remark came like a needle of impatience. "I take it we've arrived?"

The General reached into his coat and brought out his polished pipe. He clamped his teeth onto the hollow stem, sparked a match, and drew smoke. He released it in a lazy cloud. "What makes you think that?"

"Enough with the games."

Strom grunted. "You don't know why I brought you here?"

Crick.

Gehn said nothing, his eyes bright within his shadowed expression. He never pulled his gaze away from the dim and cryptic surface ahead.

The General waited, clutching the amber-lit pipe close to his face, but after some time passed without a response, he turned and made back through the knee-high foliage. "There's stew if you're hungry."

"You think that I'm something..."

Strom came to a momentary halt.

"...something with power you can use." Gehn glanced back at him. "But you're wrong."

The General came back into the firelit camp and stopped to rest his right boot on a stump. As he drew smoke from the pipe, his eyes moved toward the few remaining soldiers sitting at the center of the space, and came to land on the gently-simmering pot.

Angel's Blood is a potent substance known for its ability to induce shallow sleep and vivid dreams when consumed. It is rumored to have hypnotic effects, although such claims have been widely challenged by scholars and magi. Due to the toxin's association to witches, it has been labeled taboo in many realms, yet it remains a favorite interrogation tool.

By the light of his pipe and the fire's waning embers, Strom reread the page of the tiny book, his eyes flicking up once to scan the twitching, dozing bodies around him.

The chemical is extracted from the stalk of the elusive Wingflower plant, a species found only in the Basin of Corad. Once purified, the substance is clear, odorless and tasteless, and retains its effect even after being exposed to high temperatures.

He checked the dosage one last time before snapping the booklet shut and tucking it away into his coat. After one tap to dump out the ashes, his pipe followed.

Making through the camp's loud grunts and incoherent mumblings, the General's mind returned to the moment he'd feigned interest in the stew with a toxin-filled phial in his furtive left hand. He felt a mild rush of shame that was gone as quickly as it had come.

75

"They're coming for us." A soldier blurted in his sleep. "They're *coming*."

"Shhh-shh-shh." Strom lulled gently as he passed.

He came to the camp's outer edge and now saw a shadow in the dense ferns: a body-sized depression. Beside it, on a stone, rested an empty, wooden bowl with a fleck of boiled jerky still clinging to its inner curve.

Slowly bringing himself to a crouch, Strom waited for some indication that Gehn might still be awake, but there was only stillness. He looked back once toward the camp at the sound of a single cough, then, bracing himself on one arm, he leaned close and whispered: "*Open the gate.*"

Crick.

"*Open the gate, Gehn.*"

Gehn made no sound.

Strom frowned to himself. It dawned on him suddenly that he couldn't hear the man's breathing, and when he leaned further forward and peered down over the countless narrow leaves, he found only a flattened blanket.

"For God's sake." He muttered.

He took a deep breath and then his old muscles tensed when he spotted the figure ahead in the thin mist, standing exactly between himself and the ancient, gray surface, facing it.

The General straightened.

The figure took several steps closer to the wall, stopping directly in front of its two perfect, vertical grooves.

'He's asleep.' Strom realized.

Gehn stood motionless now, his head tilted forward slightly, as though something in the solid gray had drawn his attention, some mark visible to his dreaming eyes alone. Then, after a moment's pause, he placed his palm flat on the wall, and Strom was certain that he saw a wisp of teal flame snake up between the man's splayed fingers.

Gehn retracted his hand.

Strom's heart began to pound.

The wind hit with hurricane force, tearing through the trees and foliage and stirring the campfire to roaring brilliance.

76

Tangled, distorted shadows danced like restless spirits on the wall's surface.

Beneath the rush of the wind, Strom's ears detected a scraping, rumbling sound like stone against stone, and he saw now that a mass rose between the parallel lines to reveal a dark, square-edged opening into which Gehn seemed to stare as though it were nothing unusual.

"General!" Strom heard behind him.

The gate reached some twenty feet above the ground and stopped with a low *boom* that Strom felt more than he heard. The violent wind abruptly ceased, and silence fell but for the snapping flames.

Gehn had slipped into the yawning rectangle of dark to disappear.

Seconds later, Strom stood exactly where Gehn had, staring into the passage with a fiery torch high in one hand.

Behind him stood every last soldier, many still in their undergarments and a few carrying weapons as they simply gawked like a mob of nervous townsfolk at an enemy's door.

"I think there was something wrong with that stew." One of the men groaned, bent and grasping at his own torso.

"Are we going in there, General?" Came a second, eager voice. "That's a deathtrap if I've ever seen one."

Strom said nothing. After a last inspection of the floor of long-flattened ground, of the walls and high ceiling like smooth, moist stone reaching away into lightless corridor, he briefly looked back at the two soldiers nearest him. "Both of you, follow me."

It wasn't long before the walls pulled away on either side, and now, it was not darkness but a thick fog that obscured Strom's vision. High above, beyond the haze and the fuzzy sphere of torch-glow, traces of night sky were discernible.

For a time, they walked, and though the fog thinned, there existed only a tract of hard, cloddy earth broken here and there by patches of bright-green moss. Often, the General's eyes would catch, on the ground, a pebble-sized, darting shadow. He squinted down at one now as it sped away from his feet in intermittent, randomly-directed bursts.

One of the two soldiers stooped. His word came gradually, as though he'd come to some great revelation. "Frogs."

"Where's the city?" The other said. "Destroyed?"

"I don't think destroyed." Strom said, his mustache a mirror image of his angled eyebrows. "There aren't any ruins here."

"God." The soldier's head swiveled and pivoted, as though the surrounding haze held a forest dense with tangled, thorny vines. "No one back home is going to believe this."

"They won't know." The General corrected.

"Sir, you have to look at this."

Strom turned to see one half-armored body bent low over the ground and seemingly enthralled by the clustered patches of moss. The General spoke with crisp condescension. "Soldier."

Kneeling beside the first, the second warrior looked up now with wide, sober eyes. "General..."

Before Strom could react, the shine of his own torch waned until barely a flit of fire still clung to its blackened end. The gust of bitter cold seemed to pass through him.

"*Sir.*"

The torchlight snapped back to its former orange effulgence. After another moment spent staring at it, Strom shot his men a frosty glance. "Come on."

As he went forward, he never saw the change in the scattered moss beneath his boots: a steady wave of sunken, gray blight like the work of invisible flame.

All at once, the three of them emerged from the pale, blind void and halted. For a time, they could only stare out at the sheer size of the space before them, of the monstrous wall that encompassed them like a dark mountain range without peaks, its far reaches touching what seemed the very edges of the starry vault. Here and there from the wall's curved crown, moonlit clouds poured like waterfalls.

"Wow." One of the soldiers muttered.

Ahead, the ground fell away into a shallow and empty crater. There remained no trace of whatever the wall had once protected, as though its secret had been carried away by the very hand of God.

Even at this distance, they could see the figure standing at the crater's low center.

One of the soldiers pointed. "There."

They made down into the vast depression, never noticing that the mist followed them now and closed on them from every direction like a sprung trap.

At Strom's gesture, they stopped a handful of strides from the figure. The man, standing with his back to them and with his hands in hardened fists at his sides, appeared to be shivering.

"Gehn." Strom said.

A hostile reply came, not screamed and yet boomingly loud, as though twenty men had spoken the same words at once. "*Who are you?*"

"Strom," the General answered, "with two of my soldiers." He glanced back to see that one of the warriors had a rifle raised. With a slight shake of his head, Strom clamped his hand onto the barrel and gently pushed down.

"Gehn." The General repeated.

Gehn had yet to respond.

A sound filled the space now: an escalating ebb and flow of air that seemed to match Gehn's heaving torso, and as Strom saw the closing fog, he was certain that his eyes caught the pale vapor pulsing with the same uncanny rhythm.

Gehn's shape and the surrounding ground darkened as though a dense cloud had passed before the moon. The man bent forward and placed his hands on the front of his head, and as he gave an echoing, pain-filled cry, the mist rushed in like floodwater.

The burst was a steady and dazzling blue.

Strom stood his ground, heat washing against his face and through his hair as the flame ahead pulled apart at its veiled source and slashed out like whips in the haze. At the edge of his

79

vision, he saw the barrel of the soldier's rifle leveled toward the light. "Hold your fire!" The General commanded.

"He's a demon!"

"I said don't shoot!"

With a brilliant, fulminating *CLAP*, the fireworks ceased.

Slowly, the General raised his free hand to touch his face, to make sure that it hadn't melted as he'd so imagined; his fingers found only a thin layer of sweat.

The two soldiers drew closer to Strom as he moved forward through the creeping clouds. He saw the outline then: the man-like shape still facing away, faint blue lights shuddering here and there in its darkness like restless lightning in a thunderhead.

"God, he's..." one of the warriors started, his lips peeled back in a freakish, empty smile, "he's *one* of them."

Strom drew a deep breath. "Gehn." He said.

The flashes stopped.

"General." Gehn said at last, and though now his voice sounded like nothing more than a man's, his question simmered with demand for an answer: "How did you know?"

Chapter 8

(8 years earlier)

DEFECT

The wind came in waves. Each scattered gust pushed gently against the trees and brushed through blades of grass bright green from the recent overabundance of rain.

Egan arrived at the top of the hill and stopped his ink-black horse to stare at the two monuments before him: two shapes like great chess pieces, one taller and darker than the other, each of them as devoid of color as the sky above.

Clutching a handful of white flowers like tiny, clustered hailstones, the young king dropped down onto his own feet, his mind ever aware of the four mounted escorts watching his every move.

He touched the side of Raven's neck and then slowly approached the two columnar shapes. From up close, their subtle differences were clearly discernible, but it was the ground beneath them that drew his eyes now. While only grass adorned the foot of the polished and sharply-sculpted monument to his left, at his right, a heap of colored garlands encircled the second stone's base, some of the cut flowers so fresh that they hadn't yet been trampled by rain.

The young king turned back toward what might have been another statue: his nearest, black-armored protector. "Leave me for a few minutes."

The rider's mouth opened, but he said nothing until he'd scanned the surrounding trees. "Strom wouldn't like us letting you stray from our sight."

"Strom isn't your king." Egan firmly replied.

"...Yes, Sire." After a final hesitation, the escort turned his horse and started away down the hill. He raised his hand to signal the other three.

Egan watched them meld, one by one, into the green shadows before he brought his attention to the stark monument at his left.

Above the finely-shaped "L" in its dark, lustrous surface, the late ruler's chiseled visage stared off into the distance with a look of dauntless courage. With the sound of swaying grass, the words whispered up from the recesses of Egan's mind: "Did you hear him beg?"

Lips pursed, he came now to the second stone, smooth and vase-like, almost white in comparison to the first. As he knelt to add the flower's he'd brought to its existing collection, a wave of wind rose to shudder the white spheres on their needle-thin branches. Among the petals, a small square of paper caught the king's eye. He took it and turned it to find carefully-written words:

Mother of Dain, we know that you will watch over us from heaven just as closely as you did when you were with us on earth.

Anger welled up in Egan as he stared down past the note, his senses slowly reaching down beyond the flowers and cold blades of grass before pushing into the endless, silent black that was the soil.

After a glance back down the hill to make sure that his escorts were still invisible, the young king rose and climbed back onto his horse. Facing the thick forest that began not ten strides away, he started Raven forward with a gentle nudge. Again he urged him, and, by the third time, he was already speeding through the trees with the low branches swiping at his clothes and hair like arrows glancing off of armor. He looked back only once to catch a fragmented view of the two monuments, and what he was sure was a third shape — a silhouette of a rider on a horse — rising between them.

He'd left Raven near the base.

The ground was soaked and bare but for a few leafless tarquins that years of wind had hammered into stiff curves. Far below him, Dain rolled like a dark green sea broken by knife-edge boulders. Distant rain funnels hung as still as the strokes of a painting.

Egan's focus returned to the object in the center of his palm: a coin-sized spiral of black and white stripes with five curved, delicate spines running its edge. A yawning skull stared back at him from its rounded surface, a face so tiny and intricate that it seemed to vanish in the seashell's natural flecks.

"Threshold to the dead." He whispered.

Returning the shell to a pouch at his waist, he brought his eyes up toward the sheer drop before him.

After a parched swallow and a deep, silent breath, he started forward. Reaching out, he took the branch of the nearest tree and ran his hand along as he went, ready to grip if he lost his footing. In the light of his ultimate intention, the precaution seemed absurdly pointless to him.

An updraft swept through his hair as he arrived at the lip of dark stone and looked over it toward the ground several hundred feet below.

He fought the sudden tightness in his hamstrings, the potent urge to lower his center of gravity and move away from danger, and though he still clung quivering to the branch, he took another slow and deliberate step forward.

Then the wind quieted. The world seemed to watch and wait.

"You're not afraid." He whispered to himself, his arm almost fully outstretched now and his body slanted forward over the cliff's sharp edge and the boulders far below. He closed his eyes and saw in his mind the gaping, black mouth of the underworld.

"You're not afraid." He repeated.

He imagined what it would be like to fall, the sound of the bough springing back into place as he plummeted without a scream.

Seconds passed.

When he opened his eyes again, he spotted three specks weaving through the distant folds of green: three riders speeding toward his location.

Slowly, the young king pulled himself straight and stepped back from the edge.

He made down the ridge's shadowed side and found his ink-black steed waiting on a patch of turf, puffing nervously and flicking his tail.

"Hey, hey boy," Egan said, stroking his hand along Raven's velvet snout, "it's alright. But we've got to go."

Seconds later they were racing down through a rounded, grassy ravine beset by boulders and slender trees. Egan stiffened when he heard an echoed *pop* above Raven's rapid thudding.

He straightened now, turning his head but unable to see past the rugged, natural walls rushing past on either side. When the second and third *pop* rang out, he knew the sound for certain.

'Gunshots.'

In his distraction, he nearly missed the great, dark shape ahead like a loosed boulder in the trench's center: a nightmare built of scales and spines, tail lashing, eyes like brilliant spheres of red.

With a desperate wheeze, the horse skidded to a halt in the grassy earth. A scene appeared in Egan's mind: a flash of cobblestone and rubble lit by orange flame, and, if not for his animal's brisk turn, he might never have pulled his gaze away from the beast below.

Then they were flying back up the ravine the way they'd come, and in the utter fury of Raven's speed, the young king simply held tight.

He'd spotted the upper end of the trench ahead when, above one flanking ledge of stone, a second, spiny silhouette appeared and dropped down directly into their path.

Raven came to yet another violent stop. Now, Egan looked back to see the first creature close on them with hideous speed, spitting and snapping like a rabid dog. He could only cling to his mount's mane and wince.

The voice was calm. "*Stop.*"

In an instant, the beasts became statues but for the wind of their breaths and the twitching of tight flesh above bared fangs. They stood mere strides away, their heads low and their red eyes fixed.

Raven reared and flung his hooves at the air before dropping down into a jerking, backward circle.

"I was about your age when I fled from Capitol." The unseen speaker added, his voice tipped with a razor point of feigned passion. "I truly found myself out here."

"What do you want?!" Egan cried.

"I want you to return to your people and deliver a message."

A flicker of shadowy movement drew Egan's attention to the closest wall of boulders: not the wizard as he'd first expected, but a third creature like the other two, rising to look down at him. The young king felt his blood curdle when he saw the mangled, human shape hanging from the beast's jaws, and now he caught the movement of one tired eye as the escort's stare met his own.

Chapter 9

(Present time)

AWAKE

It was something in the morning sky that lured his eyes, a secret in clouds ablaze with molten reds and oranges that Gehn could only question.

'A sunrise in the west?'

His gaze followed the horizon line beyond the plateau's edge, starting at the sea and turning north across endless, arid flats until, at last, he was looking toward a bulging, charcoal-gray funnel that seemed to cover a third of the sky.

As he squinted to see the smoke's source, a sliver of western sun emerged, its light flooding the broken plateau and the plains beyond and spilling across a myriad of tiny rises like heaps of ash. Then the scent of charred flesh filled his nostrils and the earth began to tremble.

Gehn woke to find himself amidst the steady *thud thud thud* of hooves. Beneath him in the dust, the angled shadows of the other riders assured him that the sun was rising in its proper place. When he looked up, he was at once sure that he'd slept for miles, for at the base of the rugged, scrub-ridden foothills, he could see the beginnings of lush countryside. Half of him wanted to believe that this was the first he'd ever seen life on these fields, that the grass and the gnarled oaks ahead had sprung up like mold and fungi after a night of rain.

'Dain.' He thought.

The word felt foreign to him now.

By the time the sun had finished its full arc overhead, the company arrived at an intersecting road. Atop a slanted post, weathered arrow signs were covered with black X's and scribbled skulls, but the most obvious defacement was the warning that had been carved deep into the wood: BEWARE OF DOGNERS.

Strom turned to scrutinize a distant, wooden husk smothered in crisscrossed vines. "I remember this place when people still lived here." He turned his horse onto the eastern route and urged it forward. "Used to be you couldn't pass through without getting blocked by a herd of something."

Wind came hard against them as they rode east through field after field under the stars. At the sight of the lonely barn, they broke from the road and made for it, restless heads of grain beating at their stirrup-held feet.

They made no fire, and with an energy fueled by thoughts of fast-approaching rest, the men unpacked.

Gehn watched as Strom climbed the last high rungs of the creaking ladder. Slowly, the General came and sat down across from him on a bale. Strom swung his glinting gaze out through the hayloft's opening.

Below them, the men lounged and ate and muttered in darkness.

Gehn sat with his head low and his hands clasped onto his knees. His tone was more statement than question. "The swamp tower was a test?"

"A trigger." Strom answered, shifting his seat on the bale to pull out his pipe. "That's my theory, at least."

"Theory?" Gehn's eyes flicked back up onto the man.

Blinking down at the hay-strewn floor, Strom lit a match and puffed. "Two bodies were unearthed at the southern cliffs." Still

87

holding the pipe, he scratched lightly at his forehead with a free fingertip. "Linus charged me with their safe transport back to Capitol, to the hands of his top mage, Alcris. They were shut tight in crates for the journey, but I did glimpse them once," his stare met Gehn's, "both of them so perfectly preserved that they might've been merely asleep. I knew nothing of the king's plans for them. After his assassination, we searched the remains of the wizards' lab and uncovered two shattered cylinders. It was obvious that one had birthed the reanimated beast, but the other..." The General trailed off. He conjured a thick mass of smoke that glided away toward the opening, accelerating just before it vanished into the wind.

Gehn squinted out into moonlit field. Somehow, his early memories of Capitol seemed to be the cloudiest and most distant ones of all. He said now what he'd known even before Strom had implied it. "I was the one in the second cylinder."

"I guessed as much." The General affirmed. "I had the city scoured for a man fitting the description of a lifeless being I'd seen only for a moment. Months passed and I was sure you'd slipped away. Then the dream came."

Gehn listened. At the edge of his vision, the countless, swaying stalks resembled a rolling ocean of teal flame.

"I've never been one to jump to spiritual conclusions, but this..." The General uttered a quiet, introspective laugh as he turned his eyes toward the darkness again. He shook his head. "I've never experienced anything quite like it. Every few weeks it would jar me awake, and each time it grew more and more vivid until I was certain I could feel the mist. In it, I saw a man, faceless in silhouette against a gray sky, a sword in his hand and a fallen monstrosity beneath him. I knew it was the same creature that had slaughtered Linus in Capitol. Mind you, this was back when only *one* existed and not hundreds." Strom puffed again and waited for the smoke to disperse. "The vision was always the same. I did my best to ignore it.

"When I finally found you, you had already planted yourself into my ranks. I kept an eye on you from a distance. You proved to be the ideal soldier, but part of me was still skeptical that you would turn out to be something more. Years passed, and the wizard's destructive hounds only grew in number. Then, all at once, the dreams stopped. Feeling I might lose my chance, I put a plan together. I manufactured the scenario that had been haunting my sleep. The old tower was the perfect place."

"And the Ancient Wall?"

"That was a hunch." The General said.

A silence held between them for a time. Outside, countless heads of grain whispered ceaselessly.

Strom tapped the ashes out of his pipe but simply held it. "So, that's it." He leaned slowly back. As his wrinkled face suffused with shadow, the intent sharpened in his frozen, gray eyes. "You're one of the *Ancient* race."

Gehn said nothing to this.

"The Wall." Strom stashed his pipe and crossed his arms. "It once protected a fortress or a city, is that correct?"

"I don't know." Gehn said. "And I don't know what happened there."

Strom nodded once and sighed through his nose, but the look in his eyes retained its potency. "If something isn't done about the beasts, Dain will soon be nothing more than a pile of bones. I need to know that you're on my side, Gehn. I'm asking you to help me beat them."

Gehn only half listened now. He'd accepted the answers for their apparent logic, but he found himself delving deep into the implications of Strom's tale. Again he recalled the voice he'd heard, the calling of his own name as though to lead him.

"Gehn."

"The dreams..." Gehn said, his eyes roving blankly across the floor. "There was nothing else?" When he looked up, he met the General's stare.

"No." Strom replied. "And I couldn't tell you where they came from."

MATTERS AT HAND

The twenty-one-year-old king awakened to overwhelming sunlight. Squinting, blinking, he sat forward and found himself at the cluttered desk on his tower's balcony, facing a peaceful view of Dain. Beyond Capitol's firm and bristling walls, checkered farmland seemed to stretch infinitely north. Fleets of clouds patrolled a late afternoon sky.

All the beauty only seemed to fuel the pulsing ache in Egan's head.

Dizzily, he stood and moved to the balustrade. From here, he saw that the city gates had been opened, and that, filing down the main street now, were what appeared to be a dozen or so dark suits on horses. Even from this far, the king knew that Strom led them, but he still seized the spyglass from his desk.

Riding at the rear of the group was a man that Egan didn't recognize.

'It's *him*.' The king guessed, lowering the spyglass. He muttered the word under his breath: "Unbelievable."

Even with its doors open to the corridor, the chamber was all but pitch-dark. Gehn could discern a few shapes here, mainly a large, square table in the center of the space, evenly surrounded by sixteen wooden chairs.

It wasn't until Strom had drawn the curtain of a single tall window that the room's neglect was clearly visible. Tangled strings of cobweb gleamed in the slanted shaft of light. A heavy layer of dust rested on every surface.

"Welcome to the old war room." the General said as he moved to close the doors.

Gehn's eyes fell from the massive, black chandelier to the chamber's far wall, where several built-in shelves held hundreds of tomes.

The General went to the wall now and pulled open a drawer to exhume a dense roll of enormous maps. He brought the roll back to the table and here he flung it to unfurl like one would a sheet, letting it land on the surface with a heavy *fump* and a cloud of dust. He peeled back six of the maps before stopping on one that focused on an asymmetric mass of pen-strokes surrounded by the sharp, triangular representations of trees.

Gehn knew the place at once.

"My ultimate plan has always been to make a single push against the beasts." The General said. "It would be an all-or-nothing maneuver, nine tenths of Dain's military power condensed into a single spearhead. If there was..."

A *creak* interrupted him.

Gehn turned and saw, standing in one partly-open door, a young man with pale skin and glossy-black hair. He could see no crown, but one glance at the man's dark, plush robe upheld his suspicion.

"Your Highness." Strom said amiably.

The king offered no return smile. "Private meeting?"

"Private?" The General put his hands behind his back. "I take it the guard I sent never found you. Please, join us."

Egan stepped into the room. He eyed Gehn for several seconds before finally closing the door behind him.

"Sire," Strom gestured with his hand, "Gehn."

Gehn offered a modest bow.

"He'll be helping on the tactical side of things."

Squinting as though at some grotesque sculpture, the king came step after slow step closer. He stopped when his face was mere inches from Gehn's.

"Your Highness." Gehn said. By the smell that struck him now, the young man might've spent the day soaking in a vat of wine.

Egan tilted his head back. "You have a smudge," he voiced in a tone that dripped with something less than true concern, "on your forehead."

Gehn stared at him. "I'll be sure to take care of it."

"Mmm." A smug smile broke free from the corner of the king's lip. His eyes fell to Gehn's feet and back up again.

A clot of irritation formed in Gehn's chest.

Clearing his throat, Strom made around to the far side of the table and planted his hands down against it. "I'd like to continue now."

Egan at last broke his stare. "Of course." He moved to the table, dragged out two chairs and faced one toward the table's corner. As he sat, he propped a black-booted foot up onto the other chair.

Gehn pulled one away but remained standing at the table's edge.

The General extended a hand over the center of the map and touched a spot a few inches inside the Swamp's southernmost border of ink pines. "Here was the tower," he said, glancing up at Gehn, "just to give you a better idea of scale. Due to the dognar activity that surrounds this entire region, I believe it contains Eleazar's lair."

"So it's really true." Egan ejected with a sharpness that defied inebriation. "You're going to march us toward a shimmering victory and... deliver Dain from all destruction."

Gehn gave no answer.

His eyes on the young king, Strom's eyebrows formed a shallow V. "Perhaps we should postpone this discussion until you've had your afternoon nap."

The king turned toward the window. In the harsh sunlight, the dark, discolored blotches beneath his eyes held a look of disease. "Don't let me stop you."

Gehn spoke now as though the man did not exist. "How big is our army?"

"Five thousand six hundred men, roughly." Strom started. "Counting weapons: three thousand cannons, twelve hundred catapults and other artillery units. Plenty of mines."

"And what do the dognars number?"

"In total?" Frowning, Strom shook his head. "I don't know that for sure, but it's estimated that there are no less than four hundred of them, though they rarely travel in packs larger than forty strong."

Gehn analyzed the bog below him, every bight, every protrusion or sparseness in its tree border. No revelations came to him but for what he next expressed. "This is the worst place for us to fight them."

"Astute." Egan said with a glare.

Strom cleared his throat pointedly.

Breathing deeply, Gehn flipped to the next map in the collection, this one presenting a view so large that Dain was the size of a coin amidst many countries and continents, some labeled *Unexplored.*

Strom lightly shook his head. "There are no allies to be found. The northern kingdoms continue to ignore our requests."

"What about the dwarves?" Gehn said. "I've seen their power firsthand. Their help would be valuable."

"The dwarves are too stubborn." Countered the General. "They think only for themselves. We've not been on good terms with King Pond for some time."

Gehn's attention fell on the blank section of parchment immediately east of Dain. "And the forest giants?"

"The dwarves have a history of using them as slaves." The General replied. "We've caught Pond's imps moving a captured forest giant or two across Dain more than once. The giants will *never* be our allies if we're to have dwarves fighting alongside us. That's assuming we were lucky enough to find them in the endless wilderness that is the East."

Gehn went around to the window and beheld a section of Capitol that was all houses and long shadows. He spied a pair of far-off soldiers keeping watch over the street. A vision returned to him now: early light touching the edges of a swollen, ever-rising column of smoke. "You would risk sending your men to die in vain without knowing for certain?"

Egan, lax in his chair as though he were about to nod off, chuckled.

Strom looked toward the king and then back to Gehn. "The greatest risk I see is the one posed by wasted time." Flipping through the maps, he returned to the first one he'd presented, the one in which the Great Swamp looked a country of its own. "Right now, we need to plan according to our situation, so, tell me, pretending that we live in a world in which no potential allies exist and that our enemy only grows stronger by the day, how do we win?"

That night, at the end of a torch-lit hall, Strom directed Gehn toward a door and left him with an order to get some rest.

The guest-chamber was cramped but still elegant, a different tree-crowded scene carved into each wooden wall. Beyond a gently-steaming bath, a platter of food and a change of clothes waited on the bed, all the work of servants Gehn had barely glimpsed since entering the palace.

He soon found himself wandering the long and silent corridors, passing one closed door after another until at last he came to an open doorway filled with a warm, welcoming glow. He entered, noticing first the ten columns of polished, gold-hued granite that ribbed the space. All above and around the main wall's crackling fireplace, there hung a countless number of swords and shields and other instruments of war.

He'd inspected nearly half of the display when he heard the footsteps behind him.

"I thought I told you to get some sleep." Voiced Strom.

Gehn's attention roved from a trio of slanted rifles to several single-edged blades with large, curved teeth. "Your collection?"

"Lifetime in the making." Strom said before sauntering toward the chamber's corner where a cabinet waited.

"Do you have children?" Gehn inquired now, having noticed the small, black figurine standing alone on the mantel of the fireplace: a rounded, toy crow made crudely out of twigs and wooden shavings.

"No." The General answered.

Taking the bird and turning it in his hand, Gehn discerned, beneath its flat base, a faint message scratched into the wood:

94

"Drink?" Strom grunted with the pop of a cork.

"No, thank you." Gehn returned the plump crow to its place on the mantel and stepped back for another look at the weapon-clad wall in its entirety. When at last he saw it, the muscles in his face went slack.

It hung above the others, an enormous double-edged brand with a handle that looked to have been carved from gray marble. The mirror shine of its broad, lengthy blade held a tint of blue, and, for a moment, he was certain that his eyes caught a twinkle at its honed tip.

"Where did you get that?" Gehn asked.

Approaching with a silver cup in his left hand, Strom tracked Gehn's gaze with a glance. "*That* was given to me as a gift before I came to this part of the world. Few men would even have the strength to wield it."

"And its history?"

"It's old." The General brought the goblet to his lips and swallowed, a flicker of gritted teeth showing through beneath his mustache. "I'm sure it's seen its share of walls before mine."

Gehn's irises shone up at the object. He spoke with quiet resolve. "It was never meant for decoration."

The next morning, Strom strode up to the guestroom door where a gaunt chambermaid waited for him.

"He won't answer to my knocks." The woman said. "It's been a quarter hour."

Strom knocked. "Is it locked?" He asked, but he was pushing the door open before she could answer. "Gehn? Are you in here?"

Resting on the end of the neatly-made bed was a folded triangle of paper. He took it and opened it and began to read:

Meet me at the Green Hills Fort in three weeks with your army assembled.

95

I'll bring it back.

"Bring it back?" Strom wondered aloud, and he nearly trampled the curious chambermaid in his move to exit the room.

Not one minute later, he stared up at the two naked hooks above the wall's otherwise complete collection of weapons; the great, mirror-blue blade was gone.

"I heard the news."

The General looked back to see Egan standing at the chamber's open doorway: a silhouette against a section of sunlit palace wall.

"I hope you're right to trust this man."

Chapter 10

EAST

Wilderness.

At a hill's base, Gehn dismounted and made his way up through slender trees, their branches clawing futilely at the brown cloak he'd taken from the palace wardrobe.

He came to the top to observe a patchwork of terrain. Ahead on the flat and mostly-barren expanse, jagged rock pillars stabbed upward like pointed teeth. Shallow streams snaked carefully between them, flowing ever northward to feed a vast, crystalline lake inhabited by an array of reedy islands.

Gehn reached back and his fingers brushed the cold cross-guard of Strom's prized greatsword before finding the curve of parchment. He brought out the map and unrolled it and it billowed lazily between his hands. When he looked up from the pen strokes that comprised Dain's edge — pen strokes that his surroundings no longer resembled — the sun had broken free from the sky's scattered clouds, illuminating a line of dark green across the eastern horizon.

He had heard tales about the place he sought, and he realized as he drew closer that he'd been wrong to discount them as exaggerations. Even from a mile's distance, the forest towered ahead like an impossible, leaf-ridden cliff marching away eternally into the north and south.

He arrived at the edge at last and stopped. Drifting dust sparkled in the few penetrating curtains of light. Far beneath the boughs like twisted, muscular arms holding the canopy aloft, roots dominated the dry ground. Undergrowth was almost nonexistent.

He felt an urge to shatter the quiet.

"*Hello!*"

His echo bounded away through the trees, and no answer came.

Traveling through the place made him feel as if he'd shrunk.

"I'd like to count the rings in one of those." Gehn muttered, looking up at the trunks as his newly-acquired horse clopped.

He'd stopped at a creek to let the horse drink and to refill his canteen when the corner of his eye caught a tall, massive form in the vertical shadows: something with sunken eyes and skin like bark. He turned to look but saw only another mammoth tree.

"Hey!"

With a gentle whinny, the horse lifted its head to stare.

"I don't mean you harm!" Gehn called, watching keenly for a sign of movement that never came.

As he climbed back onto his steed, he gave the trunks a last look and muttered: "I know you're out there."

An unseen bird heralded the coming night, its long, mournful call the very sound of loneliness.

Gehn found shelter in a cavernous hollow beneath a twenty-foot stump. He remained awake for many hours, his back against a wall of splintered wood as he kept watch over the sleeping horse, his mind anticipating a predator that matched the trees in size.

He'd unsheathed the massive sword and kept it now beside him on the ground, his right hand loose around its handle as he strained for a sound in the forest's silence.

There came only the bird's infrequent, lamenting cries.

Gehn dozed in the early hours of morning. He dreamed that something watched him from between the distant trees, not a beast or a giant but a shadow in the shape of a man, a form motionless but for its hair like a black flag lashing in a windstorm. Gehn tightened his grip on the sword and the figure faded from sight.

As he stepped cautiously out of the hollow, he found himself surrounded by a circle of prodigious shapes: forest giants, staring blankly down at him. Before he could speak to them, they vanished like vapor into the dark.

He journeyed slow the next day, entering a place where bushes grew in sparse, flowering clusters and a sprawling network of vines challenged the trees' roots for ground dominance.

The sun had nearly reached its highest point when Gehn heard the thunderous buzzing. He pulled the horse around and focused onto a treetop where leaves and branches thrashed and a sudden cloud of birds screeched away through the air. He drew his blade just as the disturbance fell eerily still.

Without warning, the steed reared up onto its hind legs and took several steps backward with a neigh of protest.

"Easy." Gehn's one hand went to the animal's silvery neck while the other tightened on the sword-handle. He'd not yet taken his eyes off the canopy above.

After watching and waiting in vain for nearly a minute, he turned the horse and urged it forward into the wood.

By twilight, he'd reached the eastern edge.

From here, plains pulled away for miles to form hills, and hills pulled ever further and higher into mountains crowned with snow.

He made camp beside a boulder that had been torn from the earth by monstrous, wooden tentacles.

As he stared into the vibrant flames and at the branches being hastily consumed, he heard a whispered voice say: "Strom was right."

Sneering, he balled the cloak into a pillow and reclined on it with one hand behind his head. Above him, trunks faded into the blackness of the forest ceiling.

"*IS ANYONE THERE?*" He called.

There was no response.

Slowly shutting his eyes, he thought again of the noise he'd heard earlier: the buzzing like that of a colossal insect, and as he touched the rope that clung tight to his left wrist, he was reminded that nothing was going to snatch the horse away without taking him along as well.

He lay awake for a time, his world consisting only of the sword in his hand and the occasional, hushed sounds of his steed and the fire.

Gehn jerked straight up with a rapid breath.

Beside him, there remained only a faint patch of scarlet coals. He tried to think of what exactly had awakened him when it came again: neighing, off in the woods.

Frantic neighing.

He jumped to his feet and threw his hand back only for a loose braid of rope to snap from the shadows and fall to the ground before him. It had been cleanly severed, and, for a moment, he could only stare in shock as a rush of electric heat spread beneath the surface of his skin.

The neighing rose to a virtual screaming.

It didn't occur to Gehn just how sharp his senses had become as he dashed into the forest's darkness; to his eyes, it was as if the high branches had parted to allow the light of a full moon.

As he broke through tangles of brush and stopped in the center of a clearing, the horse's sounds seemed now to resonate from every direction, seemed to fall steadily quieter, as though the animal were being whisked away into the night.

And then, silence prevailed.

Hours later, with his back to the eastern mountains and to a sky glowing ever-brighter with the pinks and cream colors of approaching sunrise, sitting on one of the great roots that had hoisted the boulder and now held it frozen in the air, Gehn turned the rope's neatly-sliced end slowly before him. Beyond it, contrasted by the morning's angled light, the wood's recesses seemed to hold a shadow all the darker, a shadow he now *knew* he could not trust.

'Not a giant.' Gehn told himself, but he wasn't entirely convinced. According to the tales he'd heard, forest giants were herbivorous, but their physical might was matched by a reputation for unpredictability. He pictured one of the beings carrying the horse away like an ignorant child setting a lamb free from its pen, but this idea seemed to have one flaw. He let go of the rope then and eyed the shaded hollows between the trunks nearest him. 'He was in pain.'

VENOM

Gehn didn't need to look at the map to gauge just how long it would take him to reach the nearest town on foot. Swiftly and steadily he moved, driven by a goal to exit the forest before nightfall, the weighty sword thudding against his back as he crossed swell after swell of hard, pervasive roots.

It wasn't until the day had outpaced him that he finally stopped to rest.

Curling flakes of bark tumbled from his hands and his boots as he climbed the old, immense stump. He came to the top and surveyed the surrounding forest, its monolithic trees interspersed by a hundred shafts of dust-choked sunlight. He raised a biscuit to his mouth, devoured it in two bites, and promptly washed this down with a swig from his canteen.

If the forest hadn't been so silent in that moment, he would never have heard the quiet *ticktickticktick* behind him like the rapid drumming of sharpened steel points against wood.

Gehn turned to find only stillness.

For a while, he scanned the span of vertical shapes, his rigid right hand still clutching the canteen, and when he first saw the two round, dark holes in the nearby tree, he took little notice. Then he looked back and his mind distinguished the giant's staring face. Adrenaline flooded through him.

"*HEY!*"

The giant flinched.

Like startled statues, the two stared at one another. Gehn found himself transfixed by the being's lean yet powerful frame, by its clear potential.

Then it spun to flee.

"Wait!" Gehn shouted, but even as he dropped down from the stump to pursue, his quarry was but an outline between the trunks ahead, a pair of massive, square shoulders from which equally-massive arms swung.

"COME BACK!"

By the time that the echo of his call had fallen to silence, so had the tremorous *boom*s made by the being's heavy, flying feet.

Putting his hands on his hips, Gehn shook his head and flashed part of a bitter smile at the air. "Fine." He screwed the cap back onto his canteen and stowed the object at his side.

It was then that he heard the noise from his right, faint and steady: the clopping of hooves. He turned and made forward a step, his wide eyes seeking the source, and when, at first, he beheld the pale, gray shape like an apparition moving in and out of view behind the trees, his mind refused to accept the sight as real.

Into an angled cylinder of sun, the horse emerged, serene, with only a tousled mane to hint of any distress. It whickered and swished its tail.

Gradually, Gehn circled and scrutinized the animal. He saw nothing noteworthy until he'd returned to its front, where a pair of thin, superficial slashes ran just below its muscular neck.

It offered a listless blink.

"What happened to you?" Gehn quietly asked.

After a glance toward the trunks where he'd watched the fleeing giant disappear, he stroked the horse's face and now climbed up onto its back. He put his heels gently into its sides.

But the horse didn't move.

Gehn witnessed a change in the beast's hide then: a flicker of dark stripes beneath the gray, and as it turned its head to stare back at him with a clear, amber eye, he saw that he'd been tricked.

The acid-coated spike plunged deep into Gehn's back and forced a yell out of him. He attempted to reach back first, to grasp the pernicious thing now pushing liquid fire into his body. His hands failed there, and as he leaned forward and took a handful of the beast's mane, he could feel his muscles growing stiffer with each throbbing heartbeat.

The mane tore away like cobweb.

Through feverish waves, Gehn watched the once-steed melt like candlewax beneath him, witnessed its back stretch and shift into overlapping plates of black and green. Each leg bent and split in two, and as the horror settled onto eight dark, spidery appendages, a pair of pincer-claws solidified from steaming sludge.

Fighting the paralysis, Gehn managed a glance behind at the curled, segmented tail that had buried its stinger into him like a butcher's hook.

Multiple jewel eyes watched without emotion. Mandibles hissed and clicked to produce words. "*You won't be needing this.*" An enormous pincer cut the greatsword from Gehn's back and hurled the weapon into a nearby bush. The barb ripped out of his back only to come down in a second forceful stab, thrusting him forward to pin him to the hard roots.

Gehn groaned as new venom flowed. He knew that the creature would be nothing if he could only move. "My horse..." he said through gritted teeth. By this point, he felt as though only his mouth hadn't turned to hard clay like the rest of him. "I was just beginning to *like* that horse."

103

"Don't be so bitter." The scorpion clicked in its repugnant voice. It snickered. *"Your horse had the honor of giving its life to a god. You should feel so honored."*

Gehn found himself snickering back as he sensed the spark of heat growing in his chest.

As if suddenly expecting its prey to escape, the madly-clicking scorpion drove down harder with its tail and shifted closer to vise Gehn's arms in its striped claws.

"The honor's yours." The Ancient replied.

From the far trees, two very tall forms observed without word.

Their main focus had always been the shape-changer, yet now, as the taller, leaner of the two giants watched the human's slow and inevitable demise to the predator's venom, he felt the concern inside him shift. He turned and looked at his burlier companion and received an instantaneous answer: a single shake of the head. He knew why his fellow giant would want to wait, that the scorpion would be an easier target once it had gorged itself. His eyes fell to the shaft of the great, wooden spear that he clutched, the same that he himself had used only days ago to defend a pair of fawns.

He looked up again toward the grim scene. He was ready to step forward when a sudden, brilliant flash filled the trees ahead and brought his eyes to squints. White-hot flame enveloped both predator and prey, both outlines reduced to frail, azure shadows in a blinding orb. Ringing out now over the roar of the blaze was a veritable banshee chorus: the scream of the shape-changer.

Then the light vanished and a lingering veil of smoke remained, pierced and whipped again and again by the barbed tail of a charred and writhing shape.

All around Gehn, the world seemed to ripple and throb. Shivering, control oozing back into his muscles, he began to crawl toward the bushes that had swallowed his weapon. At last, he saw a glint through the cluster of leaves. When he brushed them aside, he found the object waiting like a long-forgotten artifact, like a lake's shimmering reflection.

Now, he turned to face the scorpion in its violent throes, thin smoke still rising from its blackened exoskeleton. Once more the creature had begun to shift, its body swelling and squeezing as four stalks sprouted from its oozing back and now spread into transparent wings. The claws and curling tail shriveled to leave a form like a great, grotesque wasp to squirm and buzz with furious futility.

"*RAHK TAKSAH*!!" It screamed. "*RAHK KUTAS KATAH*!!!"

Gehn raised the blade. With a wet *chack*, he split the creature's head and buried half of the mirror edge into the roots.

Wincing, he fell to his side. Darkness crept into his vision, and as he drifted off, he was certain that he saw something approach him through the shadows of the trees, something like a column made of churning, black fumes.

The giants waited in silence.

The sun had fallen some distance before the two finally moved in closer, practically on tiptoe, often stopping to slip behind trees and peer.

Beside the human lay the headless, black mutation, the killing blade angled and jutting from its head, its legs smoldering weakly like a bonfire's remnant brands. A tang of charred flesh hung in the air.

Sorrett, the taller of the two, stopped just beyond the angled shaft of sunlight that partially contained the scene. He watched the human now for any sign of movement, listened for any sound of breath. He found only stillness. After a glance back at the nervous face of his companion, Turren, he crouched and slowly extended the blunt end of his spear. With it he nudged the human's side.

The wood's scattered sunbeams fell dim so quickly that Sorrett turned his eyes toward the leaf-obscured sky. A frozen breeze touched the giant's face, and when he heard the groan and looked back down, he nearly fell backward with surprise.

Head facing downward, the human had shifted and turned to grip the roots beneath itself in a trembling attempt to stand.

As his companion swiftly retreated into the trees, Sorrett made step after slow step backward. Something in the human's movements chilled him now, a rigidity in its angled stance as it straightened with its head still hanging and its fingers hooked like vengeful claws. Darkness seemed to spread across its body like a drifting shadow cast by the canopy above, and just before Sorrett turned to retreat, the human's word came like a lengthy, wheezing breath:

"*Sorrett.*"

The giant stopped. "How...?" He uttered.

Before it fully rose, the human silhouette took the sword's handle and pulled free a blade dripping with the shape-changer's thick, inky ichor. When it angled its face toward Sorrett, the giant he was sure that he glimpsed ghostly, blue flames beneath its eyelids now. A single thread of lightning danced between those half-open eyes and the poisoned blade, illuminating an open mouth of bared teeth.

"Turren." Sorrett said as he broke his stillness and took another step backward.

With the snarl of a beast, the human charged toward him.

"Run!" Sorrett cried.

As he turned to sprint, he saw Turren leap out of hiding and hurl a massive, wooden spear at the attacker. He heard the weapon strike wood with a rapidly-resonating *chuck-uck-uck-uck.*

Then he turned and found himself running, yet despite his confidence in his and his companion's speed, the urge to look back quickly overcame him. He saw their pursuer almost immediately, some fifteen strides to the left, beyond the flying trunks: a living shadow of his own movements but for a sword cocked back in a single hand as though it weighed nothing at all.

"Look out!" Sorrett cried in the half second before the blade came spinning through the air. Ducking, he watched Turren break to the right just as the deadly wheel screamed past the

106

giant's shoulder, ripped through a low branch and plunged into the distant woods with a series of clangs.

The two giants broke out into a vast, barren clearing and chased their own weak shadows under a sky of broken clouds. When at last they reached the space's opposite end, they both skidded to a halt and turned.

From the trees the being came, no longer running but seeming to float toward them as dust and leaves and tiny stones lifted from the ground about its feet and joined the dark vapor that now enveloped it.

Turren bit off the words: "It's got no weapon."

The shake of Sorrett's head was not for agreement's sake.

Snatching the spear from Sorrett's hands, Turren stepped toward the human-thing with a growl.

Though the smoke-swathed form halted, Sorrett felt a shudder in the ground like the building wrath of a volcano. "*Turren.*" He uttered. " *Wait.*"

CRACK!

In a flash of light, the spearhead burst and flung fiery splinters into Turren's face. Staggering backward, the forest giant dropped what remained of the weapon and put his palms over his eyes, and now Sorrett was sure that he saw tendrils of blood oozing out between every crevice in Turren's hide. The swirling blackness seemed to quicken with the sound of his scream.

Sorrett had spotted the monstrous, old tree mere seconds earlier, and now, as he pushed, an escalating *creak* filled the clearing and it finally succumbed to his strength. The tree fell like the hammer of God, its thunderous *CRASH* summoning a storm of dust and leaves.

The being was nowhere to be seen.

Turren stopped screaming. The forest giant lie panting on the ground, holding to himself as if he'd just awakened from a nightmare.

Beside a naked, splintered stump, Sorrett stood, gazing wide-eyed at his handiwork. "It was a dying ta." He murmured as though to forgive himself.

Turren sat forward and stared dazedly. He gasped when he noticed the multiple streaks of crimson that covered him. "What happened?"

Sorrett made his way to the side of the felled tree, carefully scanning the tangled boughs as he went. He planted a foot against the trunk, and with a shoving kick, he rolled it back several yards, snapped branches swinging. There, amidst the mess of leaves and wooden fragments, lie a body bruised and bleeding and appearing strangely small. Of its dark transformation there was no trace.

Grunting, Turren got to his feet. "Sorrett?"

"Are you hurt?" Sorrett asked.

"I..." Turren, inspecting his own bloodied forearms, frowned. "My shoulder is on fire."

Sorrett took up the splintered spear and came over the defeated being. Drawing a deep breath through his nose, he raised the weapon high and vertical, his arm tense and his mind prepared to kill, and then, with the tip of his foot, he gently touched the body.

The being didn't move.

Lifting the wooden shaft higher, sure that the thing below him would wake and rise up with the same supernatural rage as it had before, Sorrett kicked again.

The being didn't move. Its eyes remained closed.

The forest giant's stony countenance softened. He lowered his spear.

"It's the human we were following." Turren stated, as though this was an unexpected discovery. "He kept calling out to us."

"Turren."

Turren didn't look up.

"Turren, are you sure you're alright?"

Though the giant's lips moved and his mouth parted, no answer emerged.

"Just stay here and wait for me." Sorrett said. "And don't go near him."

It didn't take Sorrett long to spot the blade angled against a vine-smothered stump, its bright steel contrasted by stripes of dark, drying blood peppered with splinters. Taking care not to touch the cursed substance, he cleaned off the sword as thoroughly as he could, and then, with several old vines, he bound it to the lower shaft of his spear.

Minutes later, he returned to find his companion absent from the scene of the fall.

"Turren!?" Sorrett called, but when several seconds passed and no reply came, the forest giant bent and took the limp and battered stranger up into one hand. He turned his eyes toward the wall of trees at the clearing's southeastern edge.

Gehn surfaced once, briefly, from the river of toxic sleep to find sight a confused fog and time a thing measured by what seemed a constant, echoing drumbeat. Then, as if by a weight chained to his ankle, he was pulled back down into the depths of that void where neither strength nor flame could help him.

Far away to the west, Strom rolled over green prairie on the metal wheels of a war-machine. To his left and right, a myriad of bayonets shone in the afternoon's fire as the soldiers carrying them marched ever northward.

In the rear rode Egan on his black horse, the young king's blood saturated with a different kind of poison; his dangling, right hand clutched a bottle of sloshing wine. Though it wasn't yet half finished, the king threw it behind him to *thud* and empty itself into the grass. He never looked back.

THENNKAL

'It can't be much further.' Sorrett thought as he ran, the pallid form in his hand seeming to shimmer in the whizzing patches of moonlight.

Night challenged his knowledge of the deep wood. It cloaked the landmarks that he would normally spot from a distance, and all at once he might stumble upon one in the dark: a rugged ravine or an old deadfall like a heap of bones, but more often than not, they reassured him that he was heading in the right direction.

Except for the ones that had carved themselves into the giant's mind, there were no roads here to betray the location of the forest's heart.

Before dawn, the giant slowed at the sight of a glassy pool. Drinking on the far edge were several deer that hardly reacted to his presence; a single doe brought her head up several inches to watch him with her round, dark eye.

He approached the pond and knelt beside it, setting his laden spear and the human down upon the bank to then plunge his arms into the water and bring handful after handful to his mouth.

Finally quenched, he wiped the cold droplets from his chin and turned again to his cargo. The being's skin-color looked to have further faded, but seeing the slight rise and fall of its chest sustained the giant's hope. Though urgency tugged at him, he couldn't help but study the creature now, the sharp angles of its face and the fur that grew so thickly at the top of the head. Before the encounter, Sorrett had viewed humans only from a distance.

'It's not human.' He reminded himself. 'It merely looks like one.'

The giant was reaching to take up the spear again when he heard the garbled, distant voice. He stood and turned to find only stillness in the dawn shadows.

"Turren?" He said.

There came no answer.

By twilight, he reached Thennkal's edge to find the place silent and still.

Stashing his spear and the blade beneath a root-walled hollow, Sorrett took the human-thing in both hands and made toward the all-but-indiscernible threshold, his eyes locked on a small mark in one of the ageless trunks ahead: a curving V shape meant to look like a natural scar. Squinting at the rune, knowing all too well its cunning purpose, Sorrett slowed as he approached. He could feel his heart drumming within him now, could feel his muscles tighten as though urging him to stop before he came too close, and when he was inches from Thennkal's trees, he turned his head and closed his eyes, waiting to hear a battle roar come rolling from the depths.

But there was only the hushed voice of the wind through the branches above.

When he opened his eyes, he saw that the carving had not changed. Then, with a ghost of a smile and a final look around, he slid into the deep wood.

Night fell.

Sorrett could hear it all around him as he went, a single perpetual drone sustained by the snores and groans of slumbering giants, a sound that reminded him of just how far he'd come with no more than a few short moments of rest. All at once, he wanted to take a place with them, to lean against a trunk and close his eyes and forget about his self-appointed task.

The sight of a distant guard stirred fresh energy inside him.

He could see the sacred clearing now, a veil of delicate moonbeams piercing the night air. He'd nearly reached the place when a voice bellowed at him from the darkness to his right:

"*What brings you?*"

"Legs." Sorrett blurted, pulling the human-thing tight to his chest. "They're broken."

The inquirer, a sentry giant, emerged from the shadows and planted the blunt end of a spear against the ground.

"It's a fawn." Sorrett added. Glancing down, he noticed a dangling boot and deftly tucked it away.

Suspicion drew new etches into the sentry's face.

"It's deformed."

Seconds later, Sorrett entered the clearing and came into the jagged shadow of Thennkal's oldest living denizen, a black, behemoth column that touched the moon now with branches both naked and immense. Only at its base was there evidence of life, for, rising from the bulging, moss-blanketed roots that gripped the bank of a pond, were several thin, green stalks that, for as long as Sorrett could recall, always seemed just on the verge of budding leaves.

He stepped up to the Arkonn, cool water rippling from his ankles, and whispered a few words in his native tongue. His prayer was met by a sound like branches bending and shifting to the will of a strong wind, and now, a slanted crevice opened in the Tree's trunk to spill dim, green light across the giant's form.

Gehn was sure at first that he was dreaming.

Here he hung, submerged and yet feeling no desperate need to breathe, eyes roving tiredly across the peaceful, green glow that wrapped him. In his back, where the scorpion had twice buried its stinger and had injected its boiling venom, a tingling sensation now spread that seemed, with every passing second, to devour a little more of that pain, to restore a little more of that broken flesh.

'Thank you.' Gehn thought, and he shut his eyes.

Sorrett sat cross-legged on the pool's opposite bank, staring at the Arkonn and fighting the increasing weight of his head. It fell once; the giant nodded off for a moment before jerking back to attention and finding that something had changed.

112

He stood and splashed across the pool to find, oozing out of the many tiny cracks in the Arkonn's ancient bark, a slimy, translucent fluid. Several inches each trickle fell before bubbling and evaporating, lacing the air with a smell so potent and unpleasant that the giant stepped back and turned his head away.

'The poison.' He realized, watching the miniature bubbles shift and crawl like lustrous, emotionless eyes. 'It's pulling it out of him.'

Sorrett woke with a surge of alarm and the sudden awareness that he was falling backward. No more than a second after he'd crashed into the water had he sprung back up to a standing position, looking all around now to see if he'd drawn the attention of the guard he'd earlier encountered. He saw no one, the clearing curiously silent but for the slapping of the small waves he'd made.

He approached the Tree, and then his eyes widened when he caught sight of a familiar shape behind the thickest arch of root: the human-thing, still unconscious, snug in a mossy crevice near the Arkonn's base.

He splashed across and was about to take the body when a voice sounded like the bark of a mokru:

"Fool!"

Sorrett spun to see the sentry descending into the clearing.

"You brought a human to the sacred place?"

"I can explain." Sorrett growled back, but now he discerned new silhouettes between those of the trees: a number of spear-armed giants encircling him, and he knew that the being's fate had left his hands.

EKKNET

Darkness surrounded Gehn.

Whatever this place, it wasn't the tranquil refuge in which he'd found himself earlier. Gravity held him once more and he lay

113

upon cold, hard ground, and as his senses returned, he heard a sound like the steady whispering of ocean surf.

'No.' He thought, listening more closely. 'Wind in the leaves. I'm in the Eastern Wood.' And with this reclaimed understanding, the events before the venom had taken him came back in a murky flood.

He rose up onto his elbows to see that he was indeed in the forest still, but it was quickly clear to him that this wasn't an ordinary section of it; here, the trees stood in evenly-spaced rows like the columns of an impossible hall. Ahead in the dimness, upon a tall stump that had been carved into a crude and rugged throne, sat a truly intimidating shape. Except for the motion Gehn caught of its head tilting slightly back and its gleaming, intelligent eyes, it might have been a statue itself.

The form leaned suddenly forward in its chair, seeming to Gehn to lean directly over him though it was in fact nearly fifteen feet away, and now, it bellowed a single question: "What do you want?"

Gehn's mouth opened to say nothing.

"Well?" The giant pressed.

Despite his tongue feeling like a stone, the words came out clearly. "To talk."

"Talk?" The towering shape rumbled. "About what?"

Gehn rocked forward. Extending one hand for balance and placing the other against the ground for support, he rose awkwardly to his feet. He could still feel a trace of the poison inside him, a sense of amplified gravity, but the injuries in his back had been reduced to mere flecks of irritation. 'The sword.' He thought, looking about himself for a moment before he remembered where he'd left it in the shape-changer's head. He guessed that he was somewhere far from that place now.

"My warriors wanted to leave you at the forest's edge." The giant squinted. "Perhaps they had the right idea."

It was a moment before Gehn caught the being's meaning; he hadn't expected a forest giant to be so articulate. "I've come to ask for your help."

The giant said nothing.

114

"I'm assembling an army against the dognars." Just then, Gehn's attention landed on two pale, toothy objects, one resting at either side of the throne's base. The wedge-shaped skulls had been separated from their lower jaws and were positioned upside down with the snouts facing inward in an ornamental fashion. "I see you're familiar with them."

The great being glanced down. When it looked up again, the mistrust in its pupils seemed only to have sharpened. "You mean the mokru."

Gehn waited.

"They have sharp teeth, but our spears and axes are sharper."

"Not for long." Gehn replied firmly. "Not unless something is done about them."

"What is your name?"

"Gehn is what I'm called. You're king here, I assume."

"King Ekknet, the only." The king angled his head back. "So you would see an army of giants and humans fighting side by side?"

"And dwarves."

At this, Ekknet gave a laugh so loud that the forest seemed to tremble. When he had finished, his eyes and smile appeared almost villainous. "*Dwarves* and *giants*? Opposing armies maybe! I was sure that you were lying before, but now I see! You're mad!"

Strom's brief word of history between the midgets and the forest-dwellers rang through Gehn's mind. He weighed the value of each race now, the dwarves' ingenuity in one hand and the giants' sheer power and speed in the other, but losing either felt to him like a considerable sacrifice. He also knew that yielding too quickly could be a mistake. "You can't cooperate with the dwarves for a short period of time?"

The giant glared for a moment. "Perhaps you don't know what the dwarves did to my kind. I'll show you. Abban!"

Another tall shape seemed to materialize from the endless rows of trees. It trudged up to the throne, its great arms hanging, each of its wrists bearing a black, bracer-like object. The giant

115

stopped beside Ekknet's left hand. Contrary to its fatigued appearance, its voice held vigor. "Tol?"

"Show him your wrists."

The newcomer raised its arms into the starlight, revealing a pair of cuffs from each of which still dangled a few large links of chain.

"The devil-steel is unbreakable." Ekknet construed. "They'll bite his wrists until his death, and ever serve as a reminder of the time that he was used like an animal. Like a *machine*, as your dwarves say." Ekknet leaned back and relaxed in his throne, leering now as if he'd triumphed over an argument. "So you see."

"You wouldn't be fighting for humans or dwarves." Gehn reasoned. "Only for yourselves."

Ekknet shook his head. "You'll be taken back to the outer woods. Don't think you'll be met with such mercy as you've seen tonight if you try to return here. It was only because of one that you were spared and brought before me at all."

Hearing the sounds of footfalls behind him, Gehn glanced back and saw two guards step into the glade. While one clutched an enormous club, the other carried what appeared to be a crate or a cage fashioned of branches and covered with broad, lifeless leaves.

Gehn saw Ekknet nod to the guards. He considered the time and effort he'd placed in his attempt to enroll these creatures, and what rose to his mouth now was the voice of his own inexorable will: "*Abban.*"

Abban's countenance abandoned fatigue for intensity. The giant's eyes reflected faint, azure light.

The two guards stopped.

Gehn extended his right hand toward Abban's left.

"Tenkat?" Ekknet boomed, gripping to his throne as if he meant to thrust himself up from it. "What is this?"

Stepping forward, Gehn took hold of the cuff that clung tightly to Abban's left wrist. Glowing orange circles spread from Gehn's fingertips now as he pulled with both hands, and though Abban's eyes further widened, the giant made not even the smallest attempt to pull away.

With a snarl, the guards sprung back into action. *Boom Boom BOOM!*

"Stop!" Ekknet cried.

There came the *thud-clank* of metal on wood.

It was only after one had flung Gehn violently to the ground that the two warriors seemed to realize that the command had been meant for them.

Stifling a groan, Gehn pushed himself up.

Near Abban's feet lie the fallen black cuff, its smoldering mouth locked in a wide yawn. At a raw and bloody trench Abban gazed now, and as the giant lifted its other hand to gently touch the liberated flesh, Gehn was sure that he caught a glitter of moisture below the creature's eyes.

Wind snaked through the canopy above.

Ekknet sat and watched in silence. Any evidence of wonder in his face had expired.

Now, Abban stepped closer to Gehn and extended his remaining metal-bound wrist. Gehn was about to reach up when Ekknet's own hand took hold of the cuff instead.

"You think that this being cares about your sufferings, Abban?" Ekknet asked. "It simply wants to control you."

"No." Gehn replied.

"Whatever power you have means nothing to me." The king's sneer steadily tightened. "I won't allow my tribe to be bought with a trick."

"I can't undo what the dwarves did," Gehn calmly said, "but this is survival. If you truly love your tribe, there's only one choice for you to make."

"Enough!" Ekknet thundered, and for several seconds only stared at Gehn before finally releasing Abban's cuffed wrist and settling back into his throne. "I'll bring your request to the elders. Until then," he looked to the two guards, "take him to the stump and hold him there."

117

The cage swayed and lurched like a boat on a choppy sea. Through the tied branches and the broken veil of leaves, Gehn saw bits and pieces of the gradually-brightening forest. Then, his eyes caught something different ahead: a dark, old stump so prodigious in size that it could have passed for a ruined castle. The cage's carrier headed for an opening in its face, leaping into this at the last possible moment to glide over a seemingly-bottomless trench and then land with such force that Gehn thought the container would fly apart. Here, in the cave-like hollow, onto the center of a vast bowl of bark and umber-hued earth, the cage touched down.

"There's only one way in or out." The giant said to Gehn before it dashed back up the steep, inner slope. Once at the top, it turned to give him a final glance. "We'll be watching."

Boom boom boom... boom boom....

The sound of the being's footsteps dissolved away.

Seconds passed. Gehn stood holding the rough, wooden bars of the cage and wondered how long it would take for the Giant King to come to a decision. He took a deep breath and looked up toward the stump's ceiling of narrow fissures and smooth, blade-like ridges.

A voice broke the quiet. "You're feeling better."

Gehn turned and looked into the hollow's depths and then reached out through the bars to tear away a section of papery leaves that blocked his view. There, beyond the hazy, morning light pushing in through the opening, sitting against the stump's inner wall with its knees to its chest, was a form both slender and massive.

"My name is Sorrett." It said.

The question remained on Gehn's face.

The giant added: "I was the one that brought you to Thennkal."

118

THE SHADOW

By the time the question came, the sunbeams were clear and angled through the stump's opening. A visible sliver of canopy blazed with green.

"Do you remember what happened?"

Gehn sat cross-legged, facing his fellow prisoner through the large circle he'd ripped in the crisp layer of vines and leaves. His attention returned to the two itching holes between his shoulders, and he spoke with an icy satisfaction. "I remember putting my blade through its head."

"The shape scorpion." Sorrett stared with round, mirthless eyes. "What about after that?"

"Darkness." Gehn's gaze fell onto the scattered strips and flecks of bark outside the cage. "Then I dreamt that something was healing me."

"That was the Arkonn," Sorrett corrected, "not a dream."

"They put you in here because you helped me?"

The giant's eyes dropped. "...Yes."

"What will happen to you?"

The giant shrugged. "I don't know. I can't remember the last time someone was punished." He looked toward his left, where his outstretched arm was vised between two great, wooden poles as thick as old pine trees, both halves of the crude shackle driven deep into the ground and bound at the top by countless vines. With the finger of his free hand, Sorrett began to draw a rune in the soft earth at his side. "When you fell to the scorpion's venom, my companion and I came forward for a closer look. You rose up and attacked us."

Gehn listened without word.

"I know you have some kind of power." The giant went on. "I saw it when you scorched that creature. But this was different. This was like you were *made* of darkness. You would've killed Turren if I hadn't crushed you with the ta." Sorrett looked at him now and squinted with concern. "What's wrong?"

"Nothing."

"You look pale."

A sudden, roaring shout sounded from the forest outside. Both Gehn and Sorrett quickly turned to stare up at the stump's opening in time to hear a string of furious, echoing calls, most clearly the words: "*Tenkat! Ta riok!*"

"What is it?" Gehn asked.

Sorrett glared intently, his right hand clenching into a fist. "Something's trespassed into Thennkal." He tried to stand now, pulling hard against his wooden fetter until his lips were tight over his teeth.

Watching as the spears of morning light began to fade, sensing the sudden drop in the air's temperature, Gehn said: "Dognars. I can help you."

After a groan from the wood as well as the giant's throat, Sorrett ripped his hand free with a *crack*. He scrambled up to the edge of the opening and looked out. "It's not the mokru. I would hear them." He glanced distractedly at Gehn. "The guard is gone. Stay here."

Warily, Sorrett went. To his left he caught a flitter of movement beyond the far, pillar trunks: armed giants, running parallel to his course and toward an unseen adversary.

He stopped behind a tree to let the warriors pass ahead, and now he came directly in front of a blinding, scarlet gleam gripped by an engraving in the trunk: one of the ancient runes that shone only when an intruder had crossed into Thennkal's border.

Sorrett's bark-like skin clenched tight as a gust of frigid wind brushed past him. He turned to face the direction from which it'd come. 'The Arkonn.'

High above the branches, the morning's once-frail clouds were dense and tenebrous.

'Why do I hear nothing?' He wondered.

He passed another red glow and nearly missed the streaked, carmine splotches on the tree directly opposite: a partial, glistening handprint made of fresh blood.

Tightening his fists, he carefully scanned his surroundings until his eyes caught an odd silhouette amidst a cluster of young trees ahead. Without a sound, he moved in closer, and now he saw that the shape was indeed a giant hunkered down on a patch of flat and rootless earth with its arms crossing its chest and each hand clinging to an opposite elbow.

A second look at the strange giant's hands brought Sorrett to a halt; from fingertip to mid-forearm, each appendage was covered so completely with blood that it might've been dipped in a basin full.

"Tsst." Sorrett tried.

The other giant remained a statue.

"Hey."

Further angling its head toward the ground, the giant muttered: "I don't know how it started."

Sorrett recognized the voice at once. "*Turren?*" He moved a few steps closer and stopped again. Despite the sudden flurry of questions in his mind, he asked only one: "Why is there blood on you?"

Turren's eyes were the dark and lifeless holes of a wooden mask. "It's coming for him."

A sneer tugged at the edge of Sorrett's mouth. "What?"

"When it's finished," Turren softly said, and now raised his face toward the gloomy recesses of the forest, "it will leave us alone."

In spite of his ever-deepening dread, the calm in Sorrett's tone never wavered. "What happened?" And now he noticed, amidst the broken patches of dried blood on the other giant's shoulder, a thin, lateral cut, nearly unnoticeable but for the bulge of jaundiced flesh that encompassed it. Two memories darted through Sorrett's mind, the first of flying trees and a blade spinning past Turren's shoulder. The second vision came from the days of his youth, when he'd once witnessed the long and ugly fate of two young wolves that had dared to scavenge on a shape-scorpion's severed leg. The creature's vile blood had been as cruel as venom. "You're poisoned." Sorrett said with realization. "The Arkonn can heal you."

"No, it can't." Turren languidly replied. "It can't help any of us now. All because you brought that stranger here."

121

"What did you do?" Sorrett demanded, a hint of anger having leaked into his voice. "Tell me!"

The bloodied giant turned partially toward Sorrett now. He seemed almost to choke on three words: "*You* did this." A single tear rolled down his face. "You should never have brought him."

Sorrett leaned back.

"Leave me."

Sorrett said nothing.

"I said *go*." In one swift motion, Turren leapt up and snatched Sorrett's throat with two crimson hands.

Tripping, Sorrett fell backward and landed hard against the roots. As he fought to pull the hands away, he knew only the hateful outline above him, a hiss through gritted, glinting teeth. With his right fist, he struck the side of Turren's head once, twice, and then he felt the giant release him. Coughing, shifting awkwardly to sit forward, he caught the muffled *thud thud thud* of the giant sprinting away.

The wood was still again by the time he made it to his feet. Looking around and seeing no one, Sorrett found himself facing a section of distant, shadowy trees.

In his struggle with the frozen air, he crossed his arms against his chest, and, for a moment, the small tremors in his limbs seemed to subside.

Step by silent step, Sorrett approached the sacred clearing. He'd come close enough now that he could make out the Arkonn's immense silhouette, but something about its lower trunk fueled his unease: a tangle of unfamiliar shapes rendered all but indiscernible under the gloom of the gathering clouds. Then he crossed into the glade and his fear changed to horror, for from here he could see the two skinned stags pinned to the tree by a single spear. Beneath their dangling hooves, filled not with red light but with dripping crimson, were four savagely-carved symbols.

For a time, the giant only stared, transfixed by the grisly defacement that his mind could not accept as real, until he heard the furtive footstep behind him and turned just in time to see the weapon's shaft before it struck.

Seconds later, flat against the ground with a foot pressed against his head, he watched a glowing, scarlet rune fall dim in a distant tree, until its light was gone.

THE SHADOW FALLS

It was a slower trip this time, the movement of the cage little more than a gentle shaking as its bearer simply marched. Despite the many, watching faces being near-featureless to Gehn's eyes, he still gleaned from them a pointed expression of enmity.

His hands yearning for the sword he'd been separated from, he pressed a palm against the outside of his right boot and felt the dagger hidden there. He looked ahead again, where, past the lofty canopy, he could see a spire against the gray: the highest reaches of a dark and leafless tree.

Slowly, the crowd of prodigious beings split, and then closed behind as he was brought into the clearing. Gehn stood up in the cage and took hold of the wooden bars. To his left, a familiar giant knelt at the edge of a pond: Sorrett, encircled by the points of several trained, angled spears. The giant turned to look at him gravely.

Upon the ground of the pool's opposite side lie two felled giants, one flat on its stomach, the other frozen in a half twist with its open fingers curled like claws. Gehn couldn't yet see their wounds, only the streams of blood that snaked between the roots and saturated the slope of moist, sandy earth touching the pond's restless water.

One giant stood within the miniature waves now, the being's back to Gehn as it struggled with what looked to be a spear that had been driven into the tree's slate-colored trunk. With a grunt, the spear came loose and the giant staggered back with a splash but didn't fall, and now, as the being turned and Gehn recognized its fervid eyes, those eyes found him.

The Giant King.

Gehn's carrier stopped and placed the cage firmly onto the ground. Ekknet approached, the king's towering height revealed in full as he came up out of the water. A pair of flayed, skewered stags wagged hideously from the end of the spear he held.

"Did *you* do this?" Ekknet boomed just as two giants rushed in to take the spear and carry it away.

"No." Gehn's eyes returned to the tree then, to the vertical stripe of blood and the four symbols that had been cut into the immemorial, gray bark. Just looking at the runes made Gehn's muscles tense and brought the hairs on his arms to stand on end, and suddenly the wrath of the giant before him felt insignificant.

"Do you know what did?" Ekknet pressed.

Sorrett, still kneeling against his will, chimed: "I already told you."

"Be silent, sul." The king commanded, his stare never leaving Gehn. "I'm speaking to the strange creature that you allowed into our home."

"He was dying. You'd have done the same."

"The power of the Sacred One isn't meant to save a demon!" Spat a giant from the crowd.

"If he's a demon, then why did it choose to save him?" Sorrett countered.

"BE SILENT." The Giant King's words filled the clearing and echoed away through the wood like a thunder clap. Seemingly satisfied with the quiet that followed, he repeated his question: "Do you know what did this?"

The longer that Gehn looked at the dark runes, the more they seemed like windows into emptiness, into a fathomless void where light simply did not exist. "This is the Arkonn?"

"Yes." Ekknet turned back toward the monumental tree.

At that moment, a gaunt, pallid giant emerged from the throng, the being's hide cracked and peeling. It made feebly through the water and, at last, placed a gnarled hand against the

124

Arkonn's trunk. "The Sacred Ta is losing its warmth." It voiced. "This is the work of an unnatural power."

Ekknet turned back to regard Gehn once more with a familiar aspect of suspicion.

"I didn't do this." Gehn said.

"No." The old one at the tree agreed. "Yet you brought the evil here with you."

Gehn said nothing.

"Well?" Ekknet squinted. "Tell us what you know."

The scene returned to Gehn's mind: a stony plain and a flameless funnel of smoke against twilit sky, but even before the vision's details sharpened and he smelled the charred flesh, he could sense the presence of the thing standing inside the black, billowing column.

"If it had a name, we never learned it." Gehn started, unaware of the faint, blue fire that now stirred in his irises as he looked down toward the pool. "We only knew it, *him*, as the Evil One, the being that corrupted half of my brothers and nearly drove us to extinction."

The giants waited.

When several seconds passed and Gehn had said nothing more, Ekknet's cavernous voice cut the stillness short: "And how do we stop it from destroying the Sacred Ta?"

Gehn shook his head and his eyes returned to the tree's bloodied violations; something told him that the giants' hallowed icon had a function they knew nothing about. "This sacrifice has given him a foothold. He will feed on the Arkonn's energy until he has the strength to manifest."

Ekknet tilted his head back, his thin upper lip taut over his teeth. "What?"

"He's using the tree as a doorway to cross into this world."

"And why would he choose *now* to do such a thing?"

Before Gehn could respond, a sound caught his ear that stoked the fire at his core and conjured corkscrewing threads of smoke from the wooden bars at his fingers. It began as little more than a rattle, sharp and steady, like the warning of a nettled

125

dust viper, and grew into a vibration that sent countless ripples across the blood-tinted pond.

The elder giant pushed away from the tree with a look of bewilderment as, above his head, the four crude symbols shifted on the bark like a crawling hive of insects.

Ekknet moved two steps closer to the tree. "Entas. Those are *our* symbols."

"Totas thettek rett," the old one read, "iros entrat ta."

"Kill him," Ekknet translated, turning back to face Gehn once more, "and I will release the ta."

Silence followed, and suddenly Gehn felt the full weight of the attention focused on him. His fingers twitched, his muscles eager to rip the wooden bars open, but beneath this impulse he knew that an escape attempt would likely only seal his fate. He could never outrun them, and he wagered that even with a weapon he'd be no match for a hundred tree-sized spears.

"Say the word, Tol." One of the many glaring faces voiced. "Better the Sacred Ta should live than this filthy curse-bringer!"

The Giant King only looked at Gehn, his expression gradually slackening until it was unreadable. "And what if I did kill you?" He asked. "This devil would actually keep its word?"

'I can't show him fear.' Gehn told himself, never blinking as he challenged the giant's stare, his face angled slightly forward. "It might." He answered. "But it would still be a mistake."

After another long silence, Ekknet turned to look at the elder, and then, once more, at the message on the trunk. He moved toward one of the trees that ringed the clearing and calmly took the great, wooden axe leaning against it. "If this being wants you dead," he proclaimed, "it will have to do its own killing." He ran his thumb along the blade and glanced at the afflicted tree again with a hardened visage. "And only after it's dealt with me."

A trembling rose in the earth.

A crack broke free from the Arkonn's dark, spear-made hole, thin at first, steadily widening as it branched and climbed its way up the stony bark and brought the watching giants to gasp and mutter. Where there had once been mere ripples on the pond's surface were now tiny, frothing waves.

126

Gehn saw his own breath come out in ghostly cones. He noticed then the bare stalks that jutted upward from the Arkonn's visible roots, and, for a fleeting moment, he was sure he caught them budding leaves of vibrant green.

As the vibration grew, the jagged fissure suddenly shot upward with the speed of a lightning bolt, splitting the tree's entire body and loosing pieces to plummet into the clearing. Ekknet helped the elder away just as the Arkonn's two, creaking halves pulled apart like hungry jaws toward the sky, and now Gehn saw a massive fragment come hurtling down like a boulder at the cage. With no time to break free, he scrambled to the rear and covered his head with his arms just as the forward section disappeared behind a squall of flying splinters.

Before he could break his way out of what remained of his container, the hands of the Giant King pulled away a portion of the wooden grid and allowed him to slip through.

With the exception of the crowd's whispers and the dying movement of the pond's surface, stillness had returned to the glade. Far above, the ruined Arkonn's halves hung in a towering V shape.

The pale elder went to the lower trunk and placed a hand on it once more, but Gehn had already guessed what the giant would discover; the stalks at the Arkonn's base had indeed sprouted an array of leaves during the chaos, but those leaves were now black and withered.

Without a word, the old giant simply looked back toward Ekknet.

"Where is this devil of yours?" The Giant King's face twitched with muzzled rage. "Is he a coward?"

Gehn gave no answer.

Wind rushed quietly through the canopy. Up beyond what remained of the devastated tree, the ceiling of drifting cloud resembled an icy, inverted ocean.

Seconds passed.

At last, Ekknet nodded to the armed warriors encircling Sorrett. "Release him. As for you, Gihn, you're not to leave Thennkal until I give the word."

DARKNESS

By the time that dusk arrived, the sky was clear, and a curious crescent moon peered in through the branches.

Gehn sat alone at the edge of shallow water now as flat as glass, its surface interrupted here and there by several sharp-ridged islands that had once been part of the Arkonn. Not a cry or a trill or a rustle of wind could be heard, only the frequent, near-noiseless *twick* of a fallen leaf touching down. One after another, they tumbled through the air, and Gehn couldn't help but entertain a brief notion that the trees were weeping.

A voice behind him: "The being you spoke of..."

He turned to see Sorrett's dim form standing just outside the clearing.

"It was *him* inside you." The giant said. "He entered you with the scorpion's venom."

Looking back toward the symbols below the Arkonn's rift, Gehn thought he could remember a glimpse of that pursuit now: a moment of consciousness ruled by incomprehensible rage.

Sorrett approached Gehn's left side and bent to place a lengthy, blue blade onto the roots with a metallic *katunk*. "Yours."

Gehn glanced at the weapon.

"What this Evil One did to the Arkonn, you spoke as if he'd done it before."

Though Gehn heard the words, their meaning never registered. As he continued to sort through the fractured and scattered images that in some places coalesced to form coherent memories, he still couldn't shake the feeling that these were merely illusions, that the Ancient Wall had put him under a spell. He realized then that Sorrett was staring at him. "...What?"

"Never mind it."

Gehn turned to regard the seemingly-empty forest behind him, a stretch of endless dark trees cut through by slanted moonbeams. "They're watching us, aren't they?"

The giant nodded as though he were ashamed to admit the truth. "Yes."

Looking back to the dark and tortured V that remained of the Arkonn and the leaves that continued to fall around it, Gehn's chuckle was nearly silent. "Your king should understand that this enemy isn't an animal that he can lure into a trap."

"There is no other choice for Ekknet." Sorrett's eyes shone in the night like globes of obsidian. "Years ago, when our king finally discovered the truth behind the strange disappearances of many giants in his tribe, he gathered his strongest warriors and left the woods, and he scoured the open lands until he found wheel tracks heading into the west. He followed them." Sorrett paused as a trio of leaves fell spinning past his face. "Camp after dwarven camp he took, too cunning for the pits and snares and too quick for the sleeper darts, freeing giants and scattering the trappers as he went, but when he came to the final camp, he found his enemy waiting for him. The dwarves had drenched their captives in oil and had strapped them with fire-barrels, and when they saw the king approaching, they warned him what they would do if he didn't turn back. It was the only way they could've stopped him." The giant shook his head. "They've never returned for another attempt."

After a second glance at the sword, Gehn took its handle and dragged the heavy object closer to himself. He turned the mirror blade to check his dim reflection askance, and now, as he looked into his own eyes, Sorrett asked him: "Are you afraid?" Just then, he noticed that the branches had stopped shedding their leaves; the last one touched down inches away from his left boot. He saw Sorrett tense beside him, and now he followed the giant's stare toward a brightening, red symbol in the trunk of a tree beyond the clearing's far edge.

The noise of a single bark raced through the once-quiet forest. The sound was muffled by distance alone.

129

Gehn felt a wave of warm energy roll down through his arms to the ends of his fingers. His hand tightened on the blade's cold hilt. "That wasn't a wolf."

"Mokru." Sorrett supplied.

A second bark was heard, this one from what seemed to be a completely different direction, and then a third and fourth, and now there rose a legion of the snarling, wordless threats.

The giant moved out of the clearing and swiftly dipped to take up his spear.

Beyond Sorrett's shape, Gehn's eyes found slight movements between the trees: warriors stirring in their dark hiding places to face the threat at Thennkal's border. Here and there amidst them, scarlet symbols burned like lanterns.

By this point, the roaring, resounding barks had escalated to a maddening din.

Gehn rose to his feet. He didn't notice the black and vaporous tendrils slithering up through a section of roots near the pool.

"It doesn't sound like we've engaged them." The giant voiced over the noise as he moved out a few more steps. "Why would they announce themselves?"

"Because it's a trick." Gehn's reply drowned in a sudden rumbling noise that rose from the very ground. Now it seemed to him that every shadow in the glade had come to life to expand and shrink and expand and shrink in a quick and steady pulse. When he heard the whispered breath, he spun and he swung the blade with such force that it nearly flew from his grip.

He saw only trees. Unlike the barking, the potent tremor had ceased. Above him and against the sharp crescent moon, the broken Arkonn had the look of a demon shrine.

"Sorrett." Gehn turned, and he found that the giant had left his sight. All around the glade he scanned, his eyes drawn to every twisted shadow cast by the high branches. Then the words seemed to come from directly in front of him like the calm and reasonable voice of a trusted friend: "Put down the blade."

Gehn's eyes squeezed to glowing slits. When he caught the soot-black shape at his left, it was too late; the hand took his

130

throat and now slammed him against a nearby trunk with such abrupt force that the sword fell from his hands with a smothered clang.

Pinned and unable to shout or even breathe, struggling fruitlessly against the cold and crushing fingertips, Gehn looked now through what seemed like the bottom of a turbid river, through smoke like roiling clouds of sediment. At the other end of the outstretched arm, he discerned the tall shape of his attacker, a lightless face with two red flares for eyes and a head of long, sable hair that seemed to float as though unaffected by gravity.

Gehn ripped at the appendage, at flesh like wet sand that wouldn't quite separate from itself. He snatched the dagger from his boot and plunged it into his foe's upper arm, but when he tried to twist it, the blade snapped.

The crippling hand tightened. Any sense of time slipped away from him. Now he heard a distant, repeating *crash* like a blacksmith's hammer from the end of a long, stone corridor, each strike accompanied by a sharp, metallic pain that flashed through his core like countless needles.

Crash. Crash. Crash! Crash!

Each strike came louder than the last, each wave of agony cutting deeper and further than the one before, until he was sure that he saw tiny splits break and bleed in the skin of his forearms.

There was no tree at his back now. No roots existed below his feet, but in their place, the blackness of an infinite abyss.

By now, each sound had become an earsplitting cannon blast. '*Help me.*' He called out in his mind.

The baleful red eyes vanished from the sheets of smoke as though his tormentor had suddenly turned away. Then, Gehn saw an unexpected shape: a towering silhouette with a slender weapon held high. The hand released his neck half a moment before the massive, wooden axe head struck.

Gehn slid down against the tree. He caught another glimpse of the axe-wielding Ekknet before a pall of smoke engulfed the giant's form like a swarm of angry flies.

"Tol entra!" Came the king's desperate cry.

131

Fresh energy flooded through Gehn's body like water through a crumbling dam. He saw Strom's prized sword waiting on a heap of roots, and as he made for the weapon, he saw a blinding, white bolt lance from its hilt to its flawless tip.

"TOL ENTRA!"

In one motion, Gehn snatched up the blade and he swung, and now he felt the razor edge slice through tissue softer than clay. The sound was like a landslide: a pain-filled roar, after which the ebon body vanished and left a hollow for swirling smoke to fill.

At once, the distant barking stopped.

Ekknet opened an eye to investigate the quiet and found nothing more than the night's natural murk. He opened both eyes now, and when seconds had passed and he'd still neither seen nor felt any trace of his attacker, he brought his head out from under his arm and cautiously straightened to his full height. Above him, between the peaceful, black masses of canopy, stars twinkled in a clear sky.

He spotted Gehn standing near the glade's edge, gently touching his throat with one hand and holding the mirror blade lax with the other. Ascending both from the weapon and from Gehn's faintly-burning irises were licks of vapor as white as steam.

"You... killed him?" Ekknet asked.

At the clearing's edge, Sorrett and a handful of giants appeared and now simply gawked.

Without turning, Gehn muttered an answer: "I sent him back."

Chapter 11

AFTER THE STORM

It was on the brighter side of dawn when they broke free from the western edge of the forest.

Sorrett raced through parched scrubland in twenty-foot strides. Standing atop the giant's shoulders, Gehn looked back across bushes and tall grass stalks swaying like waves on a silty sea. He watched the wall of mammoth trees recede rapidly behind, all shade but for the highest leaves which gleamed like emeralds in the early light. He squinted at the sun and felt it had been too long since he'd last seen it.

They stopped at nightfall.

The hill was a large and lonely thing, naked compared to the surrounding wilderness but for a single brown boulder jutting from its crest. Sorrett sat cross-legged against this boulder now, rubbing his large feet and staring, as if hypnotized, into the leaping fire that Gehn had made. "The barking scalewolves," the forest giant said, "were they real?"

Gehn stood nearby, eying a jagged range of mountains on the northwestern landscape. He'd been immersed in his own thoughts, but the question now had his full attention. He turned slightly to catch just the fringe of his companion's amber-lit shape. "Why wouldn't they have been?"

Sorrett shrugged and frowned. "If they were real, their timing couldn't have been an accident. It would mean they were serving him." The giant took a break from the massaging but kept his focus on the burning branches. "Is that possible?"

"He created them." Gehn replied.

The giant's lips parted a sliver as he contemplated this. Finally, he brought up his glossy, unblinking eyes. "Created them?"

"If you can call it that." A snap and a rustle caught Gehn's ear, and he turned to the valley below in time to see a lump of dark fur shamble out of sight behind a wall of short, twisted trees.

"He's been controlling them all along?" Sorrett had barely glanced in the sound's direction.

"Maybe for that brief moment. I don't think he can control them from the other side." Gehn made his way slowly back to the fire and to the sword he'd earlier shed. Standing opposite the forest giant now, he drew the weapon from its lengthy, leather sheath and held it as though he were about to drop it into the flames. He turned the handle until the blade became a thin, dark line between him and the throbbing, orange radiance, and he thought again of the previous night's struggle, of the strange glint he'd seen in the metal before he'd buried it into his opponent's flesh. He was certain now that the weapon had been forged by Ancients, yet this knowledge failed to satisfy him. "Ekknet shouted something when he was attacked."

After a moment's thought, Sorrett supplied: "Tol entra."

"Doesn't Tol mean king in your tongue?"

"It could, but it's more a word of respect used to address authority."

Gehn sheathed the sword and set it back down. "Who has greater authority than Ekknet?"

"The Arkonn is... *was* sacred," Sorrett bitterly amended, "but Tol wouldn't be the correct word. The Ta was a gift. It didn't rule us."

Gehn took two fat branches from the pile he'd gathered earlier. He put them into the fire. "Is there a giant word for God?"

134

"There are many." Adjusting his position against the boulder, the forest giant shifted his attention up toward a starry expanse still tinted purple with twilight. "I suppose that Tol could be an old word for God."

"And... *enetra*?"

"Entra is like a battle cry, only one for help." Sorrett started pressing on the sole of his right foot again. "Does that make sense?"

Nodding, Gehn turned toward the west just as a night bird screeched in the valley below. His mind returned to the moment of its own desperate call.

"He must have been afraid." The giant added.

"What makes you say that?"

"A true warrior doesn't call out to the Mighty One for any trivial reason. Only when he feels that there is no other hope left, not even in himself." Fierce creases formed in Sorrett's face. "What that demon did to the Arkonn," he said, "the way you spoke, he has done it before. Is that correct?"

"Yes." Gehn answered, his eyes deep in the shadows far beyond the reach of the firelight. "Only it wasn't to a tree."

That night, the Ancient dreamed of still, ruined warriors so countless that they could not be distinguished from the ground itself. Then he watched as a spark of piercing white appeared on the western horizon, and he realized, as the source of steady brilliance grew into the sky, that it was not the sun but something far more powerful, something with light that flowed and spread like water over every surface until not a shadow remained.

The voice was soft,

"Gehn."

And yet he woke with it echoing in his head. He would watch the petering coals for a long time.

135

For the next several days, Gehn knew only the wind against his face and the endlessly-rolling ground like some immeasurable grindstone beneath Sorrett's swift feet.

With every mile that passed, the land became less alien to his eyes, and, at long last, the two travelers crossed over a wall of small hills and came into lush, green fields scattered with oaks.

They were spotted only once on their journey through Dain, by a young, human rider that they passed so closely and unexpectedly that they could see the shock on his pale face.

DWARVEN GROUND

Carried by the northern wind, dense clouds battled the sun for reign over the afternoon sky. Shafts of light cut down through them here and there to illuminate sharp and scattered patches of thirsty grass below, but shade endured over the silent fortress. Even from this distance, its bristles could be discerned, its four spires like the stalks of a colossal, iron thornbush.

"Still no movement." Gehn said, flat on his stomach atop the hill with his head just barely above its crest.

Behind him, a prone Sorrett agreed. "No."

"I don't know." Gehn squinted. "I've been fooled by them before."

Unlike the fort above him, the surrounding grass was a frenzy of motion. The wind had picked up to near storm level, but the sun hadn't yet surrendered; the rifts between the clouds were brighter and thicker than before.

Alone, Gehn approached the steel monstrosity. Slowly, he went, half expecting that at any moment he'd be hailed by a volley of fiery, red blasts, but, so far, the cannon ports remained shut.

Ahead stood a pair of hulking, iron doors, both of them covered top to bottom with spikes. They were open a sliver, and yet he thought that they appeared far too heavy to have been pushed by the wind.

Before the gates and between the scattered craters, on a stretch of hard, trodden earth, there could be seen a dark and bustling heap: a gathering of crows and slate-gray carrion eagles, frequently popping up their heads to check on his position. When he was about thirty feet from them, they began to disperse, squawking and flapping wildly up into the air in every direction. The eagles were the most reluctant to leave, many of them peeling last strips of meat to carry away in hooked beaks and talons.

The dwarf lay in a long-dried crater of crimson, its unarmored regions picked nearly to the bone, its skull facing the gates and its bearded jaw wide as though calling out to comrades that would never come.

Gehn stepped around the corpse and continued toward the doors.

With a bit of effort, he pushed until one swung inward by its own momentum. He peered now into an empty shell. In the center of the dirt tract inside, amidst brittle weeds and tufts of overgrown grass, there stood what appeared to be the fort's two remaining assets: a well that had been built of square, coal-black bricks and a bucket atop its edge.

Without moving from the doorway, Gehn inspected as much as he could of the fort's interior. The only life here belonged to a pair of ravens perched on the far wall.

He turned and stepped back through the gate and gave a shrill whistle, and Sorrett's shape shot up from behind the distant, eastern hill.

"I'll bet giant hands helped build this place." There was a tinge of bitterness in Sorrett's voice as he gazed up at the structures that seemed to enclose the courtyard like fingers on an evil claw. The giant sat beside the well with his legs fully extended, holding, in one hand, a branch he'd snatched from a tree just a few miles before crossing the Ulad. With the other hand he gripped the dripping bucket he'd drawn up.

"You're fluent in the speech of dwarves and humans." Gehn snapped off another piece of dried meat in his teeth. "I'd expect your kind to reject other languages."

The forest giant snorted. "We didn't learn it from the dwarves, if that's what you think. We knew it long before their kind settled in these lands."

"Humans taught you?"

Sorrett nodded. He lifted the bucket to his lips and drank greedily, then belched twice. With the back of his hand, he wiped the stray drops from his chin. "Very long ago, back when the two races lived much closer to one another, before my kind pulled away into the safety of the eastern tas." He was about to stuff the branch's leafy end into his mouth when he noticed an acorn dangling from one of its stems. He plucked it, but simply stared at it now as though suddenly caught beneath the weight of a difficult decision. After several seconds, he realized that Gehn was watching him. "This is no place for a ta." The giant said, and then crushed the acorn between his wide, flat teeth before swallowing it. He looked out again. "What happened here?"

A gust of wind whistled across the spiny towers as if to answer him.

Gehn noticed the subtle drop in air temperature even before he felt the vibration in the earth: a series of rapid, heavy impacts.

A snarling roar rang out.

Sorrett sprang up and sprinted to the yard's eastern edge to peer over the wall.

Already snatching the last of his belongings up, Gehn said: "I take it that's real."

The giant's face went slack. "They've reached the valley below us. They're following our trail exactly."

"How many?"

"More than I've ever seen. Do you think these walls could hold against them?"

"We can't risk getting trapped." Gehn replied. "Can you outrun them?"

138

"I can try."

Returning to Gehn, Sorrett dropped to one knee and made an upraised palm beside his hip just as his companion put a boot in it and launched himself up.

Gehn had barely grabbed hold of Sorrett's head before the giant was on his feet again and zooming toward the western wall of the fortress, leaping now and nearly failing to clear its pointed, black teeth. The drop to the golden field seemed like an eternity before ending in a violent jerk that might have thrown Gehn off had he not been holding so tightly.

Then the two travelers were in the open again and heading west with the thunder of many swift, clawed feet behind them.

THE CITY OF FIRE

Early Morning.

The yellow grass had vanished in the night, and for miles around there could be seen only flat, dry plain marked by the fanglike shadows of small, dust-colored stones.

For the first time in hours, Sorrett slowed from a jog to a walk. Though he did pant, there was more irritation in his voice now than exhaustion. "These rocks are sharper than thorns." He halted to inspect the rugged sole of his right foot as he balanced on his left.

Gehn scanned the east. If anything had changed there, he could no longer tell, for a glaring, orange sphere had just pulled free from the horizon. Already, the day's warmth was unwelcome.

"If the mokru catch us, they deserve to." Sorrett released his foot and planted it on a space of sand between stones. He continued carefully. "How much further?"

The Ancient once more fixed his look ahead. From atop his two-legged watchtower, he could see exceedingly far into the desert, but still there was no sign of the place he sought. "If the map is accurate, it could be another fifty miles."

139

Sorrett waited for his own labored breaths to cease before he spoke. "Only dwarves would choose to live in such a wicked place."

Onward they went, the heat rising steadily against their backs as its infernal source climbed into cloudless sky.

With every passing hour, Gehn became more aware of the canteen on his belt, hefty with water he'd not yet touched, but thoughts of the giant's grueling task kept him from drinking even a sip.

By the time the sun had reached its highest point, the heat had transformed the surrounding air into a scalding, invisible fluid. In an attempt to make shade, Gehn had propped his cloak up over himself on the tip of his blade's hilt.

"Gehn..." Sorrett groaned. The forest giant held his head low and his right hand up before his face as though sight of the torrid wasteland burned his eyes. "I can't go much further like this."

"Here." Gehn took the canteen from his belt and dropped it.

Sorrett caught it midair. "It'll hardly be a mouthful for me." He reasoned, staring at the object that barely filled the center of his palm. "You would waste it?"

"We can't turn back." Gehn said.

As the giant splashed the water into his mouth, his walking brought them to the top of a shallow rise. In the distance now, past the quivery waves of heat, there could be descried something like an angled line that was almost white compared to the surrounding desert.

For miles, they followed the supply road; Sorrett's feet found relief here where the stones had all been crushed to dust by heavy wheels.

He came to the edge of the drop and stopped, and both he and his rider silently took in the vast basin before them.

The road continued steeply downward, changing eventually into a dark, gravel causeway that crossed the flat and sandy bottom. Here and there, from smooth dunes the color of rust, ridges of igneous rock protruded like the spines of long-dead behemoths. No less than a mile away stood the opposite cliff, and, in the center of its sheer face, there existed what appeared to be a square, iron door so tremendous in size that even the giant grunted in astonishment. Smoke plumes streaked the sky beyond.

"This is it?" Sorrett asked.

"Has to be."

The giant hesitated a moment before he knelt.

Gehn stepped off and his boots landed in the sandstone with a soft *crunch*. He moved stiffly to the brink where he kneaded his legs for a while without uttering a word. Then, he adjusted his brown cloak, clasped its chain, and at last asked: "Do you remember the place we discussed?"

"The green hills."

"Yes."

Sorrett squinched. "You're certain I shouldn't wait? What if you're turned away?"

When Gehn faced Sorrett now, he saw in the giant's stance the same resilience that he'd come to recognize; any fears he'd had about pushing his companion too hard dissipated. "If I haven't returned by sunset, then go." He turned again to the west where smoke rose from unseen factories. "And don't take the same path on your way back."

Gehn reached the bottom of the basin and started onto the causeway. At its end, the great, square door seemed to wait like a slumbering predator. Even from here, he could see the many tiny holes marking the cliff around it: cannon-ports. 'They had to have seen us back there.' He thought as he assessed the unbroken stillness ahead. Movement caught the corner of his eye. He turned to see a whirlwind materialize above the rusty

141

sand some fifty feet away, watched it gain mass and strength as it ambled the boulder-ridden flats like a forgotten spirit.

By the time Gehn came to the center of the mile-wide bowl, what had once looked like natural etches in the cliff above the gate had sharpened into the features of an immense stone sculpture: the bulging eyes and nose of an irate dwarf. He noticed then that the door had been fashioned to represent the dwarf's disproportionately large, closed mouth, complete with curved, bronze spikes resembling the pointed tufts of a beard.

Boom!

He nearly mistook the sound for a cannon's blast.

The dwarf's mouth was opening now, the monumental door falling slowly outward to reveal an equally-large, square tunnel from which thudding chains resounded.

"*You will never come out.*" An internal whisper warned as he neared the dark maw so high and wide that it could've swallowed an entire ship. "*If you turn back now, you'll have a chance.*"

The gate touched ground and the heavy noises echoed a final time. From the passageway appeared two midget suits of armor, both iron black but for the flares of copper at their joints. Gehn halted when he saw that their rifles were loosely aimed in his direction.

The plumed helmets swiveled; the two guards looked at each other from cross-shaped visors, and Gehn thought he heard a whisper between them before the one on the right continued out alone, metal boots clanking, and then stopped in the center of the massive, recumbent gate.

A cloud of dust slid between Gehn and his greeter.

Several pale braids hung over the dwarf's breastplate and partially covered an insignia there: an upraised fist inside a wreath of copper flame. Within the helmet's narrow slit, two shadowed eyes simply stared.

"What do you want?" The dwarf said.

After a few short words between him and the doorkeeper, Gehn reluctantly surrendered his blade and watched it vanish into a narrow side passage.

Then, the two metal suits led him down into the dark.

At Gehn's back, the gate ascended sluggishly by the work of monstrous chains. An instant before the faint light from the outside was extinguished, his eyes perceived something ahead like a pair of iron doors from which a pattern of glinting objects extruded: cannons. Like a molten crack in the earth's crust, they split and opened outward to reveal a stretching, torch-lit corridor of stone.

His mind circled back to the sword.

"*You'll never see it again.*" The whisperer claimed.

They passed into a dim chamber that might have been endless but for a distant ceiling where rows of square openings framed afternoon sky. Great, metal shapes loomed in the shadows of the space: idle catapults and armored carts. Gehn understood now that he'd not come into the city through its main gates.

After climbing a flight of stone stairs, the three came into a tall, court-like enclosure made up of six balconied floors. On a circular platform in its center, above the bright, amber coals of an oversized brazier, stood a monument of bronze: an enormous, upraised fist with curves of burnished, metal flame rising from its knuckles.

"This way."

Both of Gehn's armored escorts waddled left around the icon and toward an open doorway leading into another torch-lit hall. He lingered briefly, yet, in that moment, he noticed a figure, cloaked and hooded in vivid yellow, watching him from the railing of the third-lowest balcony. A silvery, wolf-tail beard hung from what little could be seen of the dwarf's face.

For a moment, the two of them looked at one another before the yellow cloak turned and briskly departed from sight.

The final passageway was more tunnel than palace corridor, cramped and rounded and windowless, widening only at its end where two gold-armored guards and a pair of ornate, bronze doors hinted at what existed beyond. A bright white pillar stood between; the doors were partly open to a sunlit space.

Stepping in front of the column of light, one of the short, golden suits slanted a spear across its breastplate, and Gehn saw that a rifle had been fashioned seamlessly into the weapon's handle. A stern word buzzed inside the helmet: "Stop."

Gehn and his escorts complied.

A voice slipped through the crack between the doors. "*Is it the giant-rider?*"

"Yes, chief minister." The golden guard answered.

A short silence ensued.

Then: "*Let him in.*"

Now, the gold suits stepped back and pushed against the heavy doors, and Gehn followed his two guides into the most opulent chamber he had ever seen.

Innumerable tiles made up a floor as smooth as a pristine lake, a checkered pattern of marble blacks and granite reds and a single stripe of bright pink quartz cutting straight through the room's center toward the eventual throne.

Two prodigious heads of stone flanked the pink pathway. Liquid flowed from their hollow eyes, down their bulging, gray faces to disappear into grooves between gritted teeth. As Gehn passed through the two fountains, he noticed a white, child-sized robe fluttering ahead across the floor. The figure's hat, scarlet and vase-like, seemed to signify authority.

Spaced throughout the chamber were more gilt-suited guards, each one standing watch at the base of one of twelve towering windows. Copper fists emblazoned the lengthy, black banners hanging from a high ceiling.

With their metal footfalls echoing and reechoing, Gehn's midget escorts brought him ever closer to the room's far end, where a triangular mountain of steps supported what could only be Pond's throne. The chair appeared to be made of pure gold, its back a rounded flare of many points meant to depict the sun's fiery mane.

To Gehn, the body lounging in the seat's pillows seemed insignificant in contrast: a silken body topped by a round, pink face and a short, light-blonde beard like a shallow U. The object resting on the king's head was more gleaming temple than crown, complete with columns and archways and inch-tall acolytes.

A final pair of guards stood a few steps down from the throne, one beneath Pond's left hand and one beneath his right. These two suits were mostly gold, but far more extravagant than anything Gehn had seen so far, with dark horns curling up not only from their helms but fanning from the edges of their disc-shaped shoulders. Rubies and onyx stones adorned the guards' golden breastplates and arms, as well as the immense, rectangular shields they governed like barricades. They tightened their defensive positions as if they expected, at any moment, Gehn might produce a hidden crossbow to send a dart at their king.

The robed dwarf in the tall, red hat made up the last few steps and took position beside the throne. He whispered something into Pond's ear before turning to peer at Gehn.

"Your Excellence," One of the black-armored escorts said, arriving at the base of the ziggurat-like dais to give a synchronized bow with his counterpart, "this human has come to speak with you."

Stopping behind them, Gehn shot a glance at a clot of nearby figures: three dwarves wearing pale, feminine masks. Each watched from beneath the hood of a brightly-colored robe of purple and teal.

King Pond spoke: "If you're here to plead with me for the release of those miserable forest trolls, you're too late." The dwarf inspected the fingernails of his stubby left hand. "They're gone."

Gehn said nothing.

"I'm told you rode in on one of them. I suppose that humans and giants are working together now."

"That's the idea."

Squirming in the pillowed seat, Pond stretched his hands out to his sides and flattened his palms onto golden armrests studded with pale green gems that perfectly matched his eyes.

Gehn guessed that this was no coincidence.

"What is your name?"

"Gehn."

"So, state your business."

"The humans are gathering a force to eradicate the dognars in a single attack. I'm here seeking your involvement."

The king squinted in a false expression of concern. "The humans are having dognar trouble?"

The words left Gehn's mouth before he could stop them. "No more than the dwarves."

Beneath the chamber windows, the golden-suited guards stirred; every single helmet now faced the visitor at the base of the dais.

The three masked figures exchanged nervous whispers.

Pond's sphene glare was half-lidded. His lips twisted into a sneer.

"I've seen the deserted citadels." Gehn bluffed; in truth, he had only seen the one. "It's clear they're backing you into a hole."

Pond laughed. "You would call the City of Fire a hole? No." He beckoned now, and one of his masked attendants hurried up the ziggurat of steps clutching a chalice in white gloves. When the king had finished drinking, he promptly shooed the servant away but kept the chalice to check his reflection in its surface. He lifted a hand to stroke his blonde, perfectly-trimmed beard and then to straighten the miniature temple on his head. "Pograd holds strong. Yog will endure."

"Their numbers are growing." Gehn pressed.

"If memory serves me, those dognar hounds are a direct result of you humans delving into powers beyond your understanding." The crowned dwarf angled his round head backward. "Why should we risk venturing out to help you fix your own mistake?"

"We could make a picnic out of it." Gehn flatly replied.

Chuckles echoed from the edges of the space.

Pond was unamused.

"Because," Gehn amended, now with a slight shake of his head, "none of us can afford for this plan to fail."

Leaning in, the dwarf in the tall, red hat whispered into Pond's ear once more, bringing a sly smile to the king's face.

"I'm always looking to expand my territory." Pond leered with new incentive. "I know that Dain's southern hills are rich with silver."

"I don't have authority to give away a piece of Dain."

Pond squinted. "No? That's disappointing. Surely there's something."

Just then, four dwarves with black masks and matching black beards appeared and approached the dais, each carrying one corner of a great rectangle of bronze. On top of the mobile platform and reaching its full length was a shining, metal object.

Gehn tensed.

"The human's blade, your Excellence." One of the carriers stated.

Sitting forward on the throne, Pond raised his right hand to beckon impatiently.

The four sword-bearers ascended several steps and stopped between the pair of massive, golden shields.

Pond inspected the greatsword with an intensity that hadn't left his green eyes when they rose once more toward Gehn. "How did you acquire this?"

Every beat of the Ancient's heart fueled a flame. Suddenly, the prospect of losing the blade felt as unsettling to him as a drawn arrow's tip brushing against his throat. "I borrowed it from a collector."

"I want it."

"It isn't mine to give."

"It isn't yours to give." Pond copied with feigned good cheer. "You truly have nothing to offer me?"

"An alliance." Gehn said.

The dwarf king leaned back into the plush pillows of his enormous, gold throne. Seconds passed and not a word was uttered. Outside the far windows, serpents of smoke twisted across the afternoon sky. Finally, Pond turned his eyes down toward the greatsword again. "You know, I've been hearing an unusual rumor."

Gehn said nothing.

"It involves a man that wanders around killing dognars with a blade. Would you know anything about him?"

Both of the plumed, black helmets pivoted to regard Gehn with their cross-shaped slits.

The Ancient's eyes lingered on the distant smoke. "Yes."

Pond stiffened.

"I know he was needlessly imprisoned in a dwarven cage," Gehn said, "only to break free."

At his answer, there rose a collective gasp from the masked attendants. Several of the gilded guards at the chamber's perimeter clomped a few steps closer.

"It's not a good look for your kind." Gehn went on, his focus falling to the polished, rose-pink tiles beneath his boots. "And when the humans learn of your reluctance to cooperate, they'll see it as fear."

"You *dare...*" the dwarf in the tall, red hat attempted to protest before his face was blocked by the king's small hand.

His cheeks flush and his nostrils flaring, Pond stared at Gehn for several seconds. Then, he relaxed, and uttered a soft yet genuine chuckle, his smirk a knife of pearl encompassed by the sharp, inner edges of beard. "So, this dognar-killer," The dwarf's visage fell cold again. "What else do you know about him?"

"Little more than you, I'm sure." Gehn answered.

After a sigh, Pond drummed his fingers on the golden armrests for a moment and then turned to the dwarf beside him. He covered the side of his mouth as he whispered.

Gehn made out exactly four words.

"...test him.................few licks..."

When the king had finished, the other dwarf shot a sidelong glare at Gehn before making down the side of the dais.

"It may only be a rumor," Pond continued, "but I can't deny that it's an exciting thought: the ability to kill a dognar up close if bombs and cannons fail. The strength and reflexes it would take..." The king looked to the sky beyond the windows as

148

though he might find the truth there. "It's said not even the giants can kill them as cleanly as he can."

Quickly but quietly, the dwarf in the vase-like hat approached Gehn's right side. Gehn detected, between the drapes of the dwarf's white robe, an object like a rod of yellow metal.

"I would give almost anything just to have such a warrior, such a *weapon*, in my arsenal." Pond added with calm finality.

Gehn did nothing to stop the blow.

The scepter's large, pentagonal head struck his right cheekbone so hard that a wave of tingles spread across the side of his face. His ear seemed to go deaf for a moment.

As the dwarf in red and white drew the rod back for a second strike, Gehn shut his eyes and turned slightly away.

Pond said: "You see, I'm a bit of a collector myself."

Smack!

By the way it felt, the object that whipped Gehn's ear this time could have been a bristling mace. When he opened his eyes again, he looked down and found his own spectral reflection in the pink tiles below, and while he tried to stifle his wrath, he could see two waxing, azure lights in the head of that hazy silhouette.

Though he moved his right hand with deliberate slowness, he easily seized the incoming scepter before it could land a third blow. As the dwarf beside him growled and struggled vainly to pull it free again, he heard the *click click click*s of rifles being cocked. Even his two escorts had stepped back to train their own weapons on him.

Gehn kept his head and eyes down. He could feel a warm drop of blood creeping down the side of his neck. The hot and vengeful energy in his tight, right hand seemed to have a mind of its own, seemed as desperate to pull away from him as a held dog eager to protect its master. It begged to be unleashed into the metal that the sadistic dwarf still clung to. "Is this how you normally treat your guests?" Gehn asked.

No reply came.

Just when the Ancient felt that he could no longer contain his power, his assaulter let go and stepped back with gritted teeth.

149

"Drop it, human." Voiced a guard.

Gehn opened his hand and the scepter fell to the floor with several *clangs*. As it rolled to a stop, he saw wisps of smoke reaching up from the metal beneath its gilt, pentagonal head.

The stillness in the chamber was tomblike. Even the figures in the feminine masks had no whispers to share between themselves.

Gehn watched the fire slowly subside and then disappear in the eyes of his reflection. "May I go?" He said, and now looked up.

The king's face was a void of expression. He sighed. "See him out."

Gehn was led back by the same two dwarves that had brought him, back through the same great, lifeless passageways and now past the many slumbering war machines that might have been stirred for his cause.

'That lunatic.' He thought as he touched the broken skin at his cheekbone.

The three had arrived at a dark section of corridor when a door opened in the wall ahead and an amber glow slashed out across the floor like a molten pathway. A silhouette moved in the opening and then stepped out into full view: a figure in a yellow cloak. Beneath the newcomer's hood was a hawk's beak nose and a lengthy, white beard that pointed toward the floor like a broadsword.

'The dwarf from the balcony.' Gehn thought. He watched as a pair of ebon suits also issued from the newly-opened door and stood like mirror images to his own halted escorts. As the yellow-clad figure took up a position between them, Gehn could see that this one was atypically tall.

Gehn's escorts gave respectful tilts. "Grayblood." One of them quietly addressed.

There was a precision to the new dwarf's voice that seemed to defy the rasp of old age. "I've got a few more questions for the human. I'll take him from here."

150

Standing like a statue, Gehn's eyes never left the hooded stranger. Even as the empty sheath seemed to burn into his own back, he remained calm.

"Yes, Mediator."

The Ancient's thoughts came and went with furious speed as he followed the yellow cloak past torch after torch, through a labyrinth of intersecting passageways and beneath what seemed to him an increasingly-oppressive ceiling.

Around another corner they went, and into a dome-like chamber with an iron ladder dropping down from a dark, round opening. Gehn heard the groan of metal behind him and turned to see a heavy door slam shut; his new escorts had closed it from the other side.

His uncertainty elevated into confusion. "What is this?"

The dwarf in yellow had stopped at the base of the ladder to touch a burning match to the wick of a lantern. He looked toward Gehn now, and, in the dim light, his old face took on a grotesque appearance, its wrinkles and its scars like the fissures of an arid gorge. Only a pair of keen, hazel eyes seemed to have avoided the touch of time. "A detour." The dwarf answered. "I can help you, but we have to move."

Chapter 12

WEST

There had first been light coming in through the crate's hair-thin cracks, but now, the cramped interior was absolute blackness.

Other than the occasional bump and then the rattling tremor that always followed exactly three seconds later, the sense of motion was somewhat relaxing, yet Gehn's mind refused to rest. He didn't know how long he'd been sitting here with his knees up and his head hunched in the lack of space, but he wanted to believe that this journey was nearing its end.

"Who are you?" Gehn had said just hours before, as he'd followed the yellow-cloaked shape up a curving, stone stairway, the lantern's glow a soft halo of gold on rounded walls.

"Call me Badger." The dwarf replied. "I saw what happened in the throne room. I'm shocked that Pond let you go so easily. There's no telling how he'll react when he learns you've gone missing."

As they turned into a crude, narrow passage, Gehn's eyes caught a flurry of motion in the walls and ceiling: large, silver cockroaches skittering away from the light and vanishing into crevices until only twitching antennae remained. In the distant blackness, a pair of glassy, yellow marbles flashed and then were gone.

"The fastest way to Irchos is by supply train," Badger said, "but Pond cannot know about it. That means I'm going to have to smuggle you."

"You're smuggling me onto a caravan?"

"Train." Badger corrected. "Steam-powered transport. Probably the most expensive piece of machinery ever built by dwarven hands, but I can't fault its efficiency. If things go well, you'll be halfway to Irchos before Pond is any the wiser."

"Why should I go there?"

Never stopping, Badger briefly turned to raise a snowy eyebrow. "You need an army, don't you? I'm sending you to the only dwarf that can give it to you."

They walked for a while without word.

Thinking now of the cities marked on his own map, Gehn broke the silence: "I don't know of an Irchos."

"Of course you don't." The yellow cloak led Gehn around another corner and onto a grating suspended over dark, restless water. Their footsteps rang quietly. "The purebloods have always resented its existence. They do their best to keep us a secret from the outside world."

They arrived at a steep stair and started up.

"If Pograd is the head of this land, then Irchos is the heart. But if you ask me," Badger shook his head as though at an old regret, "the heart should have taken over long ago."

The dwarf had led him through twisting tunnels, past the steady, muffled whine of vapor in pipes glinting in scattered shafts of sunlight.

"The train is managed by dwarves loyal to Pond." Badger said hushedly. "That means you won't be safe until you reach the desert mountain and you're offloaded."

"What if I'm caught?"

"You won't be caught. Not unless you do something stupid."

153

They made then into a tremendously-large room filled with countless stacks of crates and barrels. Gehn glimpsed a fraction of the steam-snorting iron machine out under the afternoon light, cannon mouths yawning in its thickly-armored sides. Beyond it, a forest of smoldering, steel towers stood against a mountainous sandstone fist the color of rust.

"I hope that giant of yours doesn't require a message." Badger said.

"He knows not to wait for me."

At last, Badger had stopped beside one of the hollow, wooden cubes.

Staring down now into the tight space, Gehn uttered: "You're kidding."

"No."

Gehn eyed the dwarf as though he suspected a childish trick.

"We don't exactly have much time." Badger warned. "If you'd rather ride your friend west out into the frying pan, go ahead, but I won't recommend it."

An industrial *crash* shook the chamber. Gehn turned back to peer into the maze of boxes just as a rattle of dwarven voices rose up.

"In or out." Badger demanded. "What will it be?"

Now, he was rolling through the middle of a desert that he could not see.

"When you reach Irchos," the dwarf's final words echoed in his mind, "seek out Monitar Kindal. And whatever you do, don't leave the crate."

The air had grown stale and warm by this point. The abrupt bangs and tremors had died down and now there was only a slight rocking sensation.

Gehn felt sleep tugging at him.

Ghostly vestiges of a dream hung about his consciousness like smoke in a windless chasm: images of a somber plain. He felt a steady shuddering and he knew that the train was not its source.

A second vision unfolded before him: a warrior he'd once known, hunched over hard, dry ground, fingers planted like roots as cruel, obsidian scales ripped out through the flesh of his arms.

Crack!

Gehn opened his eyes to catch the last of the sapphire threads snapping from his fingertips as the planks nearest his hand burst into eager flame. He threw his palm once, twice against the spreading, orange brilliance to no avail.

The next he knew, he'd kicked the side of the crate flat and was standing outside of it, stamping until there was only smoke rising from the blackened section of wood. Tingles coursed across his arms and hands like thousands of angry ants.

After a quick check to make certain that the fire hadn't spread, he now fully took in the dim, rectangular enclosure, low-ceilinged and tightly crowded by wooden containers.

He made his way across the corrugated floor and through neat stacks of cargo, stopping at a square of bolted, black metal flanked by clusters of gears. In its exact center, a small, horizontal opening puffed dry air and revealed a sliver of scarlet wasteland. Stooping now to peer through it, he noticed a handle at its edge. The metal hatch he opened now might as well have belonged to an active furnace; a blast of warm wind met his face and he squinted at the sight of a passing landscape flat and featureless but for its broken, snakeskin surface. Blurring past, just beyond the rail's edge, were sword-length spikes of iron.

'Dognar deterrents?' He thought.

He risked an angled look through the opening now, a look into the train's westward course, and what he saw there was a distant triangle piercing the sky, a sharp and barren mountain with a sun-crowned peak.

"Irchos." He said.

After a fruitless search of the freight car for a new place to hide, he noticed, on the floor, a crooked, arm's-length of wire. As he stooped and took it, he caught a voice bubbling just beyond the recessed door at the car's far end.

By the time that the door opened with a *clank*, Gehn was back inside his partially-charred container. He'd wrapped the wire twice around one of the less-damaged panels and now held it firmly closed from the inside. "Sorrett, I hope you appreciate this." He whispered.

Boots pattered upon ribbed metal. The sounds moved past him, fading, and after the eventual *thud* of another door, Gehn could make out only the noises of the train.

When the last trace of indigo twilight had retreated from the car's interior, Gehn's battle with sleep had become a deliberate one.

He sensed it the very moment it happened, the sudden incline in the train's path and the engine's rhythmic huffs dropping to a slow, laborious pace. He guessed by the resounding clamor that it had entered a tunnel or a narrow ravine.

He waited.

With a long, metal *screech*, the train's speed dropped yet again. By the time he heard the rattle of the side door opening, he realized that the vehicle had come to a stop. Outside, the engine hissed like a hostile mountain cat.

Clank.

Dwarven laughter.

As Gehn listened to the scraping sounds of boxes and barrels being moved across the freight car's floor, his eyes caught the bouncing flicker of a lantern in the hair-thin gaps between the planks of his container.

He tensed.

"*Hold on a second. What's this?*"

Golden light blazed in through the gaps between the panels. With a *crunch*, a section of the blackened, weakened wood broke loose and fell, and now, a pair of dark, impish eyes peered in through the hole to widen.

With a swift and well-placed kick, Gehn sent both the dwarf and the wooden square crashing into the barrels across the way.

156

He retracted his leg just as an earsplitting *bang* filled the car and a tuft of sparks leapt up from the floor near the crate's splintered edge.

"Don't move." The unseen shooter warned. "I've got another loaded barrel and its begging for a spark."

Heat throbbed steadily at Gehn's core and now rolled down his arms to his fingertips. He knew that he merely had to touch the metal grooves, but he hesitated.

He heard another pair of boots scramble into position, heard the *click* of yet another firearm. Across from him, the bearded shape he'd kicked stood up and gaped. "It's a human!"

"Same one that saw the king, I take." Said the shooter. "Alright human, come out slowly."

Before Gehn had even decided on a course of action, a heavy voice rolled in from somewhere outside the car: "Lower your weapons and stand aside."

The train's engine gave another blustery hiss.

"Stay out of this, grayblood!" The unseen shooter barked back.

"Watch your mouth." Chimed yet another voice from outside. "Or don't you know who you're speaking to?"

"I know who he is!" Replied the shooter. "But this is the king's train, and he will be the one to decide the fate of this stowaway!"

"The train may be Pond's," came the weighty voice again, "but the cargo belongs to me. Now put your guns down and let him out. I won't say it again."

Gehn heard a shifting of feet on the metal floor. After a few seconds, he ventured a peek out at the short, armored warriors inside the car with him. Despite lowered rifles, their stances were taut. Hatred radiated from the cross-shaped slits of their helmets.

He stepped out of the train and into crisp, evening air, gravel crunching beneath each boot. Rugged cliffs surrounded the fire-lit space on all sides. Standing on the dock were a handful of dwarves clad in gray cloaks, the ends of their sleek beards touching the bayonet-fitted rifles that they kept slanted at their waists. Like Badger had been, Gehn could see that they were taller than the dwarves of Pograd.

Behind the small force, at the edge of an open archway atop several steps, there stood a burly outline: a black-bearded shape with veritable tree stumps for arms and legs.

Gehn waited.

"How can I help you?" The Irchite boomed. In the angled torchlight, he seemed more demigod than dwarf, like a beast not born but forged in the earth's fiery depths. From the center of the immense mane of onyx stared a hard face smeared with ash.

"I'm looking for a dwarf called Monitar." Gehn answered.

Chuckles sounded among the gray hoods.

The furrows faded from the dwarf's brow. The smile that grew at the top of his massive beard was nearly imperceptible. His eyes rose again to the gray cloaks on the dock. "Hold the train until I give the word."

"Yes Monitor."

Then he looked at Gehn. "You, come with me."

KINDAL

Gehn followed the Irchite down a long corridor. Polished columns stood in rows here, the final two having been carved to resemble muscled arms with massive hands that forever strove against the ceiling.

In the torchlight, he could see that his host wore ragged, brown coveralls. Despite the dwarf's undeniable aplomb, Gehn had trouble swallowing the idea that here, before him, scruffy and singed, was a dwarf with real authority.

"You're Monitar." Gehn voiced.

"Monitor. It's a title." The Irchite corrected. "You can call me Kindal. And you're Gehn?"

"Yes, but I don't recall telling you my name."

"Badger sent a falcon, but the message was brief. I'm guessing that things didn't go well with Pond."

Gehn said nothing.

"Don't take it personally." The dwarf said. "He hates us all with equal passion."

As they both neared the top of a wide, stone ramp, Gehn thought he detected a kind of bizarre music in the distance, that the echoes he heard were the bells and chimes of a celebration.

'Hammers.' He realized.

He followed the dwarf through an open doorway and they were out under night sky again, only here, there were no natural walls to conceal the view or shield against the ceaseless percussion of metalwork.

Before him, nestled between two razor-edged ridges, rose the fire-lit Irchos: seven mighty layers of wall, including the bottommost wall that they now walked upon, each one higher and deeper than the last, like the steps of a stairway fit for God. Beyond the seventh and highest wall, shadowy mountainside stretched upward into a summit that seemed to touch the converging clouds.

While there were no weapons or cannon ports visible to him, Gehn was certain that they existed; the walls' smooth, tan blocks seemed to whisper of war.

His eyes returned to the summit and lingered there as he went, its highest point like a fang's broken end scraping the veiled sky.

They continued on without speaking, up stairs and through another hallway before arriving at an open door. The room beyond was simple, with smooth, dark walls, each bearing an oil lamp with a steady, radiant burn. Opposite a dead fireplace, there stood a stone block of a desk and a chair made of thick, wooden slabs, and, in the far corner, a pedestal bearing a statue head with a resemblance to the so-called Monitor.

As the Irchite closed the door, he glanced over to see Gehn looking at the bust. "Irchos Moltenspar." Kindal said as he made to the desk now, pulling off one greasy glove at a time to reveal hands just as filthy. "My great-grandfather, and the

159

founder of this city." The dwarf flopped the heavy gloves upon the desk, adjusted the chair, and sat. A charred, gold bracer clung to his brawny, right forearm. "So then." He grunted.

Thinking back to the way that his host had dealt with the dwarves on the train, Gehn asked: "What exactly does Pond supply you with?"

The dwarf only stared back. His hazel eyes held a glimmer that reminded Gehn of Badger, and the Ancient had to wonder if the two were related.

When Kindal finally spoke, his form was motionless but for a mouth almost hidden in the waves of a furry, black sea. "This is the question you came through all that trouble to ask?"

Gehn said nothing.

Kindal's smile was a thin, white spark, his sinewy voice tinged with an accent that Gehn hadn't heard before meeting him. "Pond supplies me with water." The dwarf's expression fell serious again. "The mountain has its own springs, but I've always kept a surplus. Then there are the luxuries and other things that he seems to think my people value."

"And what does he get in return?"

"First, why don't you tell me what this is about." Kindal's tone was more command than request.

"Badger told me you could get me an army. My goal is to destroy the beasts that you call the dognars."

The Irchite cocked his head back a small degree. His lips opened but no words emerged.

"Forever." Gehn added.

The dwarf remained silent for a while. As he crossed his grimy, muscled arms, his hazel gaze fell to the desk's stone surface and stayed there. "...Dognars." He muttered at last.

"I presume you know of the creatures."

"Yes. They're little more than a nuisance out this far."

"They'll get worse." Gehn said with grim certainty.

Kindal drew a deep breath through his nose. His eyes met Gehn's once more. "Gold, copper, and iron, to answer your question. Two thirds of Pond's metal intake comes straight from this mountain. There is also the rare nitron that fuels his

160

machines, mainly the supply train itself. He would be hard-pressed to get such a resource elsewhere."

'Then you have power over him.' Gehn thought.

"Now then, regarding the beasts," Kindal squinted and drummed his thick, sooty fingers on the desk. "Tell me what you had in mind."

Hours passed.

Gehn stood atop the third-tier wall, staring out over the sweeping, dark nothingness that the desert had become. Cannons hugged the lower walls like hidden talons, each glossy weapon at rest within its own rectangular cavity. From the square holes of a vent grate, a chorus of hammers escaped faintly-fuming depths.

He turned when he heard footsteps approaching, the source: a gray-cloaked guard behind a wiry, grizzled beard.

"The Monitor is ready to speak with you again."

Though the main stairway of Irchos stretched from tier one to tier six, reaching the top of the seventh and highest wall required ascending a sheer flight inside a tall, arched passage. It was at the base of this stair that Gehn's dwarven escort stopped and said: "See that you don't leave the temple path."

Gehn climbed, his eyes busy on spirals and sunbursts and other intricate patterns in the surrounding brickwork.

He came out onto a wide expanse of cream-yellow sandstone blocked in by tremendous wall behind and gripped ahead by the mountain's steepest slopes. Up here, the hammers' *pings* and *pangs* were barely audible.

Past many rows of obelisks and at the level's far end, there waited a dome-like structure supported by seven pillars that flashed in the light of a roaring fire.

As Gehn went, he couldn't keep his eyes from turning up toward the mountain's menacing peak.

The clouds above had begun to scatter.

161

He came under the pale dome and saw, atop an altar's steps, a figure facing the chaotic flames. It took a moment for the Ancient to realize that this was Kindal; the Irchite had changed from his coveralls into a noble, green garment and had wet and tied his lengthy, coal-black hair.

Gehn stopped at the base of the steps.

Kindal half turned to glance back. Like his hair, his beard was combed and tied. Not a single spot of grime remained on his face or hands, and the golden bracer on his forearm was polished to a mirror sheen. "I had a vision when I was younger." The Irchite's attention returned to the fire. "A flood spread from the north. Its waters grew higher until all of the desert was a raging, black ocean, and Irchos had become an island amidst the waves." He paused for a time. A few burning logs shifted and settled with a burst of embers. "When I told my father about it, he said it was a warning."

Gehn waited.

"I want to help you, human, but I can't make any guarantees."

"What does that mean?" Gehn asked without inflection.

"My warriors are deadly, and this fortress city makes them even deadlier, but their numbers are small. Our mobile artillery consists of a few dozen mortars and several retired catapults. We would be a mere handful of riflemen joining your force. What you need is an army," The Irchite turned his eyes up toward the rising smoke, "and that army lies in Pograd."

FORGOTTEN

He reached it before the sun rose, the sky vast and empty and dim but for a scarlet stripe of cloud on the eastern horizon. Before him was a field of rock interrupted by several monolithic crags and a host of gaunt, leafless trees that grasped at the atmosphere.

Gehn turned to regard Irchos far below and immediately felt as though he were looking over a soaring island's edge. The city's fire-lit walls resembled glittering fungi between the roots of a

162

lifeless stump, the tracks of the supply train a needle reaching away across miles upon miles of featureless wasteland.

He made across the broken slabs, brittle weeds trembling between the cracks by a breeze that seemed to lead him toward the peak's center, where the greatest shaft of rock rose like an ageless column. Several shattered pickaxes lie strewn like carcasses before it, but Gehn's attention had already fixed on the dark, rectangular cavity that had been cut into the stone's base by the work of ten thousand vigorous strikes. There, beyond several feet of natural rock, he discerned the flat surface that the tools had failed to penetrate.

He quickened his step toward the space now, an image of the Ancient Wall clear in his mind with a door splitting open like a spear of burning, azure sky.

Before the Ancient could place his hand against the gray, a frigid gust of wind cut across the mountaintop, carrying with it the echo of a gentle voice: "They're not here."

Hairs rising from the nape of his neck, Gehn looked toward the shadowed side of a nearby boulder and he saw a tall shape that he knew was no coincidence. Atop the form's apparent head, a mass of thirsty weeds lashed in the wind like a head of long, dark hair.

"I'd let you see for yourself," The voice added, "but you're not strong enough to open it."

"I was strong enough to beat you." The Ancient replied.

"You're sure that wasn't the blade's power?" The shadow countered. "Tell me, do you feel just as strong without it?"

Gehn's right hand twitched for the weapon he'd lost. He told himself that his foe lacked the means to attack him physically, but he couldn't ignore the sense of overwhelming danger that had last gripped him beneath the ruin of the giants' sacred tree.

Orange sunlight spilled abruptly across the peak, illuminating the boulder's jagged side and the weeds that clung there. The only voice now was that of the wind.

After a moment, Gehn turned back toward the thing he'd come for. He reached forward to place his palm against it, but before his fingers touched it, he could only think back to the

163

emptiness beyond the Ancient Wall. He put his hand on the petrous, granulated surface, but he felt no energy trickle from his fingertips; the door that had for centuries remained shut might as well have been a cold and lifeless stone.

NEGOTIATIONS

It was late afternoon when the train puffed into Pograd and the freight car's armored doors rolled open to pour out bearded warriors wrapped in cloaks of gray.

Minutes later, Monitor Kindal threw the chamber's doors wide to find a startled dwarf in a vase-like hat directly between him and the distant throne.

"What's the meaning of this?" The chief minister squealed, scrambling aside at the last second so not to be trampled by the oncoming Irchite.

Kindal's voice rang like a heavy bell. "Pond!"

Bending forward in his lofty seat, Pond's plump fingers tightened on the golden armrests. The dwarf's keen, green eyes twinkled beneath a furrowed brow. His lips twitched with unspoken rage.

As the king's gilded guards tensed at the chamber's far edges, Kindal flashed a low, open hand at his own gray warriors watching from the doorway behind him. He continued through the trickling statues and toward the pyramid of steps where two elaborate, gleaming suits of armor shifted their monstrous shields as though they could protect Pond from the truth.

Kindal's stare never wavered as he closed the last few yards to the base of the dais. "It's time we had a talk."

Trailed by the hushed thunder of many footsteps, Gehn followed the ruffling, yellow cloak across the checkered tiles of the palace corridor. They turned a corner now to face a great, square door bristling with dagger-sized spikes of copper and bronze.

The pair of midget suits flanking the door sprung to life. "What are you doing?!"

"Open the door." Badger said.

"On whose authority, grayblood?"

At that moment, the squad of armed, Irchite warriors appeared in the hall and stopped behind Gehn and the Mediator. They never pointed their rifles; their eyes were message enough.

After a deep *boom*, the door swung away inward to reveal a vault-like chamber heaping with treasure of every kind, but the only object to catch Gehn's attention lie alone atop a golden pile in the center of the room: a length of azure metal shining like a fallen splinter of sky.

He approached the blade, and as he reached out and took its cold hilt, he felt a sudden surge of heat inside his palm.

Chapter 13

THE ATTACK

Dusk had fallen over Dain.

To the mounted lookouts on the hills, the sprawling city of tents appeared to slumber. Only a few torches winked deep within.

Twenty-eight.

Forty-seven.

The numbers were still lingering in the General's mind minutes after he'd propped his booted feet up on the desk and shut his eyes.

It'd been nearly a month since the date Gehn had set in his parting note, and forty-seven days had come and gone since Strom had rallied the majority of his forces only to watch them grow restless. He hated waiting, but waiting on a thing that he could neither control nor keep track of brought with it a very special kind of pain.

Hearing a sudden bubbling of voices outside, he opened his eyes but remained motionless, staring blankly toward a dim section of the tent's interior. He was aware of footsteps and clinking armor just before the flap was drawn aside.

"General, there's a large force approaching from the west."

The two stopped their horses on the hilltop and beheld what seemed a fortress pushing up from the land's dark edge. Fat, spiked towers rose against a crimson sky like the heads of impossible giants.

"Dwarves?" The Captain said, sitting straight up in his jade green armor.

Strom squinted at the distant silhouettes. "Without a doubt."

"Unusual that they would cross our lines like this. They can't possibly mean to attack us."

"They're not stupid."

The Captain glanced at him. "What do you make of it?"

Strom spoke dryly, as if he knew the answer to be fact. "They're coming to join us."

Just then, a brilliant, white flare zipped skyward from the dwarven force, and now a rider could be seen on one of the hills between: a swift knife of shadow piercing a valley's trapped blackness.

"There." The Captain pointed. "That's not one of ours."

Less than a minute later, by the time a second flare was launched to replace the first, the oncoming rider had reached the base of their hill and now slowed its pace.

Despite his flat tone, the Captain had a hand on the hilt of the sword at his waist. "Ho there!"

A sharp voice answered. "*Ho! I've come to speak to the General Strom!*"

Strom could make out little of the dwarf's shape, only a strip of milky beard beneath a cloak. The General tilted his head back as if this would heighten his perception. "He's listening." He said.

The rider brought his pony to a halt midway up the hill. "I was sent to ensure a safe merging of our armies."

"Is Gehn with you?"

"Gehn's the one sent me." The cloaked dwarf turned to stare at the way from which he'd come, his outline harsh white beneath the gently-falling flare. "We've had dognars at us ever since we crossed the Yullid. So far, they've kept out of range of our cannons, but we've spotted two more packs approaching from the north."

'Yullid?' The General thought, and then realized that the dwarf was talking about the border River.

"No doubt they're gathering for an attack."

"How many in total?" Strom asked.

"I'd say sixty or seventy now."

"What's your name?"

The dwarf turned back, his face still dark beneath a hood. "Badger."

"Well Badger," Strom crisply said, "you can tell your dwarves that they're welcome here."

At his final word, there came a sudden peal of cannon fire from beyond the towers on the horizon, and a third flare shot up into the night.

Raven hadn't lost his speed.

Even bearing two riders, he flew effortlessly along the hill's spine, his black mane lashing, his hooves beating grassy earth in synch with the distant salvos.

Egan felt the young woman tighten her left arm's hold on him as she twisted for yet another look into the southwest.

"What are they doing?"

He'd not responded the first two times she'd asked this, and he gave no answer now. He swung the horse abruptly to the left and down into a shallow valley, and for a moment he felt weightless in the saddle. Then they were climbing again and his weight returned twofold, and beyond the crest of the hill he could see only starry sky.

"What are they doing over there?" She demanded, this time in his ear. "I can hear cannons, and they keep shooting those candles up."

"Drills?" Egan offered, irritated. "How should I know?"

They reached the top and he slowed Raven to a trot. The horse shook its head as if it deemed this new speed unacceptable. Steam trailed from its nostrils.

"Take me back."

The young king was silent.

"Egan, I don't want to be out here anymore. Just take me back now."

"I never asked you to come along."

"Are you going to take me back or not!?"

"Yah." He kicked his heels into Raven and then they were fast accelerating, but he made no move to steer the horse in the camp's direction. He leaned forward instead, pulling the girl with him as the starlit field rushed by several feet beneath them.

"*Egan!*"

A new sound rose up across the hills and interrupted her: a high-pitched horn blast coming from somewhere ahead. Frigid understanding washed over him, and with wide eyes he caught the shape of a rider on the next ridge: one of the lookouts, flying across their current course and toward the camp. With a sudden *boom*, a blinding, red light coruscated high in the rider's wake.

There was terror in the woman's voice now. "*What's happening?*"

Raven screamed and veered with a jerk that might've thrown them both had they not been holding so tightly. Then the camp was before them, sinking below one of the many hills between, and when the king looked over his shoulder, he caught a glimpse of something coming like a tumultuous, black flood.

Strom and the Captain were watching from just outside the taut wires and angled, wooden points of the camp's perimeter when they heard the horn.

The mutterings of nearby gunners fell silent. Helmeted heads swiveled to face the dark, open lands from which the sound came.

At once, that darkness was shattered by a series of red flashes.

"To your posts!" The Captain shouted.

"*TO YOUR POSTS!*" His command echoed throughout the camp. "*DOGNARS COMING, NORTH SIDE!*"

Young soldiers burst from tents with rifles in their hands.

169

"Red." The Captain said.

Strom knew all too well what the signal meant. He turned to the west as the dwarven army unleashed a lengthy succession of *booms* and amber blinks of flame.

Though the General could see no dognars, he was sure he felt a wintry breeze touch his cheeks. He drew air in through his mouth as if to test it, as if the taste might confirm his suspicion. "The beasts are trying to catch us before our forces merge."

Not hearing him, the Captain rode ahead along the bristly perimeter and cried again to the soldiers. "Let's remind them of why they avoid this place!"

There came no cheers in response.

Gunners hunched over sleek cannons like men braced for a sprint. Hulking catapults were aimed. Auxiliary cannons rolled forward from the camp's center.

Strom dismounted. He brought his horse through a gap in the wooden spikes and entered the anxious crowd, the Captain following suit. At last, he came up to the inside edge and climbed onto a catapult's side to regain a decent view.

A rider could be seen out on the hills, and then, a second shape like a shadowy phantom chasing close behind the first.

"General!" An officer shouted. "It's our king out there!"

Strom could barely consider this before the first of the dognars appeared, pair after pair of shining, scarlet dots in a rising, evil mass.

Gasps and fearful whispers rippled through the men. Color drained from wide-eyed faces.

Years of hard experience couldn't keep a small shudder from gripping Strom's chest. He tightened his muscles, determined to retain an air of complete calm despite the fact that he'd never seen so many dognars in his entire life. Their numbers devoured the ridge, the sound of their approach like the violent crumbling of a once-proud mountain cut through by roaring barks.

"Oh God!" Someone groaned.

"Quiet." The General said. "Catapults, prepare to fire at full range!"

170

Gunners lit the round, black bombs clutched by the war machines. They hurriedly cranked immense handles as gears the size of wagon wheels turned and rumbled *click* after *click.* "*Ready!*"

The young king had caught up to the other rider and now looked to be leading in the deadly race. Logic told Strom that they were too close to be in danger of a volley, but he was accustomed to the unthinkable. He hesitated a few moments more.

"Fire!"

The catapults rattled and hurled their flaming missiles skyward as gunners scrambled to reload them.

"One more!" Strom urged. "Fire when you're ready!"

The fireballs had reached the peaks of their arcing courses when the gunners sent the second volley to speeding flight. Then, every eye was locked again on the north, locked on the closing horde to which there seemed no end, and Strom felt a thrill of adrenaline greater than any he'd experienced in years.

The first bombs streaked down like hailstones, ripping into the beasts' numbers with earth-shuddering explosions reaching high in terrific plumes of flame.

"*Die! Die! Die!*" The word rose up again and again among the soldiers like a chant. "*Back to hell with you demons!*"

Through drifting veils of dust and smoke the surviving creatures came. They thundered over the field as if with new rage, their eyes blazing and their fanged jaws wide, their lolling, purple tongues thirsty for blood.

Strom's attention fell upon the two riders that seemed almost to lead the creatures into battle. While the lookout was breaking off to the right, Egan hadn't deviated from his beeline for the camp.

"*Get him out of the way!*" The General snapped as the second volley smashed down on the hazy hilltop to conjure columns of orange one by one. Several of his gunners clambered onto catapults and began to shout and swipe at the air.

It was a moment before the young king got the message; he turned away to the west and, by Raven's speed, was out of the line of fire almost immediately.

"*CANNONS!*" Strom was forced to shout with all of his voice over the sound of the dognars' approach. "*FIRE AWAY!*"

The first discharges were all but simultaneous, sixty or more deafening *booms* within a single second, and many of the leading beasts dropped. Claws and legs and lower jaws vanished to leave mangled horrors stumbling and skidding in the grass, but still a host of the jagged shapes had nearly reached the wall of cannon smoke.

Strom heard shrieking amidst the cacophony. He turned back just in time to see a soldier flee from his post and dash away through steadfast warriors. Looking toward the field again, he freed his double-barreled pistols and cocked their hammers back. "*RIFLES READY!! AIM FOR THE EYES AND OPEN MOUTH!!*"

And then the first monstrosity plowed into the wire-webbed barricade and its fangs stopped inches from a gunner's arm. The creature fell in a tangled fury. It snarled and thrashed as projectiles sparked off its ebon scales. At a cry, the soldiers parted for a pair of cannons being rolled forward. As the General turned his face away, he heard a single blast and felt blood spatter his neck like shrapnel.

From the haze beyond the camp's edge charged another, this one directly toward him. He raised a pistol and emptied both barrels in sequence, and with the second shot, the creature's right eye burst and went dark. Now it leapt, and Strom felt the wind of its enormous body as he abandoned his position on the catapult and hit the grassy ground hard.

Warriors screamed and scattered as the dognar crashed down onto the grass like a tumbled boulder.

Struggling to his feet, Strom looked and saw that the creature had spun back to find him with its remaining eye. It came for him again, its gaping maw like a passage into death, and just as he raised the second pistol, a brown-cloaked figure appeared from the far-right corner of his vision. There was a glimmer of steel as

172

the beast's red eye ruptured, a deep, carmine fissure open from its snout to its scaly shoulder as it collapsed in a lifeless heap.

A hand clamped onto Strom's forearm. Before he could react, he was yanked away from a set of nightmare jaws that came snapping through the wires in a blur of spit and fangs. Now, the General's cloaked savior lunged forward and swung a shining weapon so tremendously fast *CHOCK* that he would've missed it if he'd blinked.

An armored body slammed into Strom and flung him down onto a pyramid of unforgiving cannonballs. He could hear his name being cried somewhere in the chaos as he pushed himself to his feet once again and beheld, suspended in the wires before him, the halved and twitching dognar head.

Above the shouting there rose a pain-filled wail. He turned to witness a black island moving in the sea of helmets, a tail lashing up through smoke. He could see now that a soldier was pinned by the beast, its teeth ripping through armor and flesh as men stabbed vainly at its face with spears. Then the hooded figure appeared and, in an instant, the massive, blue blade plunged through the beast's neck to unleash a fountain of blood.

Another dognar rushed in from the swordsman's side.

"Lookout!" Strom roared.

The figure turned to catch the creature's snout with one hand and now kept the furiously-snapping jaws at bay as he was driven into the scattering crowd.

Strom missed the sword a mere moment before the warrior snatched a pistol from his waist and stabbed its muzzle into the beast's mouth to make a resounding *crack* and a burst of yellow sparks.

The dognar crashed down with smoke trailing from between its teeth.

The cloaked fighter swiftly reclaimed his sword just as two more monstrous shapes charged toward him, and Strom suddenly found himself squinting through silhouettes, toward the light of a violent, sapphire sun.

Badger could only watch the distant turmoil, each orange blink filling a random patch of smoke like a flash of lightning in the depths of a growing thunderhead.

Kindal's concerned voice rose behind him: "They're getting slaughtered."

But then Badger caught a new light there, blue and small at first, each writhing scintillation quicker and brighter than the last until it seemed that the camp's entire northern edge was crowned by the uncanny flame. The Irchite smiled to himself as azure radiance reflected in his eyes. "Maybe not."

With every passing second, Gehn was more aware of his own heaving chest, of his red hands tight on the handle of the red-smeared greatsword. The color was inescapable; he looked down to find himself drenched in blood. All around him lie dognars with eyes as black as caves, and though he could clearly see the wounds that his blade had inflicted on his enemies, he knew that not a single fang or talon had found him.

Gehn turned his eyes toward the north, where smoke billowed into a dark sky from what seemed a boulder-ridden expanse. There, between the scattered carcasses atop the next hill, three of the beasts stood, simply staring, and, even from this distance, Gehn could see that their eyes, like steady, scarlet candles, were fixed on him. The Ancient watched as the three creatures turned and disappeared into the night beyond the hill's crest.

A filth-freckled Strom pushed through the circle of gaping soldiers. "Gehn." He barked, and then slowly raised a handkerchief to wipe his mustache, glancing once at the cloth's collection of blood and grime and black scale fragments. "That will be all."

Egan watched the camp's northern curve with bated breath.

He started Raven along the bristling perimeter, nearby soldiers perched on unfired weapons and peering toward the

174

growing commotion of voices that had replaced the sounds of gunfire.

As the young king drew close to the battle-touched section, he saw there a thick ring of bustling, armored bodies, each of them facing a man that stood calmly and quietly at their very center.

'Gehn.' Egan realized, and as the crowd's excited noises escalated, the king felt an icy sting inside.

Egan rode out alone and stopped his steed when he could only hear the wind. For a moment, he gazed across the rolling, starlit hills before taking the crown from his head to hold it angled in his lap, and now, he looked down to his own obscured reflection in the polished, silver surface.

THE MARCH BEGINS

Over the verdant hills, the afternoon was bright and windless. A lonely oak stood some half a mile from the oncoming clouds of dust, its boughs gnarled beneath dense clusters of leaves. Two human scouts converged on the tree from different angles. Though they'd reached shouting distance of one another, they remained silent as their horses tramped. The day's heat was at its peak, and only after the riders stopped under the rare shade did they find the effort to speak.

"How far do you think we've come?" The young one asked.

Removing the cap from his canteen, the other rider splashed water into his hand, slapped it to his forehead and slid it down his face, leaving droplets in a small, scraggy mustache. "Word is we only made ten miles yesterday. I'll be shocked if we reach the Swamp within two weeks. It's those dwarf towers are slowing us down."

Both riders looked toward the southern horizon just as the tops of the mobile spires pushed into view. The muffled rumble of hooves and marching feet grew gradually louder.

"Never thought I'd see such an army."

There came a sudden rustling noise above, and the two looked up now as a handful of leaves fell swirling. The shape was barely more than a silhouette against the canopy: an immense, hairless head on equally immense shoulders that could've grown from the oak's very branches.

Cursing in stuttered yelps, the riders sped their horses out of the shade, side by side until the older, mustached scout pulled to a halt and turned back just in time to see the top of the enormous head emerge from the tree's highest leaves.

The giant revealed no more of its face than its two shadowy eyes, each glinting with its own deep-set jewel. It bellowed a question: *"Are you Eggenstroops?"*

Egan glared across the dim, purple interior of the softly-jouncing carriage. While the so-called Ancient's significance still rankled him, the feeling was a scratch on his pride compared to the damage inflicted by the General's dismissive words to him just before the camp's northward march commenced: "A king's place is behind walls, not in the center of a dangerous campaign. No one would question your bravery if you returned home to Capitol."

The carriage's bouncing stopped.

Thinking back to the break that had been taken less than an hour ago, the young king looked to the veiled window nearest him and listened in vain to the mutterings outside.

"What's going on?" He voiced.

"Giants, Sire. I don't think they mean us harm."

Even as his driver finished speaking, Egan pushed open the vehicle's door and peered out over the sunlit suits of armor both human and dwarven, past the laden, iron carts and spiked towers like ugly teeth, and toward a host of shapes like colossal, wooden effigies against the sky.

Ekknet came to the crest of the hill and stopped to take in the distant assemblage. Hanging from a pole atop the army's

176

foremost tower was a standard that caught the Giant King's eye: a tightly-clenched, orange fist. For a moment, he felt his own fists mimic that of the symbol, and he heard the wood of his monstrous battle axe utter a quiet creak.

One of his warriors came up behind him to speak in a tone just as soft. "What are we doing here, Tol?"

The Giant King had no answer. Though he looked down onto the neat rows of dwarves with their plumes and dark, polished suits, he saw them as he had years ago, drunk and half-naked, laughing atop captured giants like boulders or felled trees.

His beard like a dark flare of vines, Kindal tromped through wild grass and toward the five figures waiting for him on the field: Gehn, Strom, and three forest giants with grim expressions, one of them so mighty in size that the Irchite first thought his eyes had been deceived. He stopped beside the human General.

"Monitor Kindal." Gehn nodded toward the foremost giant. "King Ekknet. If we want to succeed as a unit, we're going to need a single leader." Gehn looked at Strom. "General, I would say that you're the most qualified to manage a versatile army."

Strom crossed his arms and stared down into the blades of fierce green.

"Are there any objections to this?"

Kindal scanned the three giants before him and his attention landed on the one standing furthest away: a warrior with shaded, timid eyes and deep trenches in its wrists that he knew had been left by dwarven cuffs. He thought of Pond on his extravagant throne and he felt his own teeth clench in bitter rage. 'Irchos should've cut your line short when he had the chance.'

"I'm not above suggestions." Strom stated. "We could still act as a team. I..."

Kindal moved forward and stopped directly beneath the giants' collective shadow. "I know what was done to you, and I'm sorry." The Irchite solemnly said, his hazel eyes smoldering beneath soot-black eyebrows. "I know it's not something easily forgiven, so understand that we accept this alliance humbly.

177

What you suffered," he looked toward the face of the warrior with the scarred wrists, "it was an evil thing."

There was stillness now as the giants looked down without expression upon the dwarf. Then, after several long seconds, Kindal caught a slight nod from the Giant King.

As he returned to his previous place beside the General and the talking resumed, the Irchite could barely hear it. His eyes fell to the golden bracer on his right forearm, and now, a word filled his mind like a whispered accusation:

"Grayblood."

Chapter 14

THE BRINK

Beneath an umbrage of countless needles and between slender, dark trunks, a pallid face watched the south.

Eleazar hadn't believed the reports at first, but now, as the fifth lofty, spear-carrying shape could be descried in the distance, something twitched in the wizard's dry throat like a restless insect in its cocoon.

He heard the low, rumbling growl behind him, and he didn't have to look back to know that it was not directed toward the approaching, enemy force. Cold breath brushed past his cheek.

His words came out in a hitching whisper: "*Let me think.*"

The Ulad was a dark, diagonal line between shallow hills. From here, its calm water seemed to flow against gravity, from southwest to northeast and out of sight, as if unseen mountains called it back. Away from the river's far edge, there stretched a field of living grass patched with dead, and from the open land's end, a legion of pines rose into perpetually-cloudy sky.

The army crossed, and when the last set of soaked, iron wheels rolled up from the riverbank and came to a stop, men and dwarves and giants peered without word at the forbidding wall of trees. A flock of crows burst from one of the scraggy, moss green tops to break the silence and flap away into the north.

179

Gehn and Strom stood some twenty strides ahead of the others. The Ancient was certain that he'd glimpsed something in the forest's depths, some spectral face like a hint of moon through black branches, but now he could see only gloom.

"We don't know how many of the beasts are left." The General stated. "That's a bad place for us to fall into a trap."

Looking back briefly at the array of prodigious warriors behind him, Gehn's mind revisited the ravaged Arkonn. After a deep, silent breath, he said: "Burn it down."

Strom squinted into the north. "Something tells me the forest people won't like that plan."

"They'll get over a few pines."

The General reached into his coat and brought out his pipe, but before he struck a match, he touched the side of his nose and inspected his fingertip, and then his eyes were drawn to the high, gray ceiling.

When, at last, Egan turned to see how far he'd come, the army was gone from sight. The hills he'd crossed had taken on a stark, unfamiliar aspect, their valleys etched with stone and raw, eroded earth as dark as shadow.

As he stopped Raven on a bald ridge and looked upriver, it occurred to him that he'd stepped beyond Dain's northern boundary. Between steep banks, the water's body tossed with frothing waves: the work of something beyond the curving wall of rock. Though he couldn't see the waterfall's fury, its roar permeated him like the sound of a ruinous quake.

Rain came down lightly at first, resembling tiny beads of glass that scattered and rolled and collected on the helmets and polished, black cannons. Then, the shapes of the most-distant trees fell away to ghostly silhouettes, and soldiers scrambled to set up the remaining tents and tarps and umbrellas in the mere seconds before the downpour reached them.

When it ended, the only light belonged to the camp's torches. A thin line of mist hugged the ground outside the forest's edge. Blades of grass gleamed with moisture.

Watchful gunners tensed when they first spotted the shape on the field: an approaching figure trudging parallel to the forest wall and directly toward the camp from the east. A helmeted head hung low over a breastplate bearing the twin foxes of Dain. Below the emblem were two tightly-crossed arms. A limp cloak hung from steel shoulders.

"*Ho there!*" A soldier cried. "*Are you alright?!*"

The figure halted, but continued to stare down at the rain-heavy grass. The response came with puffs of steam: "*Fool horse spooked, bucked me off and headed for the river. Thought for sure one of the dognar hounds would catch me out there alone. Feels like I just ran twenty miles.*"

"*You see anything?*"

"*No, but I was sure I heard something in the deep woods.*" The mostly-hidden face turned to look north for a moment. Adjusting his armored arms to better hide the holes and scratches in the old, metal suit, pulling the cloak tight against his back with armored fingers, the figure started into the camp with a final word: "*Keep your eyes open.*"

A young soldier noticed a familiar clicking sound as he neared the end of a narrow corridor of crates, and now, he forgot about the cask of wine he'd been sent to fetch. He turned his head as if he could see through the containers, a stream of various red letters and symbols sliding past his illuminated vision.

The clicking stopped just as he arrived at an open, dark space. He raised his lantern high, angling the shadows of an auxiliary catapult some twenty feet ahead. One of these shadows had a mind of its own: a hunched, obscure form withdrew from the shine and vanished behind the weapon's cocked, iron arm.

"What's going on?" The boy demanded.

A muffled voice: "*I could use your help.*"

After a moment's hesitation, the young soldier started forward. "Maybe some light would've been a good idea?" He came around the machine and found a cloaked person bent over the muzzle of a cannon with half of its protective tarp peeled back. "Little late for maintenance work, isn't it?"

The shape turned and flashed a short, metal object toward the boy's throat. Dropping the lantern, the young soldier staggered away several steps before he tripped and crashed backward into the soggy earth, his fingers fumbling desperately in an attempt to stop the warm flood beneath his chin. A string of torturous coughs escaped him, and the last thing he saw were two pale eyes staring bitterly from the darkness above.

Within the camp's western edge, on the grass and in the thick of the snores and bass mutterings of his kind, Sorrett sat thinking, his empty gaze aimed downward on his own legs stretched out before him like fallen trees.

"I believe they mean to burn it down."

Sorrett considered this statement in silence.

"Do you think they would do the same to our forest if they meant to reach an enemy on the other side?"

"We wouldn't let them." Sorrett answered flatly.

"How would this be any different?"

Looking up across the camp and into the uncounted black pines like a herd of shaggy madraks, Sorrett thought back to a time he'd ventured into the open lands east of his home. There he'd discovered, concealed by a blanket of moss and starry flowers, a half-rotted deer. "There's something wrong with these ta." He said. "They grow like weeds."

"*You there!*" A sharp voice sounded.

Sorrett swung his eyes in its direction but saw only stacks of crates beyond the circle of sleepers.

"*Over here, you dumb trolls!*"

Giants stirred and turned to grimace.

Sorrett rose to his feet, and the three closest to him did the same. He was certain that he saw movement now beside one of

182

the containers: a long object wrapped in a tarp, angling upward like a massive, pointed finger with a final *click*.

Though the burst of flame was gone in an instant, the dizzying *boom* lingered in Sorrett's ears as he staggered backward and finally noticed, in the back of the giant beside him, a yawning, crimson hole. He watched in shock as the warrior collapsed, face first, onto the grass.

"KOT RIOK!" The other two standing giants charged at the source of the smoke.

"Wait!" Sorrett urged with a backward step.

But already the crates and the covered cannon were flung aside to reveal an armored, dwarven cart containing several barrels and a string of hissing sparks.

Standing atop the northernmost tower, Gehn had turned, seconds earlier, toward the cannon's unexpected roar, and now he watched as two tall forms were instantly engulfed.

BOOM!

The explosion went off like a thunderclap, flattening nearby tents and painting half the camp with orange brilliance. Once-tranquil giants curled up or raised their arms to shield themselves.

At the foot of an ever-ascending column of smoke and flame, beneath debris coming down like lazy, fiery leaves, three large bodies lie motionless.

As humans and dwarves appeared at the scene's edge, Gehn looked to see Ekknet staring in from just outside the camp. A handful of the Giant King's warriors rushed to their leader to grunt in their native tongue, but a single, bitter word rang clearly in Gehn's ears: "*dwarves*".

Now Ekknet's eyes darkened and his upper lip pulled back to reveal clenched, gravestone teeth. The king's focus landed on the nearby crowds, and the power in his voice seemed to shake the air. "GROUP THEM!"

"*Ekknet! Wait!*" Gehn moved to the tower's edge. While he was certain that he saw the being's deep-set eyes meet his own for a moment, the madness in that face never flagged.

Giant warriors strode forward as though into battle, snarling and sending dwarves to disperse like frightened mice as humans leapt aside. One by one, the small warriors were plucked up to struggle helplessly against mighty hands.

"*Stop!*" Gehn's plea drowned in a series of gunshots and riotous screams. He turned to the forest again to check the stillness between the trees, but then, his eyes caught a distant shape emerging from the row of umbrellas and half-hidden cannons on the camp's northern edge: a rider, cloaked and hooded, heading out into the field and toward the wood at an unhurried pace.

The Ancient's lips parted.

Now the shape leaned forward on an accelerating horse, dark cloak flying.

Beckoned by the rifle that leaned nearby, Gehn snatched the weapon and swiftly put the rider in its sights. As he held his breath, his last thought before pulling the trigger was that the shot would be impossible.

Crack!

The rider jerked. The horse reared in protest, sending the figure off to tumble twice in the grass, and then Gehn's eyes were fixed on an inert, black mound. The animal went kicking away.

"It's the wizard!" A soldier shouted below. "Seize 'im!"

Armed men broke out into the field.

Suddenly, the fallen lump sprung to life and hurried toward the pines like a cloak in a windstorm.

In an action of habit, Gehn snapped the rifle open only to realize that he had nothing to feed the empty chamber. His eyes darted for a second rifle that didn't exist, and then returned to a fleeing foe that seemed to remain untouched by the soldier's desperate shots.

To Gehn, every shadow seemed to pulsate, to shrink and expand with the beat of his own pounding heart. He thought of the three lifeless giants as the sound of the screams and shouts

184

became a steady judder, and now, thin, white smoke rolled upward from the wood and metal in his clutching fingers.

The wizard had nearly reached the trees.

Planting one hand on the tower's wooden rail, Gehn vaulted himself over and watched the ground fly upward to collide with his boots. He reached the camp's edge just in time to see a soldier loose a final spout of smoke and to hear, somewhere, the growing drumbeat of an approaching giant's feet.

"Gehn!" Sorrett's voice came.

"Sorrett," Gehn sensed the giant halt behind him as he watched Eleazar meld into the murk, "stop them."

Then he started forward into the field, and when he glimpsed the pair of bright, red orbs flash between the shadow pines ahead, his rage only grew.

Strom rode down between the lines of the tents, his head turning this way and that as shapes darted in and out of view: those of soldiers dark and low, those of forest giants fire-lit and wading through the camp like creatures out of nightmare.

"General!"

"What's happening here?!" Strom demanded as the narrow-faced officer ran to him and now jogged to keep his steed's pace. Off to his left, a new flame billowed into starless, night sky.

"Someone blew up three giants and now they're all tearing the camp to pieces!"

"Where's Gehn?!"

"*General!*" A gunner farther down the row cried. "*Gehn chased Eleazar into the trees!*"

Even if it hadn't been for the trail cut freshly into the ferns and the occasional, clear footprint stamped into the moist, mossy earth, Gehn could still have tracked the wizard easily. He was a beast on the hunt, his keen ears ever detecting the muted crashes ahead, his prey's putrid scent choking his nostrils.

185

Pines flew past him. Foliage reached for him and made futile nets that swayed and smoldered in his wake. He knew now that he was gaining quickly on his foe; he could see the flickering speck of shadow ahead, and, all at once, he decided that he would not use the weighty greatsword that beat against his back. Instead, he would use his hands. He would shatter bones and tear flesh.

He burst through a final snare of branches and stopped at the edge of a vast, round clearing in the trees. White mist crawled across its floor. Stumps and branches of fallen pines jutted up like wicked, black bones.

He saw no sign of his quarry, heard not the faintest snap of a twig ahead, and so he waited, eyes twinkling, steam shooting quietly from between his teeth. Somewhere high above, an owl offered the night a rasping shriek.

Movement at the clearing's opposite end: a hunched shape forsook the cover of one tree for that of another.

Gehn charged forward over the mist. He'd made it halfway across when the figure appeared again, dark and still, seeming to face him this time.

Crack!

From where Eleazar's head should've been, a dot of yellow fire blinked, and with a *zattt,* Gehn felt pain like a red-hot spearhead plunge into his right shoulder.

The realization that he'd been shot did nothing to deter him. He knew that his prey would have no second shot, no second chance to escape justice. He'd nearly reached the wizard when his foot broke through dead branches and a hole clamped on his lower leg like hungry jaws. He stifled a cry as his palms hit gluttonous, brown muck, and then the man was speaking to him in a cold and cutting voice.

"*They warned me that you were a dangerous animal.*"

An attempt to free his leg resulted in agony; snapped, wooden ends hooked deep into his calf's mangled flesh. Looking around, he saw only a veil of haze between the pines. The figure had slipped from sight.

186

Prying the branches apart with all his strength, Gehn at last released his torn leg and stood with an angry exhale. Cleaning the sludge from his hands onto his cloak, he inspected the wound at his right shoulder, the front of his shirt already drenched in hot, creeping blood.

At the first low growl, Gehn felt a seed of doubt take root.

All around, from the shadows of the wood, the beasts appeared, first their luminous eyes, then their black and scaly bodies as they stalked slowly through the clearing's vapor on heavy, taloned feet.

The hole in the Ancient's shoulder screamed as he pulled the weapon, ringing, from its sheath. As he wondered how he'd reached such a helpless position, he heard a metallic chuckle rattle through his mind.

The dognars continued toward him in a circle, their heads low and their bared fangs like rows of daggers. Several began to snarl and bark, but not one moved ahead of another as they closed the final few yards.

Gehn shifted his boots in the ankle-deep mire. Gripping the blade's hilt tight with his right hand and loose with his left, he waited. While he could see the light of his own energy reflected in the terrors' scales, their eyes seemed only to track the weapon itself.

The first creature lunged at Gehn and dropped to a flashing arc of steel.

Now every beast rushed at him, snapping and ducking and dodging his rapid swings, and then, the first set of teeth found his right arm and he faltered. Within seconds, their fangs were on every part of him. His hand lost the blade. Struggling in vain as they ripped viciously at his flesh, fighting to keep a wail imprisoned in his throat, Gehn watched streams of blinding azure vanish like water between onyx scales. Then, before his vision faded, his eyes caught a familiar shape leaning over the circle: a forest giant with a weapon raised high.

Sorrett gave a savage cry with the downward stroke, burying the axe's head and freckling his face with icy dognar blood. He yanked it out and hacked again, taking a beast's head this time, and then the pack turned on him and would've overwhelmed him if it wasn't for the two giants at his sides now, chopping and battering until, at last, he could reach in and snatch Gehn's limp, torn body from the mire. One of the creatures leapt and snapped but took only a shred of the Ancient's right boot.

Sorrett turned to run when the crushing fangs found his lower leg and he thrust down the shaft of his axe to keep from falling. He turned to see another of the beasts coming from his right, its mouth open and its wide, red eyes fixed on the unconscious Ancient in his hand. In a blink, he whipped the axe around and clove its skull from side to side with a wet *crunch*. He fell sideways, cradling Gehn's body in the crook of one arm, and now the beast that'd hampered him released his leg to come snarling and spitting for his face.

Amidst a quivering multitude of armored dwarves, the Irchites stood with poise. Kindal had taken up space several feet out, facing the Giant King whose monolithic warriors had completely encircled the group. Light from the camp's fires peered in between the giants' dim bodies, touching the edges of their rigidly-trained spears and their faces locked in scowls.

"This is a very big mistake." Kindal asserted, his hazel eyes unblinking.

"*Silence.*" Ekknet, the largest silhouette, boomed. "*Hand over the guilty ones before I choose for myself.*"

"*Three of them for three of us!*" Another giant added, and the words were followed by growls of agreement.

"*I say we hurl three spears and see how many of the fat worms we can stick!*"

A white-bearded, yellow-cloaked Irchite pushed out of the dwarves now and stopped behind Kindal's right shoulder. "Monitor." He whispered.

188

Kindal never took his eyes from the mountainous king. He matched Badger's hushed tone. "Mediator."

"Many of us have weapons they overlooked. We could fight our way out of this still."

"They would crush us." Kindal said.

"Not if we use the poison darts."

"Out of the question." Now Kindal sighed through his nose and spoke loudly to address the Giant King. "As I've said, there are no guilty ones to hand over, but if you're going to take someone, you'll take me alone."

"No." Badger muttered uneasily at the Monitor's shoulder.

There rose a buzz of opposition from the gray cloaks in the crowd behind, and many plumed, copper-trimmed helmets turned to stare at Kindal in shock.

"*Spoken like a true slavemaster!*" A giant near Ekknet shouted. "*He thinks that his life is worth three of ours!*"

The black-bearded Irchite scanned the row of glaring faces above. "Slavemaster." He echoed, and gave a brief smirk. The Monitor's next words were as hard as stone. "My ancestors toiled under the whip for seven generations before Irchos broke them free."

The grooves in the Giant King's twisted expression slackened a degree.

"*And their children enslaved others in turn!*" A towering warrior cried.

"Wrong." Kindal corrected, his right hand a fist as his eyes touched on the glinting, golden reminder that held his forearm. "We served the same line of dwarves that you did, yet here we are, working alongside them to achieve a common goal."

"*He's lying!*" Another giant chimed.

Ekknet's predatory eyes twitched. His lips were tight over his teeth. "You would give up your life for these murderers?"

A new voice rang out now, one that, by its sound, belonged to neither dwarf nor giant: "There is only one murderer, and you're playing right into his hands!"

There was a break in the wall of massive bodies. Amber light spilled into the circle and across many blinking, bearded faces.

189

Kindal recognized the young, human king at once.

"We found the old suit he used to gain entry to the camp." Egan started, standing just ahead of a group of armored soldiers with torches held high. "And this." Moving around a two-wheeled cart on which a mound of tarp rested, he took one rumpled corner in his hand and then he pulled it away to reveal a pale, lifeless soldier with a bloodied throat. "You've been duped, Ekknet." Egan stared up boldly at the Giant King. "If you're too blind to see that now, you might as well turn your axe on all of us."

To Strom's eyes, the closest pines were barely distinguishable from the blackness beyond. The mist on the field might've been a thin blanket of snow.

He'd just noticed the silence in the camp behind him when, at the *crack* of a breaking branch, his attention returned in full to the forest's depths.

Helmeted heads jerked toward the sound of upset foliage. Rifles were raised and cannons were eagerly adjusted.

Crash crash crash crash CRASH!

"Don't fire until I give the word!" The General called. "And only if you know exactly what you're shooting at!"

CRASH CRASH CRASH CRASH!

Three forest giants burst from the wall of pines, their hides splotched here and there with mud and blood. The one in the center held no weapon but cradled something in its arms. As the beings strode across the field and toward the camp, a host of gleaming, scarlet dots appeared in the woods behind them.

"*Dognars!*" A soldier exclaimed.

"Cannons!" The General raised his arm. "Give me ten shots and no more!"

Several of the large guns down the perimeter blew smoke and flame. Clumps of damp earth erupted along the wood's edge. A pine's trunk exploded into splinters, and now the tree toppled heavily onto the grass to scatter a section of mist.

190

Having almost reached the camp, the giants halted and turned back to watch as the red eyes faded into the shadows.

By the tenth *boom*, any sign of the beasts had vanished.

"Sorrett!" Strom pierced the abrupt silence. "Is he alive?"

Egan made through the tents and toward the bedraggled forest giant kneeling at the camp's edge. Armored suits tightly encircled the creature, their helmets tilted down at something still hidden to the young king. He guessed what it was even before he could make sense from the muddle of words.

"...be in one piece?"

"...think he's breathing."

Then, he heard Strom's unmistakable voice. "Stand aside for the medics! All of you stand back!"

The throng of metal bodies shifted and opened slightly then, and Egan caught a fleeting, fragmented look at the arm on the grass, shredded and glistening red, motionless.

Chapter 15

GHOSTS

A handful of stars shone down through a rift in two layers of cloud as Egan made through the quiet camp. His eyes darted from shadow to black shadow, his imagination transforming each one into a hunched and skulking form. Wearing his finest battle armor, cape trailing and longsword at his waist, the young king felt ready for anything. He arrived at Strom's tent and pulled the flap aside to find darkness.

"I'm here." The General grunted.

There was a *pop*, and the tent's interior lit with the weak glow of a match. Strom touched its flame to the candle on his desk with tawny, leathery fingers, and then shook it out. He didn't look up.

The king stepped inside and let the flap fall closed behind him. "I'd like to know your thoughts."

Strom brought the same fingers close to his face and inspected them, rubbing them against his thumb one after another. He uttered a clicking sound. His mustache twitched. "I think that without Gehn, our success here would depend on the dwarves and giants more than ever." His icy eyes rose to meet the king's. "I fear that pushing forward would be an imprudent choice."

Egan squinted at the old General. "You're quitting." He said flatly.

192

"Retreating." Strom amended. "We can fall back to the south and rethink our options."

"Rethink?" The squinch in the king's face intensified. "You lead us all this way only to change your mind at the last second because *he* can no longer help us?"

"We might be dead now if not for him." The General's focus returned to his hand. "I'm not about to throw more lives away simply because the boy king suddenly found his fighting spirit."

Egan only stared, the words more a shock to him than a source of pain, and, for a while, his mind fumbled for a response. "...You're right that I've not always been a good leader," Egan quietly, soberly said at last, "but I won't let us run."

Only the General's mouth moved. "They're your men. If you want to lead them into hell, that's your right, but you'll be making a terrible mistake."

The certainty with which Strom spoke conjured a flutter of apprehension in Egan's stomach. It was then that the candle's light wavered and a phantom shape appeared in Strom's shadow, shrouded and faceless but for two glinting pupils of red. As the young king's hand went to his sword's cold hilt, a voice came that made the hairs on the back of his neck bristle:

"Listen to him, highness. I could raze your kingdom if I so desired."

Egan opened his eyes. For several seconds, he lay still in his bed, gazing up at the ceiling of his own tent.

Standing at the northern perimeter amidst muttering, armored gunners both human and dwarven, Strom turned at the sound of approaching hooves to behold what seemed to him a single, chimeric being: Egan, wrapped up in a robe that perfectly matched his sable steed.

"You're just in time, Sire." The General's attention went back to the stretch of broken, grass-cleared earth that now ran between the camp and the looming pines. Two dry days had come and gone since the night of Gehn's fall; from what Strom could see, the only trace of moisture was a layer of early-morning dew.

"Ready when you are, General." A gunner announced.
Strom gave a single nod.

Three catapults rattled from the swing of their powerful, iron-black arms. Now, a trio of fiery missiles streaked northward across the pale sky, each one to explode against the trees and roar with swiftly-spreading flame.

Somewhere away from the camp's edge, Gehn lay in silence. Far beneath the unbroken stillness of his closed eyelids, he now found himself on a steep and stony path, its margins still without the scrub that would one day thrive here in every crevice and patch of bone-white dust. The sun was falling at his right as he urgently climbed, his clothes torn and his weapons lost. His own breaths were louder in his ears than the ripping wind.

There came a shrill *crack* to his left, and he turned as an arrow went spinning away down the slope to disappear. Its point had taken a fleck from the rock and had left behind a dark and iridescent spatter. He tried to ignore the fact that he'd felt miniature droplets hit the skin of his forearm. "Are you hit?" He called back.

"No. Are you?"

"No."

"Don't they understand that they've lost?"

Gehn continued his vigorous ascent, searching as he went for a prominent boulder ahead, but here, the incline offered no such refuge. He stopped to look back at his dark-haired comrade and glimpsed one of their pursuers far below: a figure in white, standing suspiciously still on a level section of the path.

"Incoming." Gehn warned.

A subtle, whistling hiss filled his ears not one second before the arrow arrived. It glanced off the stone before him with a *kang* as he jerked his face away and shut his eyes.

He found the object seconds later, black and hideous, caught in the rocks like a vulture's remains. Its dripping, serrated head was as large as a dagger. He took the arrow, snapped its shaft in two, and flung both pieces away down the slope.

194

As they slipped through the gaps in the sharp boulders at the top and came into partial shade, the sound of the wind was joined by that of exploding waves. From the cliff's base, the sea seemed to reach forever south in a savage, bottomless blue. On its surface, sparse scratches of white shifted in and out of existence.

"We can ambush them."

"We're almost to the wall." Gehn said. In search of the narrow path, his eyes ran across a steady curve of cliff face. "They'll turn back if they have any sense."

The other warrior stared gravely from his place against a boulder, one hand tight on his knee and the other loose against his side.

Gehn focused on the cloth beneath that lax hand but saw no trace of blood.

The ground trembled suddenly. Loosed pebbles skittered down near-vertical rocks.

Stepping up to the gap in the boulders, Gehn peered into the arid northwest just in time to see a plume of black smoke rise from the horizon. The shockwave crossed the distance in an instant.

Boom!

He felt the earth jolt and turned to witness a vast, dark ripple shoot away across the ocean's surface and disappear.

'What's happening?' He thought, and then he noticed it at the corner of his vision: the shaded form of his comrade facing him fixedly.

The warrior lunged now, white teeth parted in a silent cry. In the blur of his fist was a small, sharp object.

Gehn caught his attacker's muscled arm and threw its owner hard against the rock wall. He saw now the wound he'd first missed; a tear in the garment of his once-comrade's side revealed a blackened, bleeding puncture.

The dark-haired warrior recovered swiftly. He charged and swung and the arrow's tip sliced air inches from Gehn's face.

In an instant, Gehn's lower palm smashed into jaw and now he sidestepped to let the warrior collapse on hands and knees several feet from the cliff's edge. He snatched up a skull-sized stone and held it ready.

"I always knew." The bested warrior spit blood to make crimson craters in the dust near the broken, poisoned arrowhead. He gave a small chuckle. "I think I saw it in a dream."

"Jump off." Gehn said. "I don't want to kill you."

"I thought there would be pain."

"Jump now and do a favor to us both! Do it before you turn!"

The dark-haired warrior looked up, and before the last spark of sapphire flame faded in his pupils, he uttered four quiet words: "He won't let me."

All at once, Gehn felt the cool, ocean air turn biting cold. He could only watch now as snakes of ebon vapor rose from the shape before him: a tightly-bent body pushing its fingers deeper into dry earth as though to scoop up handfuls. Partially shrouded by the thickening smoke, the trembling shape began to swell.

Gehn stepped back.

Again the ground shook, this time so violently that he couldn't tell if the bellow he heard was from the fracturing boulders or the horror before him. As he turned, he caught a glimpse of black scales like shards of volcanic rock ripping out through flesh, and then he was fleeing the edge of a rapidly-disintegrating cliff.

Knees-to-chest, Sorrett sat beside the medical tarp, watching the inferno and the inverted mountain of smoke. He heard a grunt and looked down toward the form covered in red-blotched bandages.

'I'm sorry, but there's no Arkonn this time.' The giant thought.

Plumes of black smoke bulged in the arid west.

196

Gehn could hear the resonant bark behind him as he made fleetly eastward across the ridge. He came now to the final tip of jagged, inland cliff and beheld his destination in full: the wall, like a colossal, gray ring towering between plateaus far below.

After a look back, he stepped over the edge and fell, and he landed nimbly on a shelf of dust and stone half-streaked with shadow. He'd nearly arrived at the next edge when the ground shuddered, and, as he halted, he noticed a change in the distant ellipse: a lambent, orange hue originating at its flat crown and gradually filling its entire surface. Great, pale curls of vapor rose about its form like impossible cobwebs.

"No." Gehn whispered to himself. He had witnessed destruction brought by only a fraction of the wall's tremendous power, and as its low hum rolled and the ground trembled in obedience, he felt a pang of hollow despair.

He recalled the words and now heard them spoken in the wind's soft voice: "*Nothing outside the wall survives.*"

When the shadows on the nearby stones stirred, he looked back to see his scaly pursuer crouched and staring like a shadowed boulder on the cliff above. He leapt aside just as the beast crashed down with a roaring snarl onto the quivering shelf. Fragments rained as Gehn ran, and then there came a flood of amber light, its source the distant wall like a dome of blinding sun.

The ground split, and then he was plummeting in a cascade of stones and dust.

In the time it took him to breathe deeply in, the truculent echoes were silenced.

Pain and feeling filled Gehn's body gradually, starting with the aches in his chest and back, spreading and collecting like disease. When he first tried to move, he thought he was paralyzed, but as his stupor faded, a feeling of pressure replaced it: the weight of many tons of rock.

By the lack of feeling in his right arm, he thought he'd lost it in the sudden, furious descent. He moved it, realizing then that both it and his head were not pinned like the rest of him but

197

occupied a pitch-black cavity that reached away into an immeasurable chasm.

He tried to shift his body forward, but the stones seemed to grow heavier, to squeeze down as if to punish him for this attempt. When at last he stilled with a frustrated breath, he noticed the bloody canyons that crisscrossed the flesh of his free arm. A vision of darkness and flying foliage returned to his mind. He remembered chasing a cloaked figure through pines before his own fall to cruel, ripping teeth.

'Am I dead?' He thought.

His ears detected a rhythmic sound then: a distant, growing *boom, boom, boom,* like the beating of a colossal heart. Something stirred in the darkness of the chasm ahead, but Gehn's focus didn't linger there, for an azure glimmer appeared just beyond the reach of his hand.

The greatsword.

He attempted again to stretch forward, and then, when his fingers were inches from the weapon's hilt, he looked up once more, and into a mass of twisting, ebon smoke touched by scarlet glow.

With a grunt, Gehn looked back toward the blade and now saw that the stones around him had begun to shift and change as though in a fire's flashing, dying light. Black, sharpened points bulged from every surface like thorns.

"Do not fear." The being above him whispered, and then a stifled cry escaped him as the pain pierced him in a thousand places.

INTO THE MAW

When the flames were finally satisfied, the few pines still standing were bare pillars of coal against a gloomy haze. Here and there on the fallen trunks, glowing patches of embers shone like the magic of mischievous spirits.

Cinders crunched. Flakes of ash swirled up from falling boots and rotating wheels. A number of giants had formed a vanguard some fifty yards ahead, visible to the others only as gray apparitions that often stopped to knock down stubborn trees.

Egan looked back once to see, high above the green hills, a screen of sunlight slicing through the clouds like a banner of farewell.

Minutes later, when the leading giants stopped, the young king rode ahead to Strom's side.

"This is where Gehn fell." The General explained.

Before them, a giant knelt down and lay a spear flat on dark mud that had cracked and hardened in the fire's wrath.

At first, Egan was sure that the one called Sorrett was kneeling out of respect, but now the being reached down, peeled away a section of the half-dry muck, and exhumed an oblong mass in which there could be seen a trace of bright, blue metal.

Hours came and went.

Egan had nearly fallen asleep in the saddle when a distant chatter of crows caught his ear.

He didn't recognize the trees ahead, but he knew that they weren't pines. The flames hadn't reached these, though they were clearly dead, their twisted, leafless branches resembling the roots of trees grown upside down. Even the giants eyed them with mistrust.

Egan rode through machines and armored bodies and until Raven's hooves had reached the edge of a cliff.

He'd thought it to be a high one at first, but now, he saw that the ground dropped only several yards before it leveled out into a dark plain oppressed by fog. Imagining the swamp's vastness, knowing that it stretched for unseen miles, the young king felt despair stir inside him like a corpse in a shallow grave.

He spotted a giant standing out ahead, mud at the warrior's ankles as it looked back toward its comrades with the expression of an uncertain child.

"Well," Strom's voice was mirthless, "it's just as lovely as I remember."

Carts and towers were dismantled. Planks and beams came together to make broad, raft-like squares.

Biting the stem of his pipe, Strom made his way slowly through the bustle of industrious bodies: men sawing, giants hauling and dwarves fastening, each one laboring with speed and efficiency. He heard Kindal shout somewhere ahead and now he circumvented a stack of scrap wood to find the burly Irchite up on one of the many raised, square vehicles-to-be, the mass of muscle and grease-black beard down on all fours, driving nails through overlapping sheets of brass.

"Get those seams tighter." The Monitor called at two dwarves working near him and pointed toward the infraction with his hammer. "I don't want to see a hair-thin crack."

Strom stopped and inspected the slanted, brass-shielded edge of the inverted sled before him.

Kindal glanced up. "General." The Irchite finished beating on a nail's coin-sized head and then stood to inspect the handiwork in its entirety. Nodding, he stamped the metal with his foot and then turned to face a nearby forest giant. "Flip it."

As the dwarves stepped off, the giant took hold of the object's edge and now raised it easily from a trio of support planks.

Strom pulled the pipe from his mouth temporarily. "Let it fall." He said. "We need to know its strength."

The being obeyed, bringing the sled vertical before shoving it away. With a rush of air, the object slammed down with a weighty *thud.*

Strom walked out onto its broad, splintery upside. "Monitor Kindal."

"General." The Irchite replied.

"How are those weapons coming?"

Minutes later, out beyond the camp's edge, a raised, heavy breastplate hung above the haze like a tribal warning of trespass, like a faintly-glistening torso impaled on a wooden spike.

200

Strom glanced once again toward the object near him: a crude, black cylinder kept level by an Irchite's hands as well as a thick rope that hugged the warrior's shoulder.

Kindal nodded.

BOOM!

In a blink, the tongue of flame was gone. Though the breastplate only jerked, Strom made out a fist-sized hole in its center now.

Kindal gestured with his eyes, and another Irchite promptly moved to the statuesque shooter and snapped a latch to open the weapon's rear, freeing a languid, white ribbon of smoke. As a polished projectile was pushed snugly into the hole, Strom noticed that the shape was more cone than ball.

"Lead core with a steel coat." Kindal voiced. "Won't tumble when it leaves the barrel. Won't easily bounce or deform on impact. Perfect for piercing."

"Genius." Strom muttered as a large, yellow powder charge followed the projectile and the rear of the cylinder was closed.

"I wish I could take the credit. The weapon itself is a little unwieldy..."

"More unwieldy than a cannon?" Strom looked at the Irchite sidelong. "When can they be ready?"

Egan unfastened the last strap and straightened to heft the finely-crafted black and silver saddle off of Raven's back. He let the object drop to the spongy ground and moved to the bridle when he heard Strom cough behind him. "Any change in his condition?" The king asked without turning, and to him, the span of silence that followed was answer enough.

"They're astonished that he's still alive." The General finally said.

Egan stared at a section of Raven's dark, silken face.

"I've changed the plans, Highness."

The king waited.

"A partition will stay here on the shore with the wounded and half the supplies as I take the main force forward. The giants will

201

shuttle whatever we come to need. Someone competent will have to man the shore base."

"I'm flattered you would consider me for such a task, but I'm coming with you."

"Your Highness..."

Egan closed his eyes and sighed.

"If something goes wrong out there, you can lead the others back to Capitol and form a new plan."

"A new plan. Yes." Egan listlessly replied. "We'll plan for a slow and steady defeat."

"Egan..."

"You won't change my mind."

"You're as stubborn as your father was."

The king looked back with a tinge of venom.

Strom sighed and his eyes fell to the ground. His form seemed the only one with color in the thickening fog. "It's a trait that suits you better than it did him." He said. He turned and began to walk away.

"Can we win without the Ancient?" The king blurted.

The General stopped. Somewhere unseen, a pair of hammers *ping*ed a perfect rhythm and then went silent. "With our new allies, I think we have a chance."

When Strom had departed, Egan brought his focus back to Raven. He removed the bridle and put his hand on the horse's snout. "Be safe."

Morning.

As though the massive, iron chains were easy ropes, giants whipped them over their shoulders. The beings in the leading row leaned forward, bare teeth tightly clamped, trunk-like legs bent and feet rooted deep in the mire.

With faintly-aching eyes, Egan scanned the warriors on the sled with him, armored men and dwarves looking anxiously toward the mist-screened north.

At Strom's shout, the giants began to pull.

The young king felt the vehicle lunge forward beneath his feet and his heart began to pound. He found his mind transported back to a series of small books from his childhood, each one having contained its own obscure, age-old tale of war. One of them, lacking its final pages, had been a source of bitter frustration for him, and often he'd studied the last, sharply-penned drawing of its heroes for any trace with which he might decipher their fate.

As he looked around now, he saw himself and his comrades as the figures in that very illustration.

'So be it.' He thought.

Chapter 16

NETHREDAS

The many amber lights of the land base had just dissolved behind them when the first warning came.

"Movement!" A scout giant blared.

The great beings released the bulky chains and took up their wooden axes and spears. Gunners readied the cannons of their own. Each flat became a porcupine of gleaming gun barrels.

A string of growling noises rolled out of the gray.

The nearby Ekknet was a dark and sneering statue. "They speak to one another."

The distant sounds stopped.

Climbing to stand atop the highest crate, Egan noticed that Strom and Kindal had done the same on their own sleds. He made sure to match the confidence of their stances.

Seconds passed, and the only activity was that of the dancing torch flames.

The next noise came from Egan's right: an explosive roar so overwhelmingly loud that it seemed to have come from fifty fang-lined mouths at once. Giants swung their heads in its direction and their hulking bodies followed. Three sleds over, a single cannon went off and briefly painted a section of mist molten orange. Several rifles spat in vain.

"Hold your fire unless you're directly attacked!" Strom shouted.

'They're trying to scare us.' Egan thought. 'If they thought they could beat us here in the mud and fog, they wouldn't hesitate.'

"Alright!" The General voiced. "Let's move!"

The army progressed in a square of staggered rows. Any sense of time soon slipped from Egan's grasp, and when he looked straight up, he was unable to catch a glimpse of that bright, white sphere through the clouds.

"Tracks!" The voice of a lookout giant boomed. "Many, reaching away in all directions!"

"Good!" Strom replied. "It's about time *they* were the agitated ones for a change!"

A smile touched Egan's lips. He recalled a wild boar hunt from his youth, a morning of mist and baying dogs and pent-up adrenaline, and he discovered that some deep part of him actually believed in a chance of victory.

It was now that a new layer of darkness swept over.

"Cover the guns!" The General commanded as though it were merely a drill.

Egan heard the order repeated from sled to sled as umbrellas bloomed above cannons and tarps flew onto crates. Torches died and flares burst to white, effervescent life. The young king managed to get his hood up just as the rain came, and as he gazed into the wind and the aggressive, silver streaks, he was convinced that the beasts would come next.

Lightning sped through the clouds above like fire through the veins of God. For an instant, giants that had once been invisible to Egan's eyes were sharp silhouettes, their outlines rougher than a ruin's broken columns.

He hadn't meant to fall asleep, so his abrupt awareness of loud voices, movement, and the absence of pattering drops came as a surprise. Shoving the heavy tarp off himself and sending water across splintery beams, Egan sat stiffly up, and what he saw made him wonder if he was awake at all.

205

The thick fog was gone. A still, spectral mist haunted the muck's surface for miles in every direction. Off in the west and below thin veils of afternoon light, a spidery tree stood alone in the emptiness.

"Highness, you're awake." A green-armored Captain said.

In one motion, Egan brushed the stray, black strands from his eyes and put his hood back. "How long..." He stood carefully, bracing his legs against the recurring, forward jolts. "Were we attacked?" He asked as he looked out across a tight, spearhead fleet. Free of the blinding haze, forest giants pulled their sleds with bold new haste, their legs coated with mud nearly up to the knees. Clustered on the vehicles, armored bodies stood facing the north with rifles held slack.

"No sign of the beasts." The Captain answered. "The rain washed any tracks away."

As Egan processed this, his eyes fell toward scattered pools of water reflecting broken clouds. Like clumps of pale, wiry hair, dead bushes stuck from ridges in the mire.

"Perhaps we've got them running scared."

The young king shook his head. "No." He looked northward and noticed that a pair of the towering scouts had slowed their pace.

"Atrok!" A third shouted. "Tet azarak!"

"Captain." Egan stepped closer to the rigid, green suit and softly inquired: "What's our giant's name?"

"Gerrok, I believe."

The king nodded. "Gerrok!"

"Yes?!" The shape hauling the sled returned.

"What's going on up there!? What are they saying!?"

"Stone ahead... stone not made by the earth!"

Egan joined the gunners at the front of his sled and squinched at the horizon. "I see nothing." He claimed. But now, as the afternoon dimmed, he descried a shape pushing up through the northern gloom: a slate-colored, triangular structure like a mountainous, long-forgotten altar. Just the sight of it made his flesh tingle with apprehension, and his mind returned to the tales of his childhood to fix on a specific rhyme:

206

Past ridges and valleys,
Beyond forests blood-red,
Lies the temple Nethredas,
Threshold to the dead.

Ever higher the ziggurat loomed above the sea of mist, until, at last, its three tiers were fully visible. While Egan could perceive a straight, receded stair that spanned from its base to its flat peak, he had yet to spot any evidence of brickwork. So far, it seemed to him as though the entire object had been cut from a single, tremendous rock.

As the force closed on the forbidding shape, forest giants tilting back their heads to take in its size, Egan heard not a single whispered word. Any hints of sun had left the high clouds, and the token warmth had followed.

Strom called for a halt.

He turned just in time to see a forest giant set Egan down carefully onto his sled. "Highness." The General said, noticing how fiercely sober the king looked. Studying the structure ahead, Egan's keen, blue eyes were like fractured glaciers, and now, Strom caught a glimmer of the late queen in the angles of the young man's face.

"I think I see an opening at the top." The king voiced.

Strom replied with a grunt.

"If this is the place," Egan scanned the surrounding bleakness, "where are the hounds?"

"That's the big question, it seems."

Another giant approached, this one pulling a small, wooden square on which the coal-bearded Kindal stood.

"Oi." The Irchite hailed. "Your wizard is quite the builder."

"I'd wager he didn't build that." The General replied, his eyes following the edges of the dire, pyramidal shape. "Let's get a closer look."

207

The sled was escorted by Ekknet and several axe-carriers.

When the giant pulling the vehicle had come within a few yards of the artificial island, he halted and stared.

"Good enough." Strom said.

A single, long plank was brought by soldiers and dropped onto the mud between. Egan followed the General down onto it, grimacing when he felt the wood shift and sink several inches beneath their weight. Directly ahead, the structure's recessed staircase rose like countless stained teeth held tight by a perfect cleft. Without even a single *caw*, a pair of crows broke from its shadows above and flapped away beneath dim sky.

"The crow's silence is louder than the banshee's scream." The young king recited quietly to himself. Suddenly, he heard Ekknet's voice behind him: "I smell death." Now Egan caught the scent, an undeniable reek of decay, and as he drew closer to the steps, he saw that their stains were not made up of the dark moss he'd imagined.

"I'd say this is the place." The General said.

The blood on the stairs had long dried, the work of ceaseless downpours having faded only its pointed, vertical stripes.

"That's a dognar highway if I ever saw one!" A soldier called.

Egan reached down and put his fingertips on the object's sloped and petrous matter. His thoughts went to the grip of an exotic scimitar in Strom's collection. 'It's like sharkskin.'

"I know this material." Strom said. "Our bombs wouldn't even mark it."

"Ancient-made?" Kindal asked.

"Undoubtedly."

Egan looked again toward the structure's partly-silhouetted top. "Do you think they are waiting in there?"

"If they are, our giants would have an easy time keeping them contained." The General answered. "I think they're smarter than that."

Just then, a peal of distant *boom*s drew every face back toward the south.

"That wasn't our group." Egan said.

208

"No." Strom added gravely. "That was the land base."

Sorrett stood beside the medical tents with a spear clutched tight in his hands. He'd heard the first of the growls not minutes before, and now, he saw swift movement past the taut gunners at the edge: a pack of shapes like jagged shadows speeding right to left across the misty plain.

With a yellow flash, there rang another *BOOM.*

"Save your shots!" A human officer screamed. "They're baiting us!"

Gehn looked up when he heard the muffled explosions, past a lightless, man-like shape that seemed to hover at the edge of the chasm before him. Beyond the being's long hair which hung like drifting, black ropes, there existed only a fractured ceiling of stone. He detected soldiers' frantic voices then, and now, he saw his tormentor also turn its red flare eyes up as if the waking world was just above.

Though the being spoke in a soft, clear voice, its words echoed in the space like the roar of a surging waterfall: "My servants are hungry for destruction."

Gehn knew agony to a steady rhythm, to countless stone fangs pushing endlessly into his flesh in tiny, excruciating increments like rats taking their time with a meal.

'It isn't real.' He tried to tell himself.

The growing weight of fatigue had nearly consumed him. His arm was a withered branch, his fingertips still inches from the handle of the sword that he hoped could save him.

But his hand was getting closer.

"Let go." The being above said with unseen lips, its words resounding with quiet malice. "My kingdom awaits you."

Gehn focused on a razor-edged blade that, even in the depths, seemed to hold a trace of reflected sunlight. With all his might, he gripped to the thought of the weapon ahead, and he knew that if his concentration slipped for but a moment, his chance would vanish as swiftly as a heavy stone down a well.

Standing beside the General atop a crate, King Egan stared southward and into the wall of cloud along with the men and dwarves and giants around him. The salvos of the land base had fallen silent.

At the edge of the sled, Monitor Kindal clutched a rifle as though it were a walking stick. "These beasts of yours are always playing games."

"Not for the fun of it." Strom supplied. "They're up to something. Stay alert. Giant!"

"Yes."

"Get us back out there with the others, please."

Egan looked into the west and he discerned, below the fading light, several remote, bush-infested islands resembling stranded animals. A rumble sounded in the north, and when the king turned back toward the ziggurat, he saw, beyond its apex, a ceiling of murky cloud coming like a colossal ocean wave.

A gray-cloaked Irchite voiced a warning before Egan could. "We've got a storm approaching."

The forest giant pulled them as though it meant to outrun the change in weather, but raindrops were already pelting the mud with escalating intensity. As darkness spread rapidly over the swamp and the fleet's umbrellas sprung up like pale mushrooms, Ekknet and his warrior giants staunchly escorted the sled away from the structure.

It was by chance that the young king turned and saw it: a slowly-rising bulge in one of the trapped, rain-battered pools nearby. His face went slack as a stony and sharp-edged shape broke up through the surface to open an eye like a fiery ruby.

"*Look out!*" Egan screamed.

The mass of sludge and muscle and fangs struck with the speed of a venomous snake, snatching a hapless, stupefied gunner to dismember with brutal efficiency, crunching armor as if it were tin. Quickly it came for a second victim, its dripping

210

claw splintering wooden planks as it tried to pull itself up onto the vehicle, its presence met by a dozen rifle blasts and shouts and finally the killing hack of Ekknet's mighty axe. *CHRACK!*

But now the beasts were emerging everywhere, shape upon terrible shape rising from the mire as though the sudden downpour had conjured them, smashing up through sleds and ripping through soldiers with murderous excitement. As guns thundered like fireworks, armed giants rushed in through sheets of rain.

"*Kindal! To your left!*" The young king cried, watching now as the Irchite lifted the bulky mauler from the sled's floor and swung its muzzle toward two charging monstrosities.

Boom!

One dognar dropped instantly, its gaping jaws plunging into the muck as though to swallow it.

The second hulk of dripping scales veered away from the roars of several cannons and then came again for the sled with its head bent low. *Crack!* The crates were thrown as though by the blast of a catapult bomb. Egan flew with them, and, seconds later, found himself half-submerged in black ooze colder than snow, dazedly trying to stand up straight again through the pounding drops. Then, he saw the forest giant's massive foot fall toward him. As he dove away into the mud, the second foot crashed down, so close to him that he could see the tiny patterns in the grooves of its bark-like hide. He heard now the snapping and snarling of a beast beneath Ekknet's battle roar.

Strom's voice: "Egan!"

Instead of turning back, the young king looked north through the falling streaks and toward that towering shape like a pagan temple, for his eyes were drawn to the structure's top by something that he first thought was a hallucination: a single dot of steady, orange light.

Egan's blood turned to ice. 'Him.' He thought, and as the sounds of the battle behind him seemed to fall away, his mind tapped into a memory like roots into a pocket of poison water: "*I want you to return to your people and deliver a message. I want you to tell them that judgment is on their doorstep.*"

211

"Help them, Ekknet!" Strom cried. "They're getting slaughtered out there!"

BOOM!

In the fireball's sudden, brilliant light, Egan caught a hooded shape beneath the high lantern: a figure whisking around to disappear into the ziggurat's square throat. The young king's eyes fell, and he noticed near him, amidst the mud and scattered wooden debris, a single, sleek rifle with its hammer cocked back.

"Let go."

The being's words seemed to echo inside Gehn, to echo and re-echo until they became one with the steady pulse that tore deeper and deeper into his flesh.

'I almost have it.' He thought.

His hand pushed steadily forward as though against a torrent. He could see the sword's hilt at the very edge of his grasp, but now, as his fingertips brushed against the object's end, he knew that something about it had changed.

"No." With his groaned word, Gehn felt hope leave him like breath from a strangled throat. He looked up, and he saw not the glinting sword he'd long reached for but a crude semblance to the object: a shadowy ridge of gravel from which his touch loosed tiny landslides.

A chuckle sounded above him, quiet though it brimmed with terrible joy, and now, as he felt his own defiance give way to his foe's torturous power, he put his face against the broken, stone floor and shut his eyes.

"You have nothing left." The being whispered. "Your pain will be unending."

The thorns of stone drove into Gehn with such sudden force that he felt as though he would be ripped apart.

There in his mind, in the center of a roiling, black storm of dread and hopelessness, he glimpsed a thing he'd somehow forgotten: the hanging V shape of an immense and broken tree. The vision brought back a giant's booming cry: "Tol entra!"

212

An echo of his own voice followed. "Is there a giant word for God?"

Gehn saw next a wide, dim plain. "It was never the blade." The Ancient whispered as a sliver of blinding light appeared on that far, western horizon, its radiance flooding his sight like a sunrise. "It was always Him."

His tormentor's words rumbled from the very stone. "He cannot help you here."

Opening his eyes and looking toward his arm now, Gehn saw, in the depths of the deepest gashes, a hint of glow like burning, blue coals. "Help me."

"*Silence!*" The being's voice came with the fury of a stampede. "*You're as weak as those who fell before you!*"

The Ancient felt heat spreading at his core as he turned his eyes up toward his enemy's dark face. "Help me," he whispered, and the final word brought with it the light of a growing, sapphire flame, "God."

And then, he couldn't distinguish between the roar of his foe and the crumbling of his stony prison.

Raindrops hammered Egan's face as he climbed, the structure's sharp and perfect steps passing by beneath him like the gears of a mountainous machine. He came to the top, the entrance before him resembling the yawning, black tomb of a tribal king, and he looked back on the chaos for a mere moment before turning again to start down into the dark.

He never saw the burst of teal light in the southern sky.

Sorrett's attention was pulled for a moment to the clouds directly above, to a thousand jittering, effulgent lines that swayed like reeds in a windstorm, and then, a voice cut through the shouts around him as though to wake him from a dream.

"*Sorrett.*"

He looked back down toward the white tents, a few stray, thin strings of lightning writhing harmlessly between the poles, and he watched as a familiar figure now donned a drab cloak and took up a greatsword.

Sorrett's mouth fell open. Though he strained his eyes, he could see no wounds in the warrior's flesh, only faint, discolored marks like very old scars. "Gehn." The giant said when his expression had hardened. "They need us."

The Ancient didn't shout, yet his answer resonated with authority: *"Take me to them."*

THE RECKONING

A white flare crackled in Egan's left hand as he descended. Its light threw a steady luster on the surfaces that enclosed him, the tunnel's floor, walls and ceiling shooting away toward the blackness of an indefinite distance. His right hand clutched the rifle, its muzzle jabbing out forward like the snout of a dog on the scent. He heard a soft rattle behind him, and when he looked back toward his own swollen and grotesque shadow, he suppressed an urge to turn the flare back as well.

The rattle echoed in his mind and became Eleazar's voice: "You didn't do as I asked."

Egan saw his younger self speeding back to Capitol by the work of Raven's hooves, his own furious tears streaming down past gritted teeth.

"You didn't tell any of them." The phantom wizard added. "Not even the General."

A tiny, bitter smile tugged at the king's lips.

Again he eyed the slate-colored material surrounding him, the floor that seemed to gently grip the soles of his muddied boots.

'Ancient-made.' He thought.

The darkness ahead grew in size and in clarity, assuming a vertical, rectangular form.

Slowing his pace, Egan raised the rifle and supported it as best he could while still holding the flare, the hungry flame having already reduced the object's length by more than half. He neared the change in the passage and was welcomed by a stench of decay

214

so overpowering that he felt his throat tighten. He came to the tunnel's end and stopped, his echoed footsteps falling away beneath the sizzle of the flare.

'Threshold to the dead.' He thought.

Three enormous piles reached toward the blackness of an unseen ceiling. Mostly there were bones, hundreds of skeletons broken and tangled, slack-jawed skulls of humans and dwarves and other nameless creatures, their shadows shifting, leery spirits in the wavering light. Here and there, interspersed amongst both fresh and brittle corpses were other forgotten objects: shields and swords and bits of armor.

Egan was about to bring out another flare when he spotted, resting several yards away within a bull's ribcage, an unused torch.

Amidst the noise of the ceaseless discharges and the sight of smoke trails flashing into existence over mud and carnage, Strom's thoughts turned once more to the missing king.

In the distance, beyond pillars of fire like a colonnade in hell, a force of dognars had returned from the dark. Like a single entity the beasts moved, veering in and out of view but ever closing on the sled's position, red eyes burning with murderous purpose.

The General turned as the cannons and maulers did, sure now as the horde charged that it would not veer again.

A snarling Ekknet appeared from the side of Strom's vision, the giant clutching a glossy, ebon sphere in one blood-smeared hand: a catapult bomb. At the touch of an eager Irchite's flare, the round object burst into flame, and now Ekknet sent it speeding like a red-hot cannonball toward the beasts.

BOOM!

Guns quieted. Humans, dwarves and giants stared, their fire-lit faces tight with bitter satisfaction. Any movement had ceased but for the new, vibrant blaze.

Strom thought of the numbers that had come boiling up from the swamp's surface, and he could only wonder as to how many of the creatures still lurked out past the rolling sheets of rain. "We haven't seen the last of them." He warned.

"General." A gunner looked at Strom from the side of an open crate. "Our munitions are nearly depleted."

"Ours as well!" Came the cry from an adjacent sled.

Strom looked out across a stretch of strewn debris, of dognar corpses like glistening boulders of onyx, and while he was aware of the other lifeless bodies half-submerged in sludge, he knew that dwelling on them could only lead to doubt. "Ekknet, bring us as many of those crates and barrels as you can."

The mud-spattered giant had to but glance at his remaining warriors. As they hastily conveyed supplies, Ekknet took up his axe and kept watch.

Soldiers scrambled to pry wooden lids.

"Has anyone seen the king?" Strom bellowed, as if Egan were an object that he often misplaced.

"I did," a weighty voice answered, "running up those stairs."

The General turned toward the stout Irchite at the sled's opposite corner: Kindal, facing the wicked, three-tiered shape.

"Are you certain?" Strom asked.

Before Kindal could respond, a series of roaring barks echoed from the swamp's murky, southern depths. Forest giants froze in their tracks as the clamor rapidly intensified.

Squinting, Strom saw only the dying pyres that spelled the ruin of the most-distant sleds. Then, a sudden, azure flash appeared beyond a wall of frenzied silhouettes, and, like a swarm of hornets, the noise became an earsplitting storm.

'Gehn.' The General thought.

"Behind us!"

Strom turned toward the north again expecting an attack, but what he saw instead cut like a small, sharp dagger into his newfound hope: a single dognar, swiftly ascending the ziggurat's stair to disappear into its peak.

With the slope of bones behind him, Egan moved again across flat and seamless floor, every step taking him further from

216

the glow of the lonely, petering torch he'd left behind, and deeper into a chamber filled with immeasurable darkness. Just as he felt an itch to spark another flare, he discerned several pinpoints of orange like night fires at the top of a distant spire, and he suddenly felt as though he'd crossed into a vivid dream.

He walked as if hypnotized. Finally, when he stopped and strained for anything that might betray his foe, he found only the quiet, steady breath of the chill air.

By the hovering glows, he saw that he stood now on a narrow path like a bridge that spanned the center of a seeming abyss. Drawing close to one edge, he quickly realized that the drop here was an illusion; a surface of still, clear liquid reached away like a lake beneath starless, night sky. Gently, he pushed the tip of his right boot into the liquid and was met by hard resistance.

'Barely more than an inch.' He thought, but now, the spreading ripples led his eyes to the monstrous, square holes spaced evenly across the bottom of the vast and artificial pool. Further away, countless hollows that had first been imperceptible to him now appeared in winks of somber, teal light like the work of immersed fireflies.

Then, against the brief, intermittent flashes of a nearby cavity, he noticed a silhouette: a drowned shape with its head and limbs hanging and a spiny tail that nearly breached the liquid's surface.

He tensed now when he saw all of the ones he'd missed, and when he spun to check the opposite pool, he found himself flanked on both sides by a silent legion.

'Are they alive?' He wondered, sure now that he caught a brief stir of movement by one of the shapes.

Curving down into and snaking between the square-shaped holes, thin tubes of bronze ran like searching roots: the first clear evidence of the wizard's mechanical contrivance.

The young king continued forward.

As he drew nearer to the row of high, amber flames, a network of pipes and metal cylinders took intricate shape in the darkness beneath them. Among the polished, gleaming outlines, glass spheres resembled dewdrops clinging to slender branches. Lengthy handles of valves protruded like blunted thorns.

Egan stopped near the path's end, the floor beyond it a broad, gray square over which several massive grids of metal hung suspended from high, horizontal beams. For a while, he stood and eyed the towering machinery as though he expected it to come to life, as though its quiet, pipe-fed flames would suddenly burn with brilliant wakefulness.

Then he heard the sound behind him, the same growl that had been echoing through his nightmares for a decade. He spun to see the beast coming like a terrible extension of the darkness itself, like a shape built from the black smoke of two baleful, red coals.

He aimed and fired but the shot sparked off its scales. He threw the gun down and swiftly drew his sword with a *shangggg*, but now the creature was on him and he could only cry out as the fangs breached his armor and plunged into the flesh of his torso. Then he knew only a dizzying blur of violence, of white sparks and steel skipping away across the stone-gray floor before he was thrown flat onto his back and the beast's crushing claw pinned him. Tips of talons brushed against his throat, and as he groaned through clenched teeth and gripped helplessly to an igneous foreleg, he realized that something had distracted his attacker.

Above his face, the jaws had closed and the scaly head had turned up toward the *clock, clock*ing of two boots. Egan glanced back to glimpse a shadowy, human contour against the mass of twisted, amber-lit metal. Already, he could feel warm liquid collecting inside his armor, but a sound came next that stole his full attention: a thunderous voice like trees snapping in a windstorm.

"*Zol vohtikos!*"

Egan's widening eyes flicked back and forth. 'They *do* speak!' He soundlessly mouthed.

"Last I looked it was a massacre." The wizard said crisply to the beast. "Don't tell me that you're suddenly losing."

Rugged lips peeled back to show glinting, spearhead teeth. The dognar's words, familiar now to Egan, echoed and rattled through his chest. "*WAKE THEM NOW!*"

218

The young king's shock gave way to budding hope. 'They're desperate.' He thought, and with this, the object he clutched in one furtive hand — the dagger he'd drawn slowly and now kept in the crevice beneath his side — held new meaning. He looked back toward Eleazar's shape and was certain that he saw the wizard's pale eyes glance down at him.

"I can't guarantee anything." Eleazar said at last. "If it fails, it would only be a waste of the remaining ichor."

The beast's answer was a fierce and steady snarl through half-open jaws.

Egan's hesitation fled. In an instant, he arced the dagger and drove it deep into a glowing eye. The roar nearly deafened him, and now he shielded his face with his arms as the creature dashed madly forward into a screaming wizard. Rolling over and pushing himself to his feet as blades of agony burned like fire in his body, Egan beheld a furor of dark movement charge into the shallow pool: the beast, clawing at its wound and lunging and snapping at invisible foes with chaotic intensity.

Ahead on the path, Eleazar crawled on hands and knees toward the nexus of pipes.

Gripping at the line of holes running along his armor, deviating three steps to stoop and take up his sword, Egan moved after him.

Eleazar wailed with a futile attempt to stand. Small smears of blood marked the floor behind the tips of his tattered, narrow boots.

"All these years I thought you were some kind of sorcerer." The young king sneered. "I never guessed you'd be taking orders from your own dogs."

The wizard's crippled scrambling stopped beside the machine's most-prominent outward extension: a tall, bronze lever standing at an angle above a thick hub of pipes. For only a moment did the man attempt to pull it, letting go just as Egan's blade came down like a guillotine and struck the metal with a burst of sparks.

Sorrett grunted as he put his foot against the horror's corpse and pulled his great spear free. Through the rain, he beheld something ahead like an island built of jagged, charcoal-black shapes, and while he clearly saw the creatures charging and snapping and ultimately dropping to add to the grisly mass, the true movements of their killer eluded him. The Ancient seemed to exist only in brief blinks, his cloaked form as fleeting as raindrops on a puddle's surface. The sword was all but imperceptible, evidenced only by flying bits of scale and flesh as the beasts' bodies split apart like boulders to an earthquake.

Suddenly the Ancient stopped in the center of the bloody, broken heap and released a savage cry, an arc of blue light flitting between him and the end of his blade.

Only a few dognars remained beyond the ever-descending gray veils. Now, they whisked around and sped away with bitter snarls.

The giant's panting transformed into a chuckle. "Kotok atrola!" He shouted after them.

Thunder rumbled in the north.

Sorrett approached the pile of fallen beasts, his eyes on Gehn's triumphant stance until something changed just at the Ancient's feet: a wisp of inky vapor that rose from the yawn of a dognar's skull, the head attached to its body by only a few cables of muscle and tendon.

Red light filled the hollows of its eyes.

"*Lookout!*"

The jaws snapped shut on Gehn's sword hand with hateful speed, clamping his grip to the weapon's handle.

In an instant, the Ancient yanked his hand back and ripped the head free completely of its crimson tethers. He fell to his side as Sorrett took the vise-like jaws in his own rugged fingers. Any flare that had occupied the fiendish eyes had disappeared.

Gehn drove his fingers into the row of spike teeth that held his bleeding forearm. "Pull."

"I'm pulling!"

A string of barks rose in the distance.

"Pull harder." Gehn urged.

Prying now with all his might, the giant turned his taut face toward the north just in time to catch distant lightning flicker in the sky beyond the battle's scattered fires. For a moment, he glimpsed a tenebrous, pyramidal shape like an uncanny mountain.

Egan had nearly forgotten the warm rivers running down his body when vertigo overtook him like an evil spell. He fought to keep the sword tight in his hand, to keep himself steady now as he tracked his crawling quarry into a forest of vertical, bronze shapes.

He never saw the wizard snatch and hurl a wrench from the shadows. There was only a blur before the object clipped the edge of his forehead in a flash of light and pain.

He stepped forward with new resolve, with his blade cocked back though he'd lost the exact location of his foe, but another wave of dizziness flooded through him and, the next he knew, the hard floor rushed upward and slammed against his left palm. As he shifted onto his knees, his eyes fell to the trickling patterns of blood that had escaped the gaps in his lower armor. He managed to plant one boot against the ancient surface below him, but his attempt to rise only ended in a partial collapse onto his side. The blade slipped from his grasp and *clang*ed firmly onto the floor.

The inflection held a trace of feigned concern: "You look pale, prince."

Egan looked up in time to see Eleazar plunge the tip of a needle into an injured leg and tear a piece of black cloak to quickly wrap the wound. He could only watch now as the wizard climbed to a standing position, and when he saw the long, angled lever that his foe moved for, the words leapt from his mouth. "I know about your father."

Eleazar stopped, his shape a semi-silhouette against amber-lit machinery.

"I know about his failed revolution," Egan added, certain that the bitterness in the dim and hooded face was not imagined, "the

221

torture he suffered as every eye in Capitol watched." The young king's nostrils flared and his dry lips peeled back as he secretly gathered his strength. Slowly, he reached out and took the weapon's hilt again without a sound. "I was told that, in the end, he cried out for the people to save him."

With a ghost of a smile, the wizard took the lever in his hand and pulled it down to unleash the hushed whine of liquid through pipes.

All around, the surface of the vast, dark pool gently stirred.

In a single motion, Egan leapt up and lunged forward, but the wizard had vanished into the darkness. He took hold of the lever and attempted to force it back to its original position, but the metal held fast as though it had somehow locked into place.

"They watched without a word." The voice came, its tone a quiet harmony of age-old resentment. "After all their whispered pleading for him to take the kingdom, they simply watched him scream."

What had been mere shifting in the surrounding liquid was now a mild storm of movement above the multiple submerged cavities. Above the turbulence, ropes of white light snapped in and out of existence between the massive, metal grids. Egan's eyes were drawn up to a flash exposing a section of high, featureless ceiling as a writhing bolt darted down to meet one of the wizard's structures.

Then came the first break in the roiling water: a scaly head emerging to issue a growling, guttural snort.

In the bolt's scintillating flash, the ziggurat's highest tier shone like a whitewashed tomb against the clouds.

Strom climbed through stinging rain, the rumble of footsteps and armor at his back drowned out by a sudden clap of thunder and several distant cannon blasts. As he came up the final steps and onto level surface, the handful of men and dwarves following him spread out and angled their maulers toward the monstrous, square opening that was the structure's peak.

"Flares." The General commanded.

222

With the first hissing burst of flame, the sound of a familiar voice seemed to reverberate behind him.

"*General.*"

He turned to see two shapes rising quickly to the top of the stair: a figure in a flailing cloak tailed by a scowling, mud-streaked forest giant.

'Gehn.' Strom thought, but even when he saw the jagged, stone-like mass hanging from the Ancient's right hand, it couldn't hold his attention for longer than a moment. A chill breeze issued now from the gaping passage, and as the General peered into it this time, his ears discerned what first seemed to him like a chant in an infernal tongue.

Hunched, clutching to the lever as an anchor to keep himself up, the king watched shape after spiny, dripping shape climb swiftly onto the ancient platform. The air was thick with the creatures' roaring barks like maledictions as they rushed toward the outer darkness: the pathway from which Egan had initially come. Their gleaming eyes seemed not to notice him.

'The surface.' He thought.

He could no longer feel the individual trails of blood trickling down his body; there seemed only to be a thick dampness hugging to him now.

'No.'

Egan looked out over the stormy surface. He focused on one of the submerged cavities and watched as a teal glow, once-steady, now shifted beneath the mass of a stirring shadow. Just as an arch of onyx scales broke free, the teal light moved, slowly and evenly, until it filled an adjacent cavity. Now, he peered out further and he saw two more glows gliding beneath the liquid like cursed spirits.

"He can only raise so many at once." The young king whispered to himself.

He looked down then, and he saw, resting in a neat row on the floor nearby, several large, straight tools. As he distinguished a sledgehammer among them, half of its head bearing a single,

axe-like edge, he glanced back at the humming metal behind him
with eyes hardened by resolve.

"Guns." Strom commanded under the tempest.

Soldiers both human and dwarven came to his sides with
maulers ready. Despite brave stances, the warriors' dripping
faces steadily slackened.

"Prepare to fire." Strom said, only just able to hear himself
now over the rising, frenzied chorus from the passage ahead.

A stir of movement appeared at the edge of his vision: Gehn,
his left arm outstretched and his fingertips lightly touching the
opening's side, as though the surface held a hidden secret. Strom
looked and saw clearly now the hideous and hateful trap – the
severed dognar head – clamped tight to the Ancient's right hand
and the greatsword in it. He blinked.

"I can close it." The Ancient said. "Stand back."

"The king is down there."

"And his people will know how brave he was."

Kang!

Kang!

KANG!

On its third strike, the tool's sharpened head smashed
through vertical strands to unleash small geysers of liquid and
steam.

"Stop!" Came the voice behind him.

With every last ounce of strength, Egan hacked at the central
column of black pipes, snapping and deforming them one by one
until they resembled crooked spider legs, shattering glass shapes
to free white sparks like flitting insects.

He glanced over his shoulder to catch three hostile silhouettes
against a descending flash of light: Eleazar, with two of the
massive horrors that had deviated from the group to come
rushing toward a new target.

Strom had always found logic to rest on. Logic offered quiet sanctuary even in the presence of spilt blood, but from the pain of the present choice he found no such escape.

"Strom." Gehn urged. "I can't fight them with this thing attached to me."

It was then that the first glimmers of scarlet appeared in the depths.

"General." One of the waiting officers cried.

Eyes wide, mustache a tense, inverted V, the General's paralysis broke with a jerk and a shudder, as though an arrow had plunged into his chest. He stepped back and extended his arm to the side in a gesture for his soldiers to do the same.

Immediately, Gehn leaned forward and pushed his left hand flat against the gray surface. He leaned into it now, splaying his fingers as he tilted his head down and closed his eyes. "Something's wrong." He said. "Something's drawing its power away."

"Gunners!" Strom called over the chaotic din.

"Wait." Gehn said.

Strands of blue light leapt out of the Ancient's flesh, writhing between his shape and the surface before him, threads flicking occasionally at first and then more and more to the dognar's severed head as though the crevices between its scales and fangs drew them like metal fragments to a magnet.

When Strom saw Gehn glance down at the trap attached to his hanging, right hand, he too looked there, and was certain that he saw red light fill a once-dark sphere.

"It's not going to close." The General voiced his realization as the demonic host came like the surge of a black ocean after a battle, their eyes like burning fragments of debris. Something in the creatures' bold fury told him that their numbers were beyond count. "*GUNNERS!*" He cried.

Egan saw the ring of smooth, vertical bars at the very heart of the machine. His final swing made contact to bring an explosive

225

arc of blinding, azure light that leapt between a thousand points of metal in a single instant.

Beneath the noise of the dognars coming up behind him, he heard the wizard's final protest transform into a scream.

The last thing that he felt was a moment of scorching heat before the darkness.

Strom jerked his hand up to shield his face from sudden radiance. Through his fingers, he squinted at the source, at a rapidly-pulsing flame where the Ancient had planted his hand against the structure's side. In its sheer brilliance, both the ziggurat and Gehn's angled shape were rendered white silhouettes against the outlying murk.

Then, in an instant, the light vanished.

Boom.

The sound was final, silencing what had been the thunder of the beasts' ascent and leaving only softly-whispering raindrops.

Gehn felt the pressure weaken on his right arm. He looked down just in time to see the scaly head fall and *thud* to the ancient surface, its jaws open and its purple tongue limp, a trace of black smoke rising from a milky, lifeless eye to swiftly vanish.

He focused on his bloodied hand and the greatsword it still clutched for a mere moment before he dropped the weapon with a heavy *clang* and stepped back. Looking across the warriors with him, first Sorrett, the giant's head bent low and his axe still ready, then the human and dwarven gunners that hadn't yet broken from their taut stances, he uttered it mostly to himself: "It is done."

At last, his eyes found Strom at the front of the group. Though the warriors began to stir and mutter, the General never moved, never looked away from the sealed passage ahead and the vertical line between its two petrous doors.

226

Chapter 17

WOUNDS

Dusk over Capitol.

From the outside, the city appeared deserted. Gone were the brilliant fires that normally embellished its outer wall, and its gates were tightly shut.

Atop the northern battlement, like a spirit in the shadows of an archway, a lone, young sentry kept watch over the surrounding land. He heard the hoofbeats before he saw the horse: the speck of a rider shooting out between the black oaks and toward the city. Fear welled up in him as his mind grasped for an explanation; such a sight almost always meant news of an impending attack, and, right now, Capitol was dangerously undermanned.

The sentry held his breath as the rider halted before the wall, horse stamping in place.

"*Open the main gate!*" Came the cry. "*They've returned to us!*"

Confused, the young sentry looked northward. "The dognar hounds are coming?" He asked, his voice just shy of a shout. But now, he witnessed as the light of a torch glimmered into existence on the horizon, then a second... a third. Rising into view, trudging between the distant glows were shapes like tall, branchless trees.

"Spread the word!" The rider called. *"Our warriors have come home!"*

Days passed.

A quiet morning found Strom standing in his chamber, facing a dying fireplace with his hands behind his back. Staring down into the amber-faced reflections in the polished floor, he heard a gentle knock.

"General."

Footsteps.

Strom never turned, never made a move or a sound to acknowledge the Captain's presence until the man had stopped beside him and now extended a thick, black book. Strom eyed it for a few seconds, following the intricate, silver veins that hugged its edges, before he realized that he knew it.

"We uncovered this."

The General took it in his hands but hesitated to open it. He guessed that it couldn't have been less than a decade old, but its look and texture still defied age. Expertly engraved in the cover's very center was a sharp, miniature E.

When the Captain had gone, he opened the book to find that the first thirty-or-more pages had been torn out. The first remaining page was blank but for a small, scribbled sketch at the bottom corner: a black horse.

Strom turned the page to find only a few lines. He recognized Egan's trained penmanship immediately.

This is what he read:

Nothing else is of any relevance.

On the chance that I do not return from this war alive and that these words somehow find their way into the hands of someone I knew, I do not want my body buried with my ancestors or my likeness made into an extravagant memorial.

All I want is a place among the warriors that died with me.

My father never understood that true royalty is not passed down by blood from father to son.

It is earned only by blood spilled for one's kingdom.

Strom looked up from the book, up toward the fireplace mantel where a small, black object stood alone: a rounded crow made of twigs and wooden shavings.

A cobweb mist hung over the hills as the General rode up through cold and quiet morning.

He followed the trail's final turn to pass through still trees and a pair of gray obelisks that, by their state of crumbling decay, had clearly been wrought by human hands. Ahead of him now on the hillside, markers stood in perfect rows like countless miniature towers of white amidst the green. He made through them on his steed, up the slight and gradual slope, and he glanced once toward two large monuments against the trees of a tall and distant hill.

He came to the last white marker at the uppermost row and dismounted. Pulling a spade from the saddlebag, he pushed it into soft earth, starting a hole equidistant from the other simple and identical stones. When he'd finished, he returned to the saddlebag and its protruding, cloth-wrapped contents, and now brought out a cylinder that was similar in size and shape to the other ones here but for a glossy, onyx surface. He set the object into the hole and pushed some loose dirt in around it, adjusting its straightness before he pushed more dirt. Then, he stepped back and merely looked at it for several minutes until his eyes fell to the motionless blades of grass.

"Goodbye, son." He finally uttered.

A quiet rush of air drew Strom's attention back up: a raven, landing nimbly onto one of the white markers to his right. The bird eyed him with twitching interest, its dark plumage somehow glinting purple even in the pre-sunrise dimness.

Then, after a *click* of its beak, the bird leapt from the stone and, with a few beats of its wings, was gone.

THE ROAD AHEAD

From a space between the trees at the hill's crest, Gehn could see the camps on the fields: white tents interspersed by dwarven banners, waded through and watched over by several visible giants. The fact that these warriors had not yet left for their own lands offered him a glint of hope for the future.

He made along the ridge now, his cloak trailing, the leaf-littered path flanked tightly by tall trees as straight and as dark as prison bars.

His mind returned to Sorrett's words from the previous night; he could still see the giant's gemstone eyes dancing in the light of the fire. "I had a vision of a distant place: a wood with crooked ta that I've never seen before. I went to one of them and put my ear up against it, and I could hear insects crawling beneath its bark." Sorrett had turned his head down to scowl to himself. "Swarms of them."

Gehn stopped at a clearing in the descending slope. He peered down past its far edge, through countless, coal-black trunks and scattered patches of green.

"What do you think it means?" The giant had asked.

Gehn's focus settled on a distant shape: a silhouette, slightly hunched, with arms bent outward in a hostile stance and a head surrounded by long, wild hair like tangled vines. He knew that it was merely an illusion, a shadowy semblance built of the twisted branches of a fallen tree, but he still felt the hairs on his neck stand up straight.

"It means there's still evil out there." He'd replied.

Sorrett had brought his gleaming, firelit eyes up again, a trace of smile having appeared at the corner of his mouth. "Then it seems your God still has plans for us both."

Gehn looked now above the tops of the far trees and focused on the jagged spires of stone just within Dain's eastern border.

230

Beyond them, in the north, he was certain that he could discern a single peak, seemingly translucent in the pallid atmosphere.

"Do you think we will find them?" Sorrett had asked as the fire's light had waned. "Your people?"

Hearing a *snap* behind him, Gehn turned to see the giant materialize from the vertical shapes. "Your stealth has gotten rusty." He said, looking back toward the spectral mountain once more.

The giant stopped and thrust the butt of his spear into the earth. "I didn't want to frighten you."

"Thank you." Gehn said. "Let's go."

Seconds later, as treetops rolled steadily past him and Sorrett's feet ripped faster and faster at the forest floor below, Gehn felt the greatsword thudding against his back, and as he set his eyes far ahead and tilted his face forward into the wind, he smiled.

POST-EPILOGUE

The chandelier's pipe-fed flames burned like a ring of amber stars.

Staring toward the distant doors, King Pond drummed his fingers on the intricate armrests of his throne and blew a long, impatient sigh.

Twilit sky filled the chamber's lofty windows. Golden-armored guards, usually perfect statues at their positions about the edges of the space and near the throne platform, stirred with restless anticipation.

"Where is he?" Pond blurted. "Does it take an hour to walk here from the main gates?"

Beside Pond's chair, the chief minister stood like a red pyramid made up of robe and tall, pointed hat. He spoke without ever pulling his beady eyes away from the doors ahead. "He should be here by now."

"Maybe you can do something useful for once." Pond brought a hand up to touch his own rounded, freshly-trimmed beard. "Get some eyes on him."

"Yes, your Excellence." The chief minister extended a short arm from between the falls of the robe and flapped his hand at the guards at the base of the throne platform. "One of you! Get eyes on him!"

"Yes, chief minister! Hey! Get some eyes on him!"

232

The dwarf king puffed a sigh through his teeth. "The grayblood thinks his time is more valuable than mine." He snapped his fingers, summoning his masked wine-bearer up the steps and to the throne. He took the jewel-encrusted chalice and brought it to his lips, but he didn't yet drink. "I'm going to savor this."

Before one of the guards could make it to the far end of the chamber, the doors there swung open to a group of Irchites: Monitor Kindal — unmistakable by the enormous wreath of black that flowed from his head and face — followed by the yellow-cloaked Mediator and a handful of gray warriors with faces shadowed by hoods and beards like broad, white swords. The dwarves' boots thundered as they approached across the vast, mirror-like floor.

Pond now took gulp... after gulp... after gulp... until the chalice was empty. With a breath of satisfaction, he simply let the cup drop to the base of his throne with several *clangs* as his masked attendant scrambled for it. "So, the Monitor has returned!" Pond called. "I give him half of my army, and he comes back with a third!"

Kindal, still crossing the chamber, replied mirthlessly. "War has a funny way of doing that. Perhaps *you* would like to lead them next time."

Pond felt a growing flutter of rage threaten his joy. He stifled it as he glanced toward the guards spaced about the chamber's perimeter. He watched them gradually bring their bladed, spear-length rifles down to hold with both hands.

"Your dwarves died heroes, as did mine." Kindal boomed, stopping several yards from Pond's throne platform. The Irchite's hazel eyes never blinked. "But before you talk to me about your loss, I suggest you check your numbers again."

"I suppose some thanks are in order." Pond squinted. "Thank you, for risking so much of mine to remove a small thorn from my side."

Kindal, still glaring, sighed. "My dwarves and I have many miles to go yet. Let's get this over with. Your business first, or mine?"

233

"My business first." Pond said, feeling joy well up inside his chest with the spreading warmth of the wine. He drummed his fingers on the armrests. "I'm afraid I have ill news, Monitor."

The Monitor waited.

Pond checked his gilt warriors again to see them drawing in with their projectile weapons leveled and trained on Kindal's group. From the main doors, more of the armored suits flowed quietly into the chamber, fanning out to join with the closing trap. Below Pond, also rigidly facing the Irchites, the shield-bearers tensed with their massive, metal rectangles as if faced with a charging horde. Unable to contain his smile, the dwarf king went on. "I'm afraid that you and your grayblood warriors never returned from this crusade against the dognar hounds."

While the cloaked Irchites readied their own rifles in response, Kindal barely glanced toward the closing threat.

Badger, the old, yellow-cloaked Mediator, spoke. "Pond, you treacherous little pig."

"You dare?!" Shrieked the chief minister.

"I suppose I should be polite?" Badger replied.

Drunk on his own impending triumph, Pond lazily raised his hand and wiggled his stubby fingers. When there was a lasting silence, he closed his fist. His eyes again found Kindal's. "Your remaining dwarves in Irchos will undoubtedly suspect my hand in your demise. They will surely cut off trade with me, but, you see, I have been stockpiling resources of my own." The king couldn't help but grin. "When I'm ready, I will march an army into the west and tear Irchos to the ground, even if it takes ten thousand bombs." The dwarf felt his smile twist into a sneer. "The mountain will be mine, and your people... perhaps I'll show them the same *mercy* that they knew ages ago."

"Enough!" Kindal voiced.

Pleased with himself, Pond leaned slowly back into his crimson-pillowed seat.

"Alright, Pond." The Irchite said, head tilted forward and amber-tinged eyes gleaming beneath eyebrows like wild, black smears of grease and soot. "You win. You have me. But leave my dwarves alone."

234

"You call that begging?"

Kindal only stared.

"I think you should try it from your knees." Pond casually suggested. He waved his masked servant over for more wine. After a gulp from the rushed chalice, seeing that the Monitor still stood, the dwarf king chuckled and said: "I don't think you understand how this game works, Monitor. You seem to believe that you can offer yourself up and still retain your dignity. If you kneel to me, right now, I may consider allowing your warriors to live for a few seconds. And then, if you continue to do as I tell you, I may let them live for a few seconds more."

Kindal only stared.

Pond's rage came as a surprise even to himself. *"Are you DEAF?!"* His words reverberated across the polished tiles like the cry of a dwarven legion.

Just then, an armored suit pushed in through the distant chamber doors. "Your Excellence! Irchites have taken over the eastern gates and battlements! They're holding Pograd open to the outside!"

The king processed this in slack-jawed silence. He was still staring toward the messenger when Kindal spoke.

"I have a question for you, Pond." The Monitor said. "When the giants were captured and made into slaves, was it your word that made it so?"

Unable to answer, Pond found himself sinking backward into the pillows as though the throne might devour him. "What is this?" He uttered. "What are you doing?"

"Or did some of your dwarves act on their own impulse, and you simply went along with it?" Kindal pressed.

"Whatever this is," Pond rapidly shook his head, "stop!"

The golden suits tightened their postures in perfect unison, jerking their aimed, horizontal weapons to eye level.

The cluster of Irchites mirrored them, the bayonets of their rifles gleaming with defiance.

"All of you that serve this king," Kindal shouted now, his eyes like burning rings of amber, "before you pull those triggers, know that doing so would be a grave mistake!"

235

Another voice rang from the chamber doors. "The city is under attack!"

A burst of gunfire sprung up outside.

Puffing, Pond's eyes flicked from the Irchites to his own circle of warriors and back again. "*No.*"

"A GRAVE MISTAKE!" Kindal roaringly repeated, his final syllable echoing in the space like a hammer's repeated crash. As the sound faded to silence, a shadow fell across the entire chamber as though the last flame of dusk had been snuffed out.

Beneath the dim glow of the chandelier, Pond turned his eyes toward one of the tall windows and pulled a wheezing gasp at what he saw: a silhouette against fading sky, almost humanlike in its proportions though it towered like a colossal statue of iron. His eyes wide with disbelief, the dwarf king looked and found every window filled with the same looming, powerful shape. He could barely hear the fearful groans of his guards and the animal-like whimpers of the chief minister beside him.

"I'd put the weapons down if I were you." Kindal advised.

The first window shattered in a storm of glass and metal. A massive leg, bristling with dark spines, swung into the chamber and slammed a foot down onto tiles strewn with debris. A second window exploded, a third and fourth and fifth, and now, the beings entered, one after another, like terrible machines of war. Spiked, bronze armor clung to their arms and legs and chests, and their fists gripped bronze spears and axes that nearly scraped the high ceiling. They wore no helmets to conceal their scowling faces.

"Forest giants." The dwarf king whispered through his teeth.

As Pond's golden warriors awkwardly dispersed and dropped their weapons and lifted their hands, a final giant came into the space, this one so great in size that the others of his kind seemed mere children. The being stopped beside the group of Irchites, slammed down the blunt end of a battle-axe to send a crack shooting through the floor, and turned its cavernous eyes in Pond's direction.

"King Pond," Kindal introduced, "King Ekknet."

236

"Kindal!" Pond screamed. "Kindal you traitorous, grayblood maggot! You filthy worm! My warriors will avenge me!"

"It was your dwarves forged the giants' armor for this." The Monitor patiently explained, glancing once toward Ekknet's countless spines of bronze. Now he squinted up toward Pond. "Your reign soured long ago."

Another forest giant appeared behind the monstrous Ekknet, this one carrying a square, iron cage from which chains and shackles hung.

"Atro katal." The Giant King bellowed, tilting his head back now so that the amber light of the chandelier found his eyes and glinted against his teeth like bricks of polished stone. "Take him."

THE
ANCIENT

Made in the USA
Las Vegas, NV
18 December 2021

38723755R00146